Terrific Luck

Arizona Heat, Book Three

Hilary Dartt

Also by Hilary Dartt

Arizona Heat

Pure Luck

Sweet Luck

Christmas Luck

Love Under the Arizona Sky

All the Stars

The Whole Sky

To the Moon

The Mint Creek Ranch

My Favorite Story

My Favorite View

My Favorite Place

The Seedling Homestead Series

A Summer of Wonder

A Dream of Home

A Promise of Forever

The Intervention Series

The Dating Intervention

The Marriage Intervention

The Motherhood Intervention

The Garden Club Series

Jasmine's Pact

Studying Sequoia

Just Holly

Terrific Luck

Arizona Heat, Book Three

Hilary Dartt

Chapter One

How many times had Cash Wilder's mama said to him, "Now Cash, that cute smile might've saved you this time, but that's not always going to work"?

She'd been right, of course; although his dazzling smile (mostly) kept him out of trouble when he was really little, it didn't keep his mom from packing her fancy red suitcase and gallivanting off to Hollywood. At which point he decided there was no use in staying out of mischief.

Intense, red-hot competition with one Opal Houston saved him. Oh, how he loved to hate her. Opal, with her curiously colored eyes —the definition of apropos. Opal, with her razor-like tongue and uncanny ability to spell every word in the English language. Opal, with her tanned arms and toned muscles.

Grown-up Cash Wilder, aged thirty-one years, quarter-owner of the Sweet Springs Ranch, chastised himself as he finished brushing his teeth and returned to his bedroom to dress. He should not be thinking about Opal Houston, teenaged or otherwise. He should be thinking about his upcoming day at the police academy. Recruits were training for Standardized Field Sobriety Tests. The grades for that day's assignments counted for a lot. He had to do well. Here he was, finally making something of himself, and he had no room for distractions.

He blamed Callie, his sister-in-law, for making him think about Opal. She'd mentioned Opal was moving back to Prescott, and he hadn't been able to keep her out of his head since. Her image was like that of a mythical creature, all iridescent and sparkling.

"Focus, Wilder." Looking into the mirror, he gave himself a serious nod.

Dressed and ready, he headed for his truck, glancing at his side of the duplex in the rearview mirror. It wasn't a bad place, but he'd come to recognize that he wanted more. He'd moved off the ranch only because his oldest brother, Sterling, left. And when Sterling left, Cash felt like the family was falling apart and he wanted—no, *needed*—something of his own. He later realized a rented duplex wasn't what he had in mind.

His phone rang and a picture of his next-oldest brother, Travis, came up on the screen. Grateful for the distraction from the distraction, Cash pressed *Answer*. "What's crackin', bro?"

"Hey, man. What are you up to?"

"The usual. Headed to school."

"I still can't believe you're gonna be a cop, man. The fuzz. After everything you did in high school. I thought the cops were, like, your sworn enemies."

He'd heard this from his brothers so many times, he could barf. Forcing a laugh, he said, "Nah, man. I told you. That was a phase. I bring to this new phase a wealth of experience and insight that will only aid me in being an effective officer of the law."

Travis snorted, and Cash resisted the urge to slam on the brakes at a red light. "What's up? Did you call for a reason, or just to give me shit?"

"Oh, right! I called for a reason, bro."

Cash waited, the rumble of his truck's engine soothing his ruffled feathers. "Are you gonna tell me what it is?"

"Uh, yeah. Obviously. As I'm sure you know, one of Lila's money-making ideas for the ranch was to offer a dude ranch experience."

"Yeah, it's a great idea."

A beat of silence passed, which meant Travis was nervous. "I was thinking, would you ever want to move back home?"

That wasn't anywhere close to what Cash was expecting. His stomach swirled with nerves. Would he? "I haven't thought about it in a while." That was a lie. Cash thought about it all the time. But he'd made such a big deal of getting away from the drama. Not just Sterling's leaving, but the reason for Sterling's leaving: their dad had gambled away his life's savings and nearly lost the ranch. "Why do you ask?"

Travis's heavy sigh came through the earpiece. "I miss you, man. I hate to think of you living in a *duplex*." He said duplex like it gave him a bad taste. "And we're going to be building all the infrastructure for the dude ranch. I thought we could build you a house while we're at it."

The wave of emotion that hit Cash surprised him. Not only because Travis said he missed him, but also because he *did* want to move home, now that they were no longer in danger of losing it. But he couldn't think about that now. "I appreciate it, man. Give me a little while to think about it, okay?"

"You got it. Just let me know."

After they hung up, Cash's mind wandered again to Opal, who'd also struck out on her own and moved away ... and who was now returning home.

When they were younger and he was still in his pleasing-the-teachers phase, the two of them were at the top of their class. Every time they did reading groups or math groups or special assignments, it was "Cash and Opal" or "Opal and Cash." Joined at the hip, constantly warring for the best scores or most praise, standing side by side in the gym during awards ceremonies.

She became a constant in his life, and looking back on their time together, she probably had no idea how much she meant to him. His home life was falling apart, his mom's wanderlust leaving his dad's anger to swirl around the house like a tornado and all four Wilder brothers adrift. Except every day at school, there was Opal, an anchor.

Cash always hoped that if he did well—got one hundred percent on every spelling test and math quiz and science project—his mom would come back. She'd realize she was missing out on four wonderful boys, and suitcase in hand, she'd walk up that walkway to the big house and come inside and hug them, one at a time. Then she'd sit on the porch swing with him and wrap her arm around his shoulders and kiss the top of his head.

He swore. "Didn't happen, though, did it?" The old hurt and resentment fired up inside his belly and he groaned, forcing himself to focus on the present moment. The trees lining the street downtown, the metallic scent of the cold air blasting from the vents in his truck, the way the sun reflected off the cupholder in the center console. Five more minutes and he'd be at the academy, where he could focus on the present.

One night, Cash's dad overheard Cash telling Sterling he wished Mom was there to tuck them in. Levi Wilder lost it. He wouldn't have his sons grow up to be soft. He raged at Cash, his face red and spit coming out of his mouth on every syllable: "Your mother isn't coming back, you hear? She left us. We're not enough for her, none of us. And you'd better get used to that right now, or you're going to live the rest of your life feeling sorry for yourself. Now buck up, boy, and get to bed."

He'd stormed out then, the vitriol in his words and tone leaving Cash speechless for once. Sterling simply wrapped Cash in his arms, almost like their mother would have done, and led him to his bed. "I ain't gonna kiss you like Mom would, but I'll tuck you in." When Cash lay down, Sterling pulled his covers up under his chin and ruffled his hair.

The very next day, something shifted for Cash. He became a whole new person. A person who now knew that no matter how well he did in school, his mom wouldn't love him enough to come back. And because Opal belonged to the old Cash, defeating her became his mission in life. Not in the good-natured way, but in a cold, calculated way.

Thankful he was pulling up at the police academy and would be forced to stop thinking about her, he sighed as he parked and gathered his things.

By junior high, Cash continued to excel in academics even while his anger manifested outside of school. One day he was beating Opal in the school spelling bee and the next he was sneaking his dad's whiskey and sharing it with the neighborhood kids in the cornfield. One day he was earning the highest math score in the class, besting Opal by a mere percentage point, and the next he was breaking into the hardware store to steal as many sleds as he could carry, so he and his brothers could make the most of overnight snowfall. One day he was leading his team to victory over Opal's in the rodeo competition and the next he was "borrowing" Old Man Hendrickson's tractor and taking a joyride around town. All three of those transgressions he'd had to confess to the examiner during his police academy interview.

Where Opal was concerned, he'd gone ice cold. At first, he could see the hurt in her eyes. But as time passed, that hurt turned to fire—the fire of competition and possibly hatred.

Taking another deep breath, Cash walked through the sliding doors of the police academy.

"What's up, bro?" Tommy Rowland met him in the lobby, raising a hand for a high five. "You ready for today?"

"I think so." He grimaced.

"Come on, man. First of all, you'd probably never imagine me saying so, but this is the funniest day of academy. Plus, you've aced everything else so far. What are you worried about?"

Cash shrugged, unaccustomed to being vulnerable. "I don't know. Mosley keeps saying this is a huge deal. The academy's the first thing that's been important to me in as long as I can remember. I don't want to mess it up."

"I get that. But I'm confident you're not going to mess it up." He cuffed Cash on the shoulder.

"Thanks, man."

Falling into step, they walked across the lobby and through the door into the main classroom. Tommy went off to greet the others, and Cash settled in at his desk with his notebook. He and Tommy had known each other since Tommy moved to Prescott in eighth grade. And although Tommy'd thought Cash was joking when he said he was going out for the police academy, he quickly became Cash's biggest mentor—and fan.

Cash watched as Tommy laughed with a couple of the other recruits. His stomach in knots, he opened his notebook and flipped through it, searching for the page where he'd written notes about the field sobriety testing. His own neat, blocky handwriting still caught him off guard. Throughout his youth, his brothers had teased him for his chicken scratch. But when he'd applied for the police academy, he'd made a point of slowing down and giving himself fresh, more adult penmanship.

He stopped flipping pages when he found the one he was looking for.

Three Phases of the DWI Detection Process: vehicle in motion, personal contact, pre-arrest screening.

SFST Battery Test: horizontal gaze, walk and turn, one leg standing—the foundation for impaired driving enforcement

"At attention!" Commander Mosley stalked into the room, his push-broom mustache leading the way.

Cash scrambled out of his desk and joined everyone else, who jumped to attention, feet together, hands in fists at their sides.

The officer in charge of the entire academy class, Commander Mosley had a barrel chest and a voice to match. Each eyebrow was half the size of his mustache, and those three patches of fuzz took up almost all the real estate on his face. The visible skin was fire-engine red whether he was teaching, yelling, giving instructions, or telling a raunchy joke. Cash found him terrifying.

He looked at his watch, his mustache twitching.

"What goes in hard and dry, and comes out soft and wet, folks?"

"What, sir?" They'd learned quickly that Mosley liked to tell jokes—and demanded his audience participate.

"Gum! Not what you were thinkin', is it? Get your minds out of the gutter, boys!"

The first time Commander Mosley told a joke, the recruits responded with silence. Mosley hollered, "Well if you aren't gonna laugh at my jokes, you're gonna have to run! Give me fifty pushups and then take two laps."

So this time, everyone guffawed, covering their mouths, slapping their thighs, and wiping their eyes. The corners of Mosley's mouth twitched upward, barely visible, and he lifted his right hand. Immediately, silence fell. "Now, as you know, we're doin' the practice field sobriety tests today."

When no one responded, Mosley stomped his foot. "Say, 'Yes, sir.'"

"Yes, sir."

He nodded. "Good. Our subjects are already here, and should be damned well inebriated. Well—" a half-laugh made his upper body bounce, just once—"some of 'em. The lucky ones."

A few people chuckled, but Cash didn't dare. A badly timed chuckle could land the entire class on the track for multiple laps.

"We're goin' in there in just a minute, but I wanted to give you a couple of tips first. Are you listenin'?"

"Yes, sir."

"First tip is, don't screw this up." His eyes crinkled—the equivalent of a smirk. "Take a few minutes to refresh yourself, check your notes and such, before we begin. Got it?"

"Yes, sir."

"That's it. That's the tip. Dismissed. See you in the conference room in ten minutes."

Cash relaxed his posture and sank into his seat with a deep breath. Every time his eyes glazed over while reviewing his notes for what felt like the millionth time, he checked the clock and forced himself to focus.

Finally, it was time to go and the recruits got to their feet, the anticipation evident in quiet chattering and laughter as they filed out of the classroom and down the hall.

The group became subdued as they entered the conference room, and once Cash got inside, he knew why: the group of "suspects" stood in a circle at the far end, apparently oblivious to those entering.

One of them, visible only from the back, was particularly striking. She wore some kind of high-heeled sandals, which gave her calves the most touchable, kissable shape. (*Kissable?* Cash had never imagined kissing anyone's calves before. He must be delirious from nerves.) Her legs were muscular and perfectly tan, and her denim shorts hugged her ass, accentuating the curve of her waist. Long, blond hair hung to the middle of her back, and Cash had a vision of running his fingers through it.

He hoped, fervently, that he wouldn't have to interact with her. The last thing he needed was a distraction. *She's already a distraction.*

"Welcome!" Mosley's voice boomed through the space.

He stood between the two groups of people—the suspects and the recruits—and everyone turned to face him. Cash tore his eyes from the blond woman before she turned around, imagining himself caught and completely humiliated if they made eye contact.

Into the silence that followed, Mosley barked, "We're about to get started. I'd like you all to break off into groups of four: two suspects with two recruits. With low murmurs and some shifting, everyone obeyed. Cash found himself paired with his fellow recruit Ricky "Big-G" Gonzaga, and a couple of guys who introduced themselves as Juan and Fred.

Juan, stone-faced and serious, glared at them and crossed his arms (which accentuated huge pecs and biceps). Cash couldn't help but wonder if he was trying to hide impairment or just bored, dragged along by a friend. As soon as Fred grinned and said, "Short for Frederick Cahill, Junior," Cash *knew* he was impaired. He looked like a college kid—he wore athletic shorts, a t-shirt, and a baseball cap and had probably started shaving only within the past year.

Ricky rubbed his hands together. "This is going to be fun. Are you guys ready?"

Juan shrugged, indicating he couldn't care less, and Fred gave a high-pitched giggle.

Cash looked at Ricky, who raised his eyebrows and said, "Let's start with Juan."

Juan answered their questions without breaking a sweat or

changing his expression. He rattled off his age, height, weight, occupation (teacher), and favorite hobbies (bowling and flag football) without missing a beat.

This guy hasn't had a drop to drink. Cash held up his forefinger a few inches in front of Juan's nose, and asked Juan to track his finger with his eyes, without moving his head. Just as he moved his finger to one side, Cash noticed a slight nystagmus and glanced at Ricky, who raised his eyebrows again—this time in surprise.

"How's he doing?" Fred's head appeared above Cash's shoulder and he laughed.

"He's doing great."

"Now we're going to have you walk in a straight line, turn around, and walk back." Ricky used his hand to indicate the direction Juan should go. "Walk heel-to-toe both ways, okay?"

Juan grunted in response and proceeded to walk away from them in a perfect straight line without a single wobble. Fred cheered.

"This guy must practice at home." Ricky talked out of the side of his mouth, but not quietly enough. Juan heard him and for the first time, he smiled as he walked back toward them.

"Now for the one-leg stand," Cash said.

Juan pulled one foot back, balancing on the other like he'd been practicing it as part of a performance. Again, Fred cheered.

"If I hadn't seen that nystagmus, I'd say he's as sober as a judge." Ricky picked up the breathalyzer and asked Juan to blow into it. "But sure enough, this thing says he's at point oh nine. Just one tenth of a percentage above the legal limit."

Juan grunted again.

"Wow, man." Cash lifted a fist for a fist bump and Juan flashed a second smile. "You almost had us fooled."

"I'll try something different for the next guys."

"My turn?" Fred popped up in front of Cash, almost like a jack in the box.

"Your turn," Ricky said. "Follow my finger. Don't move your head."

Fred's gaze followed Ricky's pointer finger without a single jerky movement. Ricky's glance this time said, *Can you believe this?!*

Just like Juan, he aced the walk and the one-leg stand.

"You're completely sober," Cash said to Fred, who giggled again.

"I know, right? I was trying to trick you guys. Did it work?"

"I'll admit, it worked." Cash offered a fist bump, which he returned with gusto. "You probably don't want to try that in a real DUI situation, though."

Juan laughed. "I won't, dude. Don't worry. This is just for fun."

"Looks like everyone is about done with their first victims." Mosley, who'd been walking around the room watching the testing, stood with his feet wide apart and surveyed the scene. "Let's do another round. Suspects, you stay where you are. All recruits, move over once, clockwise. No, not that way, Beard. The other clockwise."

Cash and Ricky took a few steps clockwise. The first thing Cash noticed about the new suspects was the pair of shoes one of them was wearing: sandals. *Oh, no.* His caveman brain took over, causing his gaze to roam from those sandals—and the perfectly painted shell-colored toenails—up the toned legs and to the curved waist and the full, gorgeous breasts encased in a loose tank top with a low-cut v-neck. Next, the smooth skin of a chest and neck, and luscious, kissable lips.

And then a pair of almost-iridescent light blue eyes.

That's when Cash realized he was looking at the unforgettable, beautiful, mesmerizing face of Opal Houston.

Those heart-shaped lips curved into a smile and those sparkling eyes glinted with something devilish. "Well, hello, Cash Wilder."

Oh, my stars.

Not only was Opal back in town, but she was right here in this very room with Cash. And she was prettier than ever. So pretty, his breath caught and he found himself speechless. Only after what must have been at least thirty seconds did Ricky elbow him. "Wilder. Get a grip, man."

Opal offered her hand to Ricky and introduced herself, and Cash could swear his speech was a little slower than usual when he told her his name.

"This is my sister, Pearl." She tilted her head toward Pearl, who looked like Opal's opposite except for those eyes. She, too, extended her hand for a shake.

"Pleased to meet you," Ricky said, elbowing Cash, who finally gathered his wits and said, "Yes, pleased to meet you," while pumping her hand like one of them had just won the lottery. He'd won some kind of lottery but wasn't sure if it was a good one or not. He vaguely remembered reading a story in high school where the "winner" of a lottery was stoned to death.

Apparently sensing that Cash was incapacitated, Ricky turned to Pearl. "Would you like to go first?"

"Sure." Her response was carefree and casual, and Cash wondered how that was possible. Did she have no idea how his consciousness was reacting to Opal right now?

Ricky started firing questions at Pearl, and Cash watched. Eyes on her sister too, Opal said to Cash, "It's been a while."

"It has." He chanced another look at her and when their eyes met, he felt something light up inside him, hot and intense.

"Seems to me, the last time I saw you was at high school graduation when you started playing music in the middle of the ceremony. What was it? 'Born to Run' by Bruce Springsteen?"

He barely registered the words she spoke. Her voice was like honey or velvet or the smoothest bourbon or maybe a combination of all three and he was drunk on it. *Maybe somebody should do the standardized field test on* me.

"Cash?"

"Sorry." Somewhere in his consciousness he registered that he was scratching the back of his head. The sounds and sights of the conference room had faded away and everything was Opal Houston. "Callie mentioned you might be moving back. And here you are."

"Might be." Something like regret or pain passed over her features, but she settled her expression and then smiled. "You're not as skinny as I remember you being."

"Is that a compliment?" He hoped it was.

"It is." The smile hadn't left her face and he knew then and there he'd do anything to see it again and again.

"Well, thank you."

Next to him, Ricky cleared his throat. Cash's head whipped around. Ricky, too, was smiling, an "I-caught-you" smile Cash would have punched right off his face if they were related. Cheeks quite suddenly burning, Cash said, "All done?"

"All done here." Ricky clapped him on the shoulder. "Want to examine the other Ms. Houston now?"

Boy, do I. His gaze made an involuntary trip down her body and he stopped it firmly on her feet before he let it roam back upwards. Just like her calves, her ankles were so *kissable.* Was he actually getting an erection right this very minute, in a room full of other future police officers and a bunch of strangers?

Cash could kick himself. He should not be thinking about anyone this way, least of all Opal Houston, and especially not right now. He imagined what his brother, Travis, the levelheaded one, would say: *Get your head on straight, man.*

For the next seven solid minutes, he focused on performing the standardized field test exactly as he'd learned. For the next seven solid minutes, he pretended he didn't notice the soft curve of Opal's throat, the sweet vanilla scent of her skin, or the rosy pink in her cheeks. Even though the field test showed she was drunk—just over the legal limit—he pretended he didn't notice that, either. Because if she'd paid him a compliment, he'd prefer to think she'd done so while she had all her wits about her.

Which was ridiculous.

Chapter Two

Opal Houston (technically, she was still Opal Getty, but she'd be ditching her married name soon) might be just the other side of tipsy, but she knew a good-looking man when she saw one. And Cash Wilder had grown up into just that. *Although,* she thought, as she followed his instructions for standing on one leg, *"good looking" didn't quite do him justice.*

She balanced on one leg, her ankle slightly wobbly, while she thought of synonyms for good-looking.

Hot.

Devilishly handsome.

Beautiful.

God-like.

Gorgeous.

Foxy.

Exquisite.

Super-duper attractive.

Giggling at that last one, she lost her balance. Cash Wilder, stunning man and scoundrel, caught her by the elbow. Their eyes locked again and she had the sudden urge to grab onto him, spill her guts, beg him to comfort her.

Which was stupid. Asinine. Foolish. Ill-advised.

She wrenched her arm free and teetered again, and although his eyes crinkled at the corners when he put both hands on her shoulders to steady her, she also saw concern there.

"I'd say you're quite intoxicated, Ms. Houston." His voice was a drawl, and somehow his smile erased the tension that had crept in while she was supposed to be having a little fun with her sister.

"I'd say so." She could only hope her smile was as cute and disarming as his.

If only she'd known Cash was going to be there, she would have insisted she and Pearl do something else. Then she wouldn't be locked into this stare-down with him.

Fortunately, the mustached guy in charge chose that moment to holler, "Okay, kids. That's time! Suspects, thank you for your time today. You've performed an important service for our recruits by giving them invaluable real-life experience in Standardized Field Testing. Recruits, well done. Take ten and I'll see you back in the classroom at fourteen hundred hours."

"Bye, Officer Gonzaga." Pearl batted her eyelashes and Opal grabbed her hand to drag her out. "Aren't you going to say good-bye to Cash, Opal?"

Her face almost certainly on fire, Opal suppressed a groan, gritted her teeth, and said, "Good-bye, Cash."

Before they'd even made it out of the police academy's conference room, Pearl was whisper-yelling, "Wow, he sure grew up handsome, didn't he?" and Opal was looking for a fire extinguisher to spray on her own face.

"Geez, Pearl, you're not even drunk."

"But *you* are, and you told Cash Wilder he's not as skinny as you remember. Which, my darling sister, is akin to saying you like his muscles. You were *flirting* with him."

Finally through the foyer, Opal inhaled as the automatic doors slid open and she and Pearl stepped into the fresh—albeit too-warm —air outside.

"Will you stop it?"

Pearl laughed, carefree, and Opal had a sudden vision of Cash punching his brother Sterling in the face in junior high because Sterling had laughed (much in the same way Pearl was laughing now) when Cash dropped his lunch tray on the cafeteria floor. Opal remembered being scandalized. Girls rarely punched each other. Now she knew, though, thanks to Pearl's two kids, Wyatt and Will, that boys roughhoused all the time.

"Why, does Mr. Wilder have your panties in a bunch?"

Heat waves rose off the parking lot pavement and Opal lengthened her stride as they walked toward the sidewalk. "I wish I could punch you in the face, Pearl."

"No you don't." Pearl, with her long legs, caught up easily and linked her arm through Opal's just as they turned onto Pleasant Street, which was shady thanks to the trees that lined it. "You love me."

Suddenly so grateful for Pearl her throat ached—especially in the wake of her separation from Boone—Opal rested her head on her sister's shoulder. The image of the bright green leaves shimmered before her. God, her moods were shifting every which way today. "I do love you. And I'm a little pissed that you embarrassed me like that in front of a guy I haven't seen in a decade and a half."

"It's all in good fun. You're not the only one who needs to relax, you know." They'd come to the end of the first block and they both stopped to watch for traffic.

Opal rolled her eyes, glad Pearl couldn't see her. What could possibly be causing stress for Perfect Pearl? Perfect Pearl with the perfect husband, perfect children, and perfect house? She wasn't the one going through a divorce from a man who was trying to leave her with absolutely nothing. Not that the conversation was worth having. The coast was clear and the two of them, still arm in arm, stepped off the sidewalk to cross the street.

"I'm sorry," Opal said, squeezing Pearl's arm. "I was just caught off guard by how..."

"Hot?"

"Yes. I was caught off guard by how hot Cash Wilder is, now. And I was embarrassed that you pointed it out."

She glanced up to see Pearl wrinkle her nose and giggle. "He *is* hot. And honestly, you should be thanking me for opening that door for you."

"Pearl! I don't want or need that door opened right now. I'm not even divorced yet."

"But you and Boone have been emotionally divorced for, like, ever. I thought you might be ready to move on if the opportunity presented itself. And it did, so." She shrugged. "Anyway, weren't you and Cash two peas in a pod back in school?"

They stepped back onto the sidewalk just in time for a kid to come whizzing by on roller skates. Pearl stepped expertly aside, pushing Opal out of the way and shouting, "Leonard Acosta, your mom is going to kill you if you don't go home and put on a helmet."

A few seconds later, Leonard whizzed by in the other direction. "Sorry, Mrs. Marshall."

"It's okay, sweetheart." Her voice was syrupy sweet. "No mother wants to see a child crack his head open."

He waved a scrawny arm, made a hard right turn, and by the time they'd reached his driveway, he was heading back to the sidewalk, buckling his helmet under his chin.

"Good boy, Leonard. I'll be sure to tell your mom I saw you wearing your helmet. But don't let me catch you without it again."

Opal watched the whole exchange with interest. "When did you become so *motherly?*"

Pearl laughed. "Oh, I don't know. Couldn't quite put a date on it. It just happened naturally once I got to know all the neighborhood kids."

They'd reached Pearl's driveway and as always, Opal admired her adorable Craftsman-style bungalow with its tidy yard and white picket fence. Inside, the floors shone and the air conditioning blasted. Opal shivered as the cool air dried the sheen of sweat that had accumulated while they walked.

"So?" Pearl got down two glasses and poured iced tea from a pitcher she took out of the fridge.

Accepting one of the glasses, Opal said, "So, what?" even though she knew what Pearl was getting at.

Sure enough, her sister rolled her eyes. "You and Cash. Weren't you guys practically best friends back in school?"

"I wouldn't say we were best friends." She sipped the iced tea. "This is good."

"What would you say you were, then?"

Opal sipped again. "Our relationship was situational. We were both at the top of our class. At first, that meant we worked together on all the extra assignments our teachers dreamed up for us. Later on, it made us the ultimate competitors. Looking back on it, I think we both had demons, you know?"

Pearl nodded.

"Cash's mom left when he was a little kid. I think at first, he hoped that if he was perfect in school, she'd come back. He used to make comments about it. He'd say she was coming for the awards presentation or the spelling bee or the science fair. Later, when he realized that wasn't going to work, he had a devil-may-care attitude and did whatever he wanted. Not that that reduced his competitive spirit at all."

"And yours?"

Opal laughed. "You know. Our parents were—"

"Insane?"

"Yeah." She smiled at Pearl over the top of her glass. "Insane. They were so worried about us succeeding that they wanted us to do *everything*. I was convinced that if I did enough, I'd *be* enough. I was starving for achievement. If only I could be the best, do the most, surely Mom and Dad would be proud of me. Preferably Mom and Dad, but barring that, maybe a teacher or a principal or a college. You know?"

"Oh, I do. How do you think that worked out for you?"

"Although I feel like that question is a bit mean-spirited, I'll humor you with an answer."

Sliding onto a barstool and crossing her legs, Pearl said, "Thanks. If we didn't have to pick up the boys in a half-hour, I'd say we should put a couple of shots of vodka in these iced teas and follow this conversation wherever that takes us."

Opal slid onto the barstool next to Pearl's and waved her off. "Another time, then. You and I can have a sleepover at my place and Leslie can watch them."

"Maybe."

"What do you mean, 'maybe'?"

Pearl's gaze darted off to one side.

"Don't be all shifty-eyed with me." Indignant, Opal sat up straight. "He's their dad."

"You're right. We'll plan a sleepover. It will be fine."

Pearl changed the subject—quite skillfully—and rushed off to start a load of laundry and change the sheets on the bed in the guest bedroom. Then it was time to go get the boys, and for the entire drive, Pearl chattered away about how she hoped Wyatt had gone one! Single! Day! without getting into a fistfight on the playground.

"The principal, Kathy—we're on a first-name basis now, believe me—would have called, I'm sure, but you just never know. Maybe they've taken pity on me and they're holding him in the principal's office because I've had to come get him early so many times."

As soon as they pulled into the pickup line though, Opal spotted her nephew, his distinct auburn hair glowing in the afternoon sunlight. She pointed at him. "Looks perfectly happy to me."

Pearl exhaled. "What a relief. And where has Will gotten to? He's probably on the playground. No matter how many times I tell him to wait with his brother, he does his own thing." Hysteria edged Pearl's voice.

Opal put a hand on her arm. "I'll get them."

"No, no, you don't have to. Parents aren't supposed to get out of the car."

"I'm not a parent, I'm an aunt."

"Still—"

Opal didn't hear what she said next because she was already out of the car, shutting the door, and jogging over to where Wyatt stood along the curb. Someone with authority—the woman had a stop sign in one hand—raised her free hand. "Um, excuse me, ma'am. Parents are required to stay in the car during pickup."

Flashing the woman her most brilliant smile, Opal said, "It's okay, I'm not a parent. I'm an aunt."

Upon hearing her voice, Wyatt turned toward her. "Aunt Opal!" And then he was running toward her, his gangly arms and legs looking so much longer than they had when she'd seen him just a couple of months before. He leaped at her like he was still a toddler and she caught him, arms around his waist, and spun him while his laughter rang in her ear like the most magical music. Actual tears smarted in her eyes.

"I missed you, buddy." She set him down and he grinned up at her. "And it looks like you're missing a tooth."

"Sure am. Hector Hendrickson knocked it out last week."

Her eyes widened and before she could consciously school her expression back to neutral, he gave her a gentle punch on the arm. "Don't worry, Aunt Opal. It was a baby tooth. The dentist said it's no big deal. Just came out a little earlier than it originally planned."

"Huh. Well, that's good."

He shrugged. "Yeah, but the tooth fairy was mad."

"How do you know?"

"She took my tooth and left a note under my pillow. Said she wasn't leaving me money because I lost my tooth fighting."

He looked so forlorn, and Opal struggled to keep from smiling. "Let's hope you lose the next one naturally, then."

"Yeah."

"Come on, let's go find your brother. Take me to the playground."

As Pearl predicted, Will was on the playground. He was climbing up a ladder on the side of a dome-shaped structure, happily oblivious to the fact that his mom was bordering on a breakdown in the car.

"Will!" Wyatt sounded stern and more like a parent than a brother. Which made Opal think he'd had to track down his brother on more than one occasion. Will, the younger of the two, continued climbing. Just as Opal's blood was starting to boil (she pictured Pearl's closed-off expression when they'd talked about Leslie watching the boys overnight, and her voice cracking with near hysteria in the car), Wyatt hollered, "Aunt Opal's here."

He turned around, clinging to the rungs, and smiled as if he'd just woken up Christmas morning and every gift tag bore his name. "Aunt Opal!"

He leaped off the structure and just as his brother had a few minutes before, charged Opal and jumped into her arms. He smelled so good—of sunshine and dirt and little boy—and she squeezed him tighter before telling him he was a stinky little boy, setting him down, and grabbing his hand.

"I'm taking you straight to your mother because she's waiting for you. Aren't you supposed to be waiting with Wyatt at the curb?"

Will's eyes went wide and he glanced at Wyatt before hooking his pointer finger into his lower lip—a habit he'd developed as a toddler. Despite the fact her blood had heated up only seconds ago, his sad expression softened her and she squeezed his hand. "Don't worry. You're not in trouble. I was just giving you a friendly reminder."

Then he smiled again and reminded her so much of Cash Wilder, she was transported back in time. The three of them returned to Pearl's car and she helped the boys load their backpacks into the trunk (not that they needed help, but an aunt got to spoil her nephews, didn't she?). Then, while Wyatt and Will told Pearl about their days, fighting for air time, Opal found herself reliving some of those elementary-school days.

Because she and Cash both excelled in school, they were placed together for everything. As kids, the boy-girl dynamic didn't cause any discomfort. They worked together practicing more advanced spelling words, reading more advanced books, and completing more advanced math worksheets. It only made sense for them to sit next to each other.

Opal and Pearl never wanted for any of the material things. Their parents' hay operation provided for all the food and plush furniture and name-brand clothing the girls could want. But it also kept their parents busy and exhausted and emotionally unavailable.

Not that Opal could put that into words as a little girl, but she did realize she always felt a gnawing sense of loneliness.

So whenever she arrived at school in the morning and Cash greeted her with that smile, dimples and everything, she suddenly felt like she belonged. Like someone really saw her. He always noticed when she got new shoes or a new backpack, and often offered to share the best parts of his lunch with her.

At some point, their paths seemed to diverge.

Opal, certain that her perfect test scores, perfect grades, and perfect attendance would impress her parents sometime, immersed herself in every single activity she could. If academics wouldn't do it, maybe sports would.

Before she realized what was happening, she was applying for Ivy League universities and getting in and becoming a corporate lawyer and marrying the handsomest man in all of New York. She'd been so focused on checking off the boxes that she didn't realize she and Boone Getty should never have gotten together, much less married.

And again, before she realized what was happening, he was demanding a divorce and had hired the most prominent divorce attorney in the state with plans of taking all their assets for himself. It was only thanks to Callie Barrett, a friend from her hometown, that she had enough to her name to buy a piece of property and fund a fresh start.

"Aunt Opal?"

Wyatt's voice came from the backseat and she turned around to face him. "What?"

"Did you hear me?"

"No, I'm sorry. I was daydreaming. Off in lala land." She glanced out the window to see that they'd already turned onto Pleasant Street and would be back at Pearl's house in a couple of minutes.

"I said your phone's ringing."

"Oh!" Only then did she hear it and when she saw her real state agent's name on the screen, she snatched it up and answered.

"Good news." Lucy Marino sounded excited—a change from her typical, professional demeanor.

"What?" Opal's heart started racing.

"The sellers accepted your offer on that ranch property."

Pearl grabbed Opal's wrist and squeezed.

"They did?"

"They did!" Lucy actually squealed and Opal joined in. She could hear her nephews asking what was going on, but she couldn't answer right away—her throat was clogged with emotion.

She was moving back home.

Chapter Three

One month later

Suffering from a post-event hangover, a gritty-eyed Cash surveyed the scene before him. The Sweet Springs Ranch still had it in terms of being an excellent party spot, he'd give it that. Travis and his fiancée Lila had gotten married in Las Vegas the week before, and they'd thrown a huge reception just last night.

June, Sterling's wife, had organized the event to perfection, and now she commandeered the cleanup like an actual drill sergeant.

"Cash! Why don't you go ahead and start taking down the string lights?"

His head pounded and he figured he probably had an actual hangover in addition to an energetic one. The night before, during the reception, Hayes suggested everyone take a drink whenever someone said "awesome." Cash shook his head, remembering the sudden spate of *awesomes* they all infused into the conversation.

I'm going to be an awesome dad. Goosebumps rose on Cash's skin when he remembered Hayes's announcement. Hayes and Callie were having a baby. Cash's throat constricted. His brother, a dad. *Me, an uncle.* Some of his friends who'd had the honor of becoming uncles called it the funnest job in the world. "You get to do all the fun stuff with the kid, and then hand him back over to his parents."

In the midst of the cheers and congratulations and delighted laughter, Cash was already picturing all the fun things he would do with his little niece or nephew. Fishing, horseback riding, getting ice cream. He wondered how old the kid had to be before he or she could sit in a saddle.

He'd retrieved the ladder and set it up next to one of the posts the string lights hung from. He climbed up and unfastened the end of the wire, then climbed down and moved the ladder near the trunk of the giant cottonwood tree.

"Need a hand?" Callie looked up at him, hands on her hips.

Quite unexpectedly, Cash felt that lump in his throat again, and even the prickle of tears forming. "You're going to be such a good mom, Cal."

If his own rush of emotion had surprised him, hers surprised him even more.

"Thank you, Cash." An actual onslaught of tears—far more than the prickle he'd just experienced—rolled down her cheeks. Laughing, she swiped them away. "I still can't believe it. We waited so long to tell everyone, and now that we have, it's even more exciting!"

"You know that kid is going to be the most spoiled kid this side of the Mississippi, right?"

She laughed again. Nodded. "Yep. And I love that."

"And to answer your question, no thank you. I can get these lights by myself. Shouldn't you be resting or something?"

She waved him off. "Oh, go on, now. I'm growing a baby. I'm not an incapable nitwit."

Cash shrugged and climbed the ladder again. As he freed the wire from the branch, Callie took the end of the string lights and began coiling the strand. "You excited about graduation?"

An involuntary sigh escaped as Cash climbed back down to the ground. "I'm nervous."

He'd never admit as much to his brothers, but Callie was like a sister to him, and sisters had a gentler way of being.

"What are you nervous about?"

He moved the ladder again, and she followed, carrying the loop of string lights. "Oh, you know. I don't have to tell you how I've been drifting for a few years. This is pretty much the first thing that's felt important to me in as long as I can remember. I really want it to go well."

"Oh, Cash." When he set down the ladder she grabbed his arm and squeezed. "You're going to be great."

Something about the confidence with which she spoke made him believe her, and he felt another onslaught of emotions. *Geez, man. Get a grip.* "Thanks, Cal."

They finished up the lights, and he took the coil from her. From across the yard, June hollered, "You can hang those in the garage, Cash. You'll see the hooks."

He saluted her. Laughing, Callie went off in search of another task and Cash headed for the garage.

Thirty-two days had passed since Cash and his fellow recruits practiced their Standardized Field Testing at the police academy. He told himself he knew that only because Commander Mosley kept a countdown on the whiteboard in the classroom. But the truth was, he knew that because for some reason his stupid brain was keeping track of how much time had passed since he'd seen Opal Houston.

He stepped inside the garage and waited for his eyes to adjust, then found the hooks on the far wall. It was amazing how much had changed since June landed at Sweet Springs Ranch.

It wasn't all due to her. Sterling had come back at the same time to help with the fundraiser to save the place from foreclosure, and it was as if that event had completely changed the energy at Sweet Springs. Under June's direction, the garage had been cleaned out and organized, the big house was almost restored to its former glory, and somehow, the family was back together again. It had changed the energy inside of Cash, too—had made him want to make something of himself, of his life.

Now, just thirty days remained until his police academy graduation. Then he'd spend three months with a Field Training Officer. Then he'd be an actual cop. The thought at once excited and terrified him. He hung the string lights on the hook and went to find everyone else.

The sound of tires skidding in the driveway made him pick up his pace. Lila had moved from Alabama to Arizona to escape a stalker, and even though police had arrested someone just weeks before, it was entirely possible another one existed. He heard a vehicle, one with a loud engine, heading away from the house, and increased his pace. He couldn't let them get away. A cloud of dust obscured his view of the driveway, and a rush of adrenaline obscured his view of everything else.

Somehow he managed a quick headcount and realized everyone was present, gathered in a group next to the big house. *Lila's safe.* But then tunnel vision took over as he watched a giant moving truck turn on to the road, trundle several yards to the north, and then turn into the property next door.

Infuriated beyond reason—a little voice in the back of his mind was telling him he really should slow down and find out what was going on, but he ignored it—he followed the truck, striding to the road and then north. Meanwhile he got hotter and hotter under the collar, in more ways than one. The walk was taking longer than he expected. He was starting to sweat.

The truck's engine cut, the driver's door slammed, and the back door creaked as it rolled open. Metal slammed as the driver pulled out the ramp. In hindsight, Cash would realize that if someone was opening up the truck, he or she was not an intruder and had some sort of actual mission here.

But in that moment, he continued striding, arms pumping as he reached the driveway and turned into it. Music started blaring. Hard rock. As if all the dust and tire noise wasn't enough, now this imbecile was playing hard rock on a Sunday morning. His head pounded in time with his steps and the beat of the music. His face felt hot. Sweat trickled down his back. He literally saw red.

He rounded the corner and spotted the truck, its ramp down. And then he saw someone backing down the ramp, maneuvering a dolly with a couple of boxes on it. The legs that belonged to that someone looked familiar. Startlingly so. He hadn't seen those legs in thirty-two days. Well, not in person, anyway.

He'd imagined them plenty of times.

Opal Houston rolled the dolly down the ramp, then turned to roll it around the truck. She was wearing denim shorts and a light blue tank top and he couldn't help but imagine touching her skin.

Somewhere in the haze of his memory, Cash remembered her saying she might be moving back to Prescott. He also clearly remembered the pain he'd seen in her expression when she said so. Now, though, she looked relaxed, at peace. *And so, so beautiful.* His body taking over since his brain was almost incoherent, Cash's movement ceased and he watched her, just for a few seconds.

Her music was so loud, Cash was positive she hadn't heard him approach, and sure enough, she jumped when she finally saw him. That, too, infuriated him. How could she be safe in this world if she wasn't aware of her surroundings?

"Cash!" She put a hand on her chest, which moved up and down as she caught her breath.

"Opal Houston, you're a damned fool! You're lucky it was just me coming up your driveway. What if it was someone else?" It was like some stress goblin had taken over. His arms waved, his body canted forward, his face contorted.

And Opal, that ethereal, frustrating woman, just smiled. She looked at her watch, tapped its face, and the music went silent.

"What are you saying?"

Cash could scream. But his words came out even, measured, hyper-controlled. "I said, Opal Houston, you're a damned fool! You're lucky it was just me coming up your driveway. What if it was someone else?"

A smile, slow and seductive (was it supposed to be seductive, or did that just happen naturally?), spread across her face. "Are you worried about me, Cash Wilder?"

Cash could scream. Again. "I *wasn't*! I was coming over here to see who tore into our driveway in a cloud of dust and then came over here and started blasting horrible music. And when I got here and saw that it was you, and you had no idea I was here because you're blasting your horrible music at a completely ridiculous volume, I thought you should know that someone could sneak up on you."

How could she look *amused*? Her lips twitched and he couldn't help but think how kissable they looked and he wanted to kick himself.

"I guess it's a good thing you're here, then."

Cash dropped his forehead into his hand. "Woman. You almost gave me a heart attack. Twice."

Mouth pressed into a line to stifle a laugh, she smiled with her eyes. "You're absolutely right. And I'm sorry about the dust and the noise. I was distracted and pulled into the Sweet Springs driveway by accident."

Quite suddenly, Cash deflated. The anger and righteousness dissolved, giving way to humiliation. A furious blush rushed up his neck and onto his face and again he wished he could kick himself.

"It's fine. I may have overreacted."

Her lips twitched again. "You may have."

Desperate to salvage the situation—and his pride—he took a deep breath, did a mental reset, and finally slowed down enough to properly check out the scene. The back of the moving truck was absolutely stuffed to the brim. Boxes and boxes were stacked floor to ceiling, and he could make out a couch, a dining table, and a bookshelf.

"Looks like you could use a hand."

If his sudden one-eighty in attitude surprised her, she didn't show it. "I could, but I also wasn't expecting one. A second dolly and set of muscles—uh, *hands*—would definitely speed things up, though."

Did she mention my muscles?

He'd forgotten he was wearing a tank top. A flame of satisfaction flared to life in his core. Acting entirely of its own accord, Cash's body marched itself down Opal's driveway, along the main road, and up the Sweet Springs Ranch driveway. He strode right past his brothers and the girls (and his unborn niece or nephew, he thought with a quirk of his lips), and retrieved the dolly from the garage. On autopilot, he made the reverse trip, silently repeating

What are you doing? in time with the sounds of his hurried steps on the gravel. The memory of how he'd treated her during high school crossed his mind, but he dismissed it for now. Could bygones be bygones?

Opal had turned down the music and Cash felt like he should comment on that, thank her, but decided not to. He'd already made such a fool of himself. The last thing he needed was to come across like a crotchety old man. *Who cares how you come across?*

Maybe I do.

As he approached the back of the truck, Opal held out a glass bottle which Cash immediately recognized as the lemonade of his childhood. He and his brothers would ride their bikes down to the market on weekends and buy them.

"Thanks." The bottle was already sweating, and Cash wasted no time twisting off the lid. "I love that sound."

Opal twisted off her lid and smiled as it popped. "Me, too."

They both drank, and Cash simultaneously enjoyed the sweet-tart flavor of the cold drink and Opal's profile as she tipped her head back to reveal her throat. He didn't realize he was staring until she grinned at him and said, "Got a staring problem, Wilder?"

Caught.

As had become habit, he offered her a flirtatious reply. "Stargazing's my hobby."

Her laugh was like a symphony. He'd pay hundreds of dollars and stand in line for hours to hear it again. "Now I can see why I've heard you've got a way with the ladies."

While he contemplated what she'd heard exactly, and from whom, she put the lid back on her lemonade and set the bottle at the base of an old oak tree. And so what if he admired the length of her legs, from her waist down to her ankles, while she did? He followed her back to the truck and gestured for her to go up the ramp ahead of him. She grabbed a dolly and he hopped into the back to help her load it. "Want me to wheel it down the ramp?"

She shook her head. "Thanks, but I've got it. I've become pretty self-reliant."

There it was again. The same expression he'd noticed thirty-two days ago at the Standardized Field Testing. Regret? Pain? Just like she had then, she quickly schooled her features to neutral.

She wheeled her load down the ramp and to the front door, which already stood open. Meanwhile, Cash pulled his empty dolly up the ramp and stacked four boxes on it. He nearly collided with Opal as she came out of the house and she stepped back to let him in.

"Where should I put these?"

She threw up her hands. "Somewhere. Anywhere. Doesn't matter."

Holding the dolly with one hand, he leaned forward to examine the sides of the boxes. "These aren't labeled."

She winced. "I know. I think that was my fatal mistake."

He got the sense Opal's packing hadn't been a time of great anticipation. No, she'd probably done it in a hurry, throwing items into boxes and taping them shut as fast as she could. "I don't think it's going to prove fatal. In fact, it could be fun. Kind of like Cracker Jacks. Remember those? Every box had a prize, but you never knew what you were going to get."

Although she rolled her eyes, he could see traces of a smile. "I love your perspective."

He inclined his head. "I'll be here all day."

He'd only been joking, but she rushed to say, "No! I don't expect that at all. I'm just so grateful you offered to help me unload."

Suddenly feeling playful, Cash leaned against the dolly, his elbow propped on the handle. "Actually, this could get interesting. If I help you unpack, I won't know whether I'm going to get a box of dishes, or a box of lacy underwear."

She snorted. "Fortunately, you don't have to help me unpack. My sister and my nephews are coming over in a little while. And—" she raised an eyebrow, provocative— "I don't own any dishes."

Cash told himself he should not, under any circumstances, be imagining Opal's lacy underwear. Or her in them. And he absolutely should not be getting aroused at the visions he conjured up.

Then she was breezing by him, leaving him in a cloud of feminine scent (he picked up something vanilla, and something soft, almost like baby powder), and he glanced upward, offering thanks for the fact that they were no longer sharing the same space.

He wheeled his dolly through the entryway and into the living room, over to where Opal had stacked her set of boxes. For the first time since realizing she was moving in next door to the Sweet Springs Ranch, he had a moment to wonder why. The Opal he'd known was a chronic overachiever. Several years back, when he heard she was getting hitched, he figured she'd be an excellent wife. She'd excel at marriage just like she did everything else.

Which begged the question, what went wrong? Why was she back in Prescott, alone in this big, empty house? Shifting the dolly out from under the stack of boxes, he headed for the front door.

"We have to stop meeting like this." Her smile told him she didn't really mind. He stepped back to let her in; this time, she was the one with the big load—but she stopped in the doorway and propped her elbow up on the dolly. "I was surprised to see you at that field testing event the other day."

This wasn't the first time he'd heard the words, or something similar. He felt himself turning prickly, a porcupine with its quills flexed. "No?"

She smiled, and then she laughed, and this time the sound was like sunlight bouncing off a million crystals. "Don't get prickly with me, Cash Wilder. I didn't mean it as a criticism. In fact, I'm proud of you."

That made his heart do a one-eighty. She was proud of him? The tension eased out of his shoulders. "Thanks. And sorry. It's just that so many people act surprised when they find out I'm going to the police academy."

"It's not because they think you can't do it, you know." She moved toward him, chucked him lightly on the chin, enveloping him in her scent again. "It's because they only know the mischievous side of you. The side that got everybody's attention when you were a teenager. You know how it is. You can go along your whole life being almost perfect, and nobody says a thing. But the second you do something different, step over the line even with the tip of your toe, everybody has something to say."

Almost like she'd experienced the same phenomenon.

"But I know the real you, and I know you're going to be a great cop."

He didn't know why his eyes smarted at that. But they did, and he had to fight the urge to literally sprint out of Opal Houston's house. Instead, he found himself wrapping his hand around hers.

Something odd happened in that moment. While they stood there, holding onto each other's hands, gazing into each other's eyes, Cash felt a bone-deep connection. Not a casual, flirtatious connection, like he did with many of the women he met at the bars, but something that reached down into his very soul. The sound of an old-fashioned car horn blared, making them both jump, and putting an end to that confounding moment.

"Sorry." She dropped his hand and pulled her phone out of her back pocket. She glanced at the screen and then at him. "It's my sister. I've got to take it."

While she talked, he returned to the truck with his empty dolly and brought in another load.

Opal ended the call and put the phone back in her pocket. "My sister should be here soon. Expect a tornado of energy."

"From your sister?"

Opal shook her head. The bemused smile she gave him told him she was more entertained than annoyed. "No. From my nephews."

"As you know, I'm quite familiar with energy tornadoes. If we hurry, maybe we can get everything unloaded before they come, and you can put some of that energy to use unpacking all these boxes."

Chapter Four

Opal had approximately forty-seven seconds to contemplate what had just happened between her and Cash. Not that she could form a coherent thought. Words and phrases buzzed around inside her brain like the ball in a pinball machine. *He's grown up nice. I wonder if he single. He is so off-limits. God, he is so good-looking. Dangerous. Risky. Divorce. Failure.*

The sound of tires crunching on gravel saved her. She was already smiling when she reached the door and her nephews came barreling up the walkway, flinging their arms around her before taking off to explore the property. An exasperated but laughing Pearl made it to the door a few seconds later. "I swear, they run everywhere they go."

"That's what little boys do. Come on in."

Pearl gasped the second she stepped through the door. "Oh my gosh, Opal! It's beautiful. You're going to love it here!"

Her sister's words brought a rush of relief. Her shoulders sagged and she let out a sigh. "Thank you. I didn't realize until this very moment how much your approval meant to me."

Pearl wrinkled her nose. "My approval? Why? You've never needed my approval for anything."

Opal held up a finger. "Always fearless and self-reliant. That's me. And look where it got me. Seems like I should have asked for your approval more often."

"Oh, Opal. You might have hit a few snags in the road, but really, look where it got you. Back home with this beautiful house, set up for a while. And, you're still young and hot, so now you can get my help finding your next husband."

Opal's nostrils flared, her eyes shot her sister a death glare, and Pearl threw her head back and laughed. "Too soon? Okay, too soon."

She let her gaze roam around the main living area, taking in the kitchen, dining room, and living room. "This is gorgeous. I can't wait for the full tour. And also, how did you get those boxes unloaded so fast?"

Opal's own gaze rested on the boxes—she didn't dare look at Pearl. "Cash came over and helped me."

Of course, her sister didn't miss a thing. "Cash *Wilder?*"

Opal felt the heat creeping up her neck and tried to stop it. Could a person stop herself from blushing? No. No, she couldn't. "Yeah. You know, his family lives next door. He heard the moving truck come in, came over to say hi, and offered to help. He said we should get everything unloaded so we could have the boys help us unpack."

She finally risked a glance at Pearl, who arched one eyebrow. "Now tell me. Was he as good-looking today as he was a month ago?"

Dammit. The blood in her cheeks got even hotter. "You know, I don't think I'm going to say."

A hooting laugh escaped from Pearl's mouth. It sounded like it came all the way from her toes. "Okay then." She hollered for the boys, who came running, and she commandeered them to start unpacking boxes.

"But these aren't even labeled." Wyatt's forehead crinkled in a way so like Pearl's, Opal had to laugh.

"I know they're not. But think of it like Cracker Jacks. There's a surprise in every box."

The two boys looked at each other, obviously perplexed, and

Opal figured they'd always think of her as the crazy aunt. "Tell you what. Let's open a few of the boxes until we find some you can unpack all in one place."

She handed each boy a pair of scissors, and she and Pearl used box cutters. Every time someone opened a box, they called out, "towels" or "sheets" or "books." Within a few minutes, she'd moved several boxes over near the linen closet and several into the kitchen. She set the boys to work on the towels, sheets, and blankets while she and Pearl went into the kitchen.

"I told Cash I didn't have any dishes." She hefted a giant box onto the counter.

Eyes squinted in confusion, Pearl pointed at the box and said, "But that entire box is packed with dishes."

This time, it was Opal who laughed out loud. "I know."

She relayed how that conversation had played out, and Pearl shook her head. "That poor man. You know that right now, at this very minute, he's picturing you in your lacy underwear."

"I hope so."

Two hours later, the four of them had unpacked all the boxes, and the pizza delivery guy knocked on the door. They gathered around Opal's dining room table—one of the only items Boone had allowed her to take—and Opal divvied up the pizza.

"Can you imagine if Dad was here?" Wyatt, his mouth full, grinned devilishly.

Pearl's eyes widened, and she gave just the tiniest shake of her head. Opal noticed, but apparently Wyatt didn't, because he plowed on. "He'd be so mad."

Will giggled, but it came out as more of a strangled sound than anything else. He tilted his head forward and growled at them from under angry eyebrows. "This place is a mess! You'd better get this cleaned up right now, Pearl."

Pearl tried for a laugh, and she might have been able to pass it off if Opal hadn't grown up watching her every move.

"Your dad doesn't like a messy house, huh?"

"Hates it." Wyatt swallowed his food and wiped his mouth with his hand. Opal handed him a napkin.

"I think he hates *us*." Will's chin wobbled. Pearl set down her slice and reached across the table to put a hand on Will's. "Hey, now. He loves you guys. It's just that his work—"

Wyatt waved a hand. "Is very stressful. We know. And when he comes home, he wants a nice, clean house."

"He doesn't even talk to us anymore." Will's lower lip jutted out. "He comes home, screams at us, and then goes into his den."

Who even has a den anymore? Opal looked at Pearl, who shrugged.

"And then, when we go to bed, he screams at Mom."

Pearl's eyes widened and Wyatt added, "You guys think we can't hear, because it's whisper-screaming, but we can."

Opal couldn't believe what she was hearing. No matter how hard a guy worked, his kids should know he loved them. And besides that, Pearl was and always had been a tidy person. If the house wasn't completely spotless, it was pretty damned close.

Pearl looked mortified. Her cheeks were drawn in, making her cheekbones stand out. It was an expression she'd worn as a child whenever she was embarrassed. Opal remembered one dinner where their dad had realized Pearl had a failing grade in math. She sat there, cheeks sucked in, unable to eat or speak because she was so mortified.

Opal imagined wrapping her hands around Leslie's neck. She'd always sensed he was a very particular guy. In fact, he'd wear only a certain brand of silk boxers, if she remembered correctly. But it sounded like he went beyond particular. It sounded like he was a real asshole.

"Fortunately, your dad isn't coming over here for dinner."

Although the days were getting shorter, when the boys asked if they could go out and explore, Pearl agreed.

"Let's go outside too, so we can keep an eye on them." Opal hefted a dining room chair and motioned for Pearl to do the same. "We can set these up on the back porch for now, but I just realized what my first purchase is going to be."

"A porch swing?"

"A porch swing. And a pitcher set with glasses. So we can make iced tea, swing, and watch the boys play."

Pearl lifted a second chair and followed Opal to the back door. "Having you as the second parent sounds like a dream."

Opal didn't respond right away. She focused on setting up her chair where she'd have a maximized view of the yard. "Look. They've already found a tree to climb."

"Perfect. They'll sleep well tonight."

Once they'd both settled in, Opal decided to say what had been on her mind since they ate pizza. "Is everything okay between you and Leslie?"

Her "Of course" was knee-jerk and high-pitched—and inauthentic.

"Really?"

Pearl didn't answer, and in the quiet that stretched between them, taut as a tightrope, Opal listened to the sounds of the crickets chirping and the wind rustling through the tall grass in the backyard. She could press her sister, throw some more questions at her, but that never worked with Pearl. With Pearl, you had to wait. So that's exactly what Opal did.

For a moment, she was able to forget about the horrible chain of events that led to her being here. For a moment, she was able to focus on the way the golden sunlight bathed the property, illuminating sparkling dust motes and making the place look magical. She was able to imagine—for the first time in forever—her own children running amok, yelling and laughing and jumping.

Was all that possible?

As late as that very morning, Opal felt like everything she wanted was out of reach. She felt like she'd had the one chance and completely botched it. Her marriage to Boone should have been perfect. God knew she'd tried. But despite her best efforts—and they were gargantuan, weren't they?—she hadn't been able to make it work. It was a one-in-a-million chance and everybody knew those didn't come along very often.

She found herself smiling at that. Only for a second, until images from the last few months of her marriage started parading through her mind. Waiting in the dark when Leslie came home late, and his shocked look when he saw her. Running through related vocabulary words: *surprise, astonishment, stupor.* Cringing as he slung horrible insults at her, his own collection of vocabulary words: *boring, lifeless, dull, nothing.*

But now, in this perfect golden moment, she thought maybe she could start over ... in fact, maybe starting over was just what she needed.

"No. Everything is not okay between me and Leslie."

I knew it. Gloating also didn't work with Pearl, so Opal simply nodded. "What's been going on?"

"I don't know. He's just—different. It's like he's turned into a different person. Not a nice one."

Something like panic took hold of Opal, and her throat constricted. "He doesn't hurt you or the boys, does he?"

"No, no, no." Pearl swallowed. "He wouldn't. Not physically, anyway. But lately, he's just been making all these digs, you know? Comments. To me, to the boys. *About* me to the boys. It's almost as if he doesn't *like* us anymore."

Opal's heart ached. How anyone could not like a spouse—well, that was complicated. But how anyone could not like their own children? And children as adorable and witty and lovable as Wyatt and Will? "That doesn't make a damned lick of sense."

"I know." Pearl sighed. "It's bizarre. Like the boys were saying, he complains if the house isn't spotless. But it's not just complaining. It becomes personal criticism, you know?"

"I can only imagine." Opal waited a beat. "You guys didn't have a fight or anything?"

"No. I mean, nothing big. There are the odd comments about why I haven't washed his underwear or taken his suits to the dry cleaners, but no big blow ups or anything." Pearl made a dismissive gesture. "Listen to me, talking about my problems when you're fresh off an ugly divorce. What you went through is so much worse than what I'm going through."

"It was explosive, that's for sure." Opal wanted to cry, remembering the screaming matches and the slammed doors and the secrets she'd discovered him hiding. "But that doesn't mean you can't confide in me. To tell you the truth, it's nice to think about something other than my own problems."

"Then let's think about Cash Wilder."

Opal smirked. "If you didn't have to drive home soon, I'd say we should open a bottle of wine and talk about Cash Wilder."

"Next time, I'm coming over on a weekend and we're having a sleepover."

"Deal."

They shook on it and Pearl stood, stretching her arms above her head. "But unfortunately, this is a school night and I need to get those rowdy boys home and to bed. I'm actually glad Leslie's not coming home tonight." She slapped a hand over her mouth. "That's awful to say. But honestly, these days, it's so much nicer when he's not around. And I haven't been able to say that out loud."

Opal stood too and opened her arms for a hug. "You can say whatever you want to me. Whenever you want."

"I know."

They stood there, hugging, for several long seconds, until the boys clambered out of the tree and flew across the yard. Opal could see the apprehension in their expressions as they approached. Little boys were often in tune with their mothers' emotions, and Opal wondered just how much hurt Wyatt and Will had observed in Pearl recently.

"Get in here!" She motioned for them to turn the embrace into a group hug, and they both grinned in relief before plowing into the women.

After thanking them profusely for helping her unpack, she helped Pearl herd the boys to the car and waved at them until they were out of sight. Feeling a bit melancholy and quite lonely, she returned to her chair on the back porch, hoping she could recreate that feeling from a few minutes before, the feeling of possibility ...

The sun had sunk even lower in the sky, and the light was fading to a purplish gray. The crickets had quieted and the smell of wet earth and decaying leaves rose from the cooling ground.

On one hand, Opal couldn't believe she was back in Prescott. Back in the small town she and Boone had yearned to leave.

Had she really wanted to leave?

She thought she had, and for a while when they lived in their big-city apartment on the twentieth floor of a swanky, modern building, she'd felt perfectly at home. But had she?

A bird—the evening light made it hard to tell what kind—flew across the yard and landed in the tree the boys had just climbed.

How many times had she told herself to think positive or make the best of things or that things would feel better when ...

Countless times.

She felt so stupid. The signs were there and she missed them. Boone had never loved her. And maybe she'd never loved him.

The sound of footsteps coming around the house surprised her, pulled her out of her deep thought. She sighed, not expecting or wanting company. But this was a small town, and she'd have to get reacquainted with the way people came and went.

When Cash walked around the side of the house, wine bottle in hand and hair still damp from the shower, her heart did a little stutter step.

"Hey." She stood up to greet him, but then suddenly wished she'd remained seated because she didn't know quite what to do with herself. Should she hug him? Should she shake his hand? Should she tear off his clothes and have her way with him?

Fortunately, he removed the guesswork and thrust the bottle at her. "Here. I brought you a housewarming gift."

She took it, hugged it close to her body. "Thank you. Pearl and I were just saying how nice it would be to sit on a porch swing and enjoy a bottle of wine. Only, she had to drive home and I don't have a porch swing." With one hand, she gestured at the dining chairs behind her.

"A porch swing is nice. We used to have one. I spent a ton of time on that thing."

"I can't picture you ever sitting still long enough."

He shrugged and she was surprised when he didn't smile. "It was kind of my mom's thing. She'd sit out there with us, one at a time. Talk to us about the day, the horses, the cows, aliens, whatever."

"That's a sweet memory."

"It is." His eyes looked sad, and she wanted to reach out to him. "Well, I'll leave you to it. Looked like you were lost in thought. I didn't mean to interrupt."

He'd started to walk away.

"Actually, Cash?"

He turned, eyebrows raised.

"Will you stay? Have a glass with me?" She held up the bottle, an offering.

Then he smiled. "Sure."

"Come on in."

He followed her in and even though they'd known each other since childhood, she didn't know how to share the space with him. Somehow, he put her at ease, propping a hip on her counter and taking the bottle from her again. "I wasn't sure if you'd have an opener unpacked yet, so I brought one."

When she opened the cabinet to find glasses, he laughed, a single short bark. "You said you didn't have dishes. Were you just messing with me, Opal Houston?"

Something about his use of her maiden name—as if she'd never been Mrs. Getty—seemed so *right*. It erased those years with Boone and all the hurt of the past couple of months.

"I was." She shrugged. "Just being funny, that's all."

"But do you have lacy underwear?" She could see he immediately questioned whether he should have asked her that. But he didn't apologize. He just waited her out.

She took the bottle back, then poured two glasses, all without looking at him. Finally, she made eye contact. "Wouldn't you like to know?"

Was she smiling a coy smile? She was. And he was smiling right back at her. She handed him a glass and he gestured for her to lead the way back out to the porch.

"How much longer 'til you graduate?"

"A month."

"How are you feeling about it?"

He sighed. "Excited. Nervous. Like I hope I don't screw it up."

"You won't. I mean, you probably will—everybody screws up—but I'm fairly confident you won't screw up anything major."

"Thanks. Hey, cheers to new beginnings."

"Cheers."

They tapped their glasses together, sipped their wine. Opal felt a release in her chest, a deep relaxation setting in.

"How is your sister doing?" Cash wanted to know.

"Overall, she's doing fine. She's a great mom. I know we talked about her two boys. Wyatt and Will. As much as it pained me to come back home, tail between my legs, it's worth it if I know I get to see them more."

Cash nodded. "Those two are hellions, aren't they?"

At her look, he held up his hands. "I meant it as a compliment! Goodness knows, I was a hellion in my time. Pearl's boys, they're adorable hellions. But I've seen them ... in the grocery store sneaking candy out of the bulk bins, at the barber shop, taking two lollipops instead of one."

Opal gasped. "Does my sister know that?"

Cash dropped his head into his free hand. "I never should've said anything. It's not like they're torturing animals. Little boys are entitled to some fun, aren't they?"

Opal sipped her wine. "A little *fun*, yes. But a little thievery? I don't think so."

"Don't tell her. I couldn't stand being a snitch. I was telling you because I thought it was funny."

He looked so solemn, she decided to keep her nephews' mischief to herself—for the time being. "Fine. But if you ever see them doing it again, you have to stop them. Make them pay for the candy. Or put back the extra lollipop."

Eyes twinkling, he said, "Deal." After a few beats of silence during which Opal watched the sky go from lavender to dusky blue, Cash said, "You said Pearl is doing *fine* overall. But you said it like the word was coated in straight vinegar. What did you mean?"

She should have known he would pick up on that. She shook her head. "Oh, nothing major. It just seems like the Houston girls might not be cut out for marital bliss."

He raised his eyebrows. "Trouble in paradise? I always thought Pearl and Leslie seemed like such a great couple. Based on outward appearances, anyway."

"Exactly. He's as handsome as she is pretty."

"I'm not sure about that."

Opal considered. Leslie was handsome, if a bit snake-like. "I guess that's subjective. Anyway. While we were eating dinner, the boys made some comments about how particular their dad is about the house being clean. And how he whisper-yells at her after they go to bed. When they went out to play, Pearl elaborated. It's not just a clean house. He sounds like a real jerk."

Cash winced. "That sucks."

"I know. Pearl is the nicest person I know. And honestly, her house is spick-and-span. It would probably pass a white-glove test. If I was forced to choose one person whose toilet I was willing to drink out of, it would probably be hers."

"Well. I never would have imagined those words coming out of your mouth."

Opal smiled. "Okay, Leslie being mean to my sister brings out another side. But you get the idea."

"Yeah. I do. And that's too bad. Seems like he's out of town a lot, right?"

"Right. For his job."

Another span of silence stretched between them. Finally, Cash spoke. "You know, it's really too bad. I know my mom had her own reasons for leaving, but I never got the sense that my dad tried very hard to get her to stay. I always told myself that if I was lucky enough to have a woman fall in love with me, I would do everything in my power to hold onto her. If Leslie can't do that, I guarantee he's going to feel like a damned fool."

Opal nodded, a rush of emotions making speech impossible. It wasn't just the words Cash used. It was the fact that he managed to sum up so succinctly exactly what Opal had been thinking. Suddenly, she felt way too close to Cash Wilder. "I hate to say this, but I guess we'd better call it a night. I have an early morning. I'm sure you do, too."

Cash stood. "I do. Should I rinse my wine glass?"

Opal took it from him. "It's okay. I'll do it. Thank you for the wine. Maybe we can finish the bottle another night."

"Yes. Let's do that."

They stood there looking at each other for a moment too long and then he seemed to snap out of a daze. "Right. I'll let myself out. Have a good night, Opal."

She watched him go, checking out his butt in his jeans until he reached the front door and turned around to offer her one more smile.

That night before she fell asleep, she savored the words that danced through her mind, each of them an adjective describing Cash Wilder: *charming, pleasant, captivating, spellbinding, intriguing.*

Chapter Five

The night after sharing a glass of wine with Opal, Cash found himself at A Cold One, raising a pint with his brothers.

"To Travis, as he enters his last days of regular nights at the bar!" Cash lifted his glass and the others followed suit. After they'd all taken drinks, Cash settled back into the corner of the booth. Since enrolling at the police academy, he'd made what his brothers called a surprising transformation. No longer was he out on the dance floor, mixing and mingling with the ladies. No, these days, he was an observer.

During week one at the Academy, Commander Mosley had stood at the front of the classroom, his fist on his hips, his feet planted wide. "Now tell me, ladies and gentlemen. What is the most important skill you will need in your job as a law enforcement officer?"

Silence.

"Tell me, ladies and gentlemen. When I ask a question, what do I expect?"

Sarah Vasquez, another recruit for the Prescott Police Department, answered in a meek voice (which they'd all learn was not her regular voice, by any means). "Answers, sir? You expect answers?"

He put a finger on his nose, then returned his fist to his waist and gave a single nod. "You bet your ass I expect answers. Now, I'm not going to act like you guys are a bunch of little kids and tell you there's no such thing as a stupid answer. Because there is. So give me answers, and make sure they aren't stupid." His gaze moved from one side of the room to the other, coming to rest on each recruit before moving on. He cleared his throat. "So. Tell me. What is the most important skill you will need in your job as a law enforcement officer?"

"Quick thinking?" someone ventured.

Commander Mosley gave another curt nod, produced a dry erase marker from somewhere, and wrote *Quick thinking* on the whiteboard. "What else?"

"Problem-solving?"

He wrote it on the board. "Any other ideas?"

"Being level-headed?"

He wrote that down, too. "Keep them coming."

A few more people called out answers, and Mosley wrote them down. After, "Running fast," at which some people snickered, Mosley rotated around, a potato-shaped ballerina in a music box, and said, "Well, congratulations. Almost none of those were stupid answers. And still, no one got the *right* answer."

He stared at them, waiting, as if he could somehow convey that right answer from his brain to theirs. After a long span of silence, he finally said, "It's observation." He rotated again and wrote the word in on its own row in all caps. With a flourish, he put the lid back on the marker and set it on the tray at the bottom of the whiteboard. He rotated again. "Ladies and gentlemen, all of these skills are important. But observation is the tool that sharpens each and every one of them. The more you observe, the more information you catalog away. The more quickly you can think and act and make decisions. It might not do much for your running speed." Here, he looked pointedly at the recruit who'd suggested fast running was a vital skill. "So I encourage you, starting now, to watch. In your daily life, in all your encounters, watch. Notice. How people behave. What they say. What they don't say. How they act. *When* they act." He paused. "Now is the time to begin."

And so, several weeks later, Cash sat in the booth at A Cold One and observed. He noticed the way Travis hadn't stopped smiling since he'd announced he and Callie were having a baby. He noticed the way some of the girls in the bar let their eyes roam over the guys, almost like they were fishing, pausing when their gaze hooked someone else's. That made him feel infinitely less special when it came to the attention he often received there.

"Where'd you go?" Sterling wanted to know.

"Just thinking about the police academy." Not that he couldn't share his thoughts with his brother, but the bar, with its loud music, loud conversation, and party atmosphere, was hardly the place.

Sterling smiled. "Almost done, right?"

Cash smiled, too, even as a swarm of bees took up residence in his stomach. "Yep."

"Is that why you've barely touched your beer or moved out of your spot? Didn't you see the group of ladies come in?"

"I saw them." *And I saw what a fool I've been making of myself.*

Sterling's attention fixed on the door. "Now *there's* a group of women."

As June, Callie, and Lila came in, Cash observed how each of his brothers perked up. Each of their smiles grew a little wider. He observed a tugging in his own chest. And then, he observed Opal walking in, too.

"I didn't know they were coming here," Sterling said. "June told me they were planning on something a little more high-end."

Nevertheless, it was obvious none of the couples wanted to spend too much time apart. Within a few seconds, the girls were at their table. Travis and Hayes slid toward Sterling and Cash to make room at the end of the booth, but June held up her hand. "We're not coming to intrude on guys' night. We just thought we'd come, have a drink, maybe play some darts."

They turned to go and Cash found his own gaze involuntarily finding Opal. She was already looking at him, and when she smiled, he observed another, different kind of tugging at his heart.

Once the girls were out of earshot, Hayes said, "Hmm."

Cash looked at Hayes, but found all three of his brothers were looking at him. "What?"

"Oh, nothing." Hayes looked at the bar and then back at Cash. "Only that I saw that little moment between you and Opal."

"What moment?" Cash pulled the bar napkin out from under his glass, crumpled it up, and threw it at Hayes. "There was no moment."

The rest of them rushed to agree: "No, not at all." "Who said there was a moment?" "He doesn't know what he's talking about."

"I call it a moment if it makes your cheeks rosy."

Cash observed his own broodiness when he said, "My cheeks are not pink."

And then, just like the jerks they were, his brothers were laughing, slapping their knees, wiping their fake tears, mimicking him.

He suddenly wished he hadn't chosen the corner spot.

"There's no escaping, is there?" Travis's voice was gleeful.

Cash shook his head.

"I heard you had a glass of wine with her last night. Just one glass."

Cash didn't bother wondering where Sterling had gotten that tidbit. Nothing was sacred in this family. "You guys want to play game of pool?"

"We can't." Hayes could barely contain his laughter. "Tables are full."

"Which means—" Sterling grinned, maniacal—"you're stuck here with us."

Sure enough, all the pool tables were in use. And, apparently, so were all the regular tables, because the girls returned and asked if they could set their drinks on the guys' table while they played a round of darts. Cash did his best, but he absolutely couldn't help observing the way Opal's jeans hugged her curves and the way he could see just the tiniest bit of her creamy skin above the waistband.

And then the girls were gone, and again, all three of his brothers were looking at him. He looked at each of them, said, "What?" and while he took a drink of his beer, they all responded, cool as cucumbers, "Nothing."

Because his brothers were watching his every move, Cash forced himself to look around the bar, even though all he wanted to do was watch Opal. It just so happened his gaze was on the door when Leslie Marshall walked in. He scanned the room, and Cash wondered—uncharitably—whether he was scanning for good-looking women, or just getting the lay of the land.

A Cold One wasn't exactly Leslie's style. From what Cash had heard, Pearl's husband preferred swanky spots with velvet seat coverings, not sports bars with beer posters tacked to the walls. Leslie didn't pay Cash any extra attention, but his upper lip curved into a sneer when he saw Opal.

I guess there's no love lost between them.

For her part, Opal seemed blissfully unaware of her brother-in-law's presence. She cheered as Callie scored twenty more points on her next throw. While June and Lila took their turn, Opal and Callie returned to the guys' table to sip at their drinks.

"Who's winning?" Hayes wanted to know.

Callie smirked. "You think we're keeping score?"

Hayes shook his head. "I *know* you're keeping score."

Opal winked at Cash. That shouldn't have made him heady with lust, but it did. Callie leaned closer, conspiratorial. "We're winning. But don't tell June and Lila."

She and Opal high-fived.

Opal finished off her beer. "Anyone else ready for another round?"

Sterling and Travis lifted their empties.

"I've got this round," Cash said, even though his beer was still half full. Let me out, fellas."

After a shuffling of bodies, Cash was out of the booth, walking side-by-side with Opal toward the bar.

Leslie Marshall was already there, elbows on the shiny wooden bar, one ankle crossed over the other. Cash had the urge to spill his beer on Leslie's expensive pants, but he wouldn't. He couldn't, now.

That kind of behavior might not get him kicked out of the police academy, but it would definitely put a blight on his record.

Opal veered off to one side, her desire to avoid her brother-in-law comical. Cash followed her and positioned himself between them. Even with a few stools' distance between himself and Leslie, Cash could hear the guy's booming voice loud and clear when he asked Jerry, A Cold One's owner, for a Brew Dog IPA.

Jerry, who'd been instrumental in the fundraiser that had saved Sweet Springs Ranch, wrinkled his nose and said, "No, I'm sorry, man. We don't have that. Here's what we've got on tap."

He ran a hand along the tap handles—all of them denoting what Jerry referred to as classic American brands—and Cash turned to watch Leslie's reaction. He sneered and literally turned up his nose before announcing to his friends, "This is why I don't usually frequent places like this. All they serve is crap. I'll take a Jack and Coke. I guess."

Jerry shot Cash a look, grabbed a tumbler, and scooped in some ice. With none of his usual flourish, he dumped some Jack into the tumbler before grabbing the soda hose and topping it off with Coke. He slid it across the counter while wearing the unfriendliest expression Cash had ever seen on him. "Want to open a tab?"

"Nah, I'm a one and done here."

God, how Cash wished he could punch that guy right in the mouth.

Jerry came over to his spot next. "What can I get you, Wilder?"

Cash inclined his head toward Opal. "Ladies first."

"Cash Wilder, you are sweet as pie," she said, infusing her voice with an extra dose of Southern charm. Then, she leaned closer to him. Jerry raised his eyebrows and Cash looked away quickly, not wanting to share in the acknowledgement that he and Opal Houston were standing here, at the bar, together.

She ordered a beer for herself and one each for June and Lila, and then a Shirley Temple for Callie. "So she can still have something fancy," she stage whispered to Cash.

Cash ordered beers for his brothers, longing to chug the rest of his first one and order a second for himself but knowing he'd regret it. Jerry arranged all the drinks on a tray and Cash carried it back to the table.

This time, his brothers scooted toward the corner, which left him sitting at the end of the booth—with an escape route and a perfect view of the women playing darts. He also had a view of Leslie Marshall hunched in a corner with his friends. The whole group of them watched a game of pool, obviously waiting for a turn. After a few shots, Leslie meandered closer to the pool table, his dark eyebrows drawn down and the corners of his mouth drawn upward, like a villain in a cartoon.

As the pool game came to a close—only the eight ball remained —Leslie lurked closer and closer, so the guys playing started to notice and shrink away from his presence. Cash was tempted to shrink away from his presence (or walk right up to him and escort him off the property), and he was several strides away.

Finally, the game ended and the players handed over their pool cues. Leslie, a satisfied smirk on his face, laid his cue across the table and racked the balls while his goons watched. Of course, he went first.

Chapter Six

How her sister had managed to marry the absolute worst (most dastardly) man in Prescott, Arizona, Opal didn't know. Pearl wasn't *actually* perfect, but on the scale of terrible to fabulous, she definitely fell pretty darned near the fabulous end.

Although Opal spent most of her energy on the darts game with Callie, June, and Lila, Leslie occupied the rest of her attention. He oozed slimy charisma, smiling a sleazy smile at the girls with the lowest-cut tops. He also oozed an icky, condescending vibe, rolling his eyes if his billiards partner made a bad shot and giving the other pool players dirty looks if they celebrated or booed.

The straw that broke the camel's back? When Leslie, in all his glory, did something that reminded Opal of her ex-husband, the one and only Boone Getty. He was preparing to shoot, leaned over the table, one arm extended onto the felt and the other crooked, holding the cue. An unsuspecting, oblivious bar goer—some poor sap in his twenties, Opal would guess—walked behind Leslie at the exact moment he drew back his arm to shoot.

Leslie's elbow collided with the other guy's arm. That arm happened to be attached to a hand holding a very full beer. So full, in fact, that the foam was actually running over the glass's edge and down the hand. When the elbow and arm collided, the beer spilled. It splashed over Leslie's entire back half—from his shoulders to his shoes.

Leslie whirled around, fury contorting his face and coloring it purple. He looked exactly like some horrifying creature out of a children's fairy tale and out of nowhere, Opal's brain superimposed Boone's face onto Leslie's. Her stomach roiled with the sick feeling her stomach used to get when he'd go into a rage. The beer-holding guy dropped the glass and held up both hands, apologizing, and Leslie dropped his pool cue and cocked his arm as if preparing to punch the guy. One of his friends grabbed him by the elbow before he could swing, and he flung him off.

Opal decided she'd had enough. Her anger propelled her out of the bar and into the parking lot. If she'd been thinking clearly, she would have grabbed a pool cue, but as it was, she could hardly hear her own inner voice. Some other entity had taken over and before she realized what she was doing, she was standing next to Leslie's ugly car, her leg pulled back, her chest heaving, her face hot.

You can't kick his car.

It was his prized possession and kicking it would be so satisfying. She felt her lips curving into a smile at the thought.

But it would hurt, probably. And also, the process of getting any damage repaired would undoubtedly affect Pearl. She'd have to chauffeur his ass around like the king he imagined he was.

No, she wouldn't kick it.

A thought occurred to her. She could disable it somehow. Yes, make it undrivable for the evening. (Was undrivable a word? Inoperative. Unworkable. Out of order.) A significant inconvenience, but without damage he'd have to get repaired. Enough of a nuisance to let him know someone was watching him.

An imaginary lightbulb illuminated above her head. *Ding.*

"I'll flatten your tires, you pathetic excuse for a man."

She glanced behind her to make sure no one had come out of A Cold One, and when the coast was clear she moved around to the other side of the car. Working as quickly as her fingers would let her, she unscrewed both valve stem caps. Then she used her new house key to press down on the valve stem core. *Hiss.* The air blew out, foul-smelling, and Opal turned her head. The hissing was so loud, she knew she wouldn't be able to hear anyone leaving the bar or walking across the parking lot.

The tire didn't look like it was deflating—not even a little.

Her sense of time was distorted. Had she been out here for three minutes or thirty? It didn't matter. Flattening his tires would be worth it. Certainly the girls would notice her absence, though. She'd said she had to use the restroom, but if she took too long, someone would go in there to check on her.

Her fingers ached from pressing down so hard on the key. After what felt like an eternity, the tire walls began to bulge out. "Yes!" Now that the deflation was visible, it seemed to be happening faster. If she could hold on for just a few more seconds, the rim would be resting on the ground. Then she'd run back into the bar and act as if she'd come out of the bathroom. Maybe. But she'd have to come back out. Deflating just one tire was no good. She had to do them all. What other excuse could she make for returning to the parking lot?

Easy. She could fake a stomachache. If she told the girls she was having stomach issues and made a certain face, eyes slightly rounded to imply, *You know what I mean,* they'd assume she had diarrhea. She could live with that.

Less than five minutes later she'd said good-bye to everyone and was back beside Leslie's car, kneeling next to the rear passenger tire. After a few seconds, she sat back on her heels, still pressing down on the key, and recited all the words she'd use to describe Leslie.

Douchebag.

Contemptible.

Rotten.

Vile.

Nefarious.

That exercise made the time pass more quickly, and the second rim was nearly touching the ground. Now for the tires on the other side. Still crouched in her position, she considered how she could stay out of sight. She never would have imagined shimmying under someone's car would seem thrilling, but in that moment, it did.

Doing her best to act casual, nonchalant, she walked around to the other side of the car and removed the first valve stem cap, then paused to walk the length of the parking lot and back. A few seconds later she'd removed the final cap. After one more glance around the parking lot, she got down in push-up position and slid underneath Leslie's car. With a smooth dexterity that surprised her, she reached around the outside of the tire, found the valve stem, and pressed down on its core. Again, when the hissing sound of the air escaping the tire obliterated her sense of hearing, she panicked. All she could do was hope no one would notice her if they came out of the bar.

Just as the third rim settled down on the squished tire, Opal heard the bar's door scrape open, and then the sounds of footsteps and voices floated through the air. Her breath caught and she held it. She pulled in her arm and tucked it underneath her body. Her stomach churned and her heart raced.

Oh, no.

What if the group emerging now was Leslie's group? It was dark. If he didn't see her, chances were good he'd get in the car and run her over. Although, maybe not. His had cost almost as much as a mortgage—he'd bragged about it. Certainly it had low-tire-pressure indicators.

The voices and footsteps came closer, and Opal started seeing stars. Remembering she'd been holding her breath, she exhaled and took a gulp of air. When they were one or two cars over, the people stopped walking. Their shoes scuffed on the pavement as they stood and talked. Maybe she'd be safer, less visible, if she moved to the center of the car. As it was now, from the right angle someone could definitely see the whole left side of her body. As quietly as possible, she scooted over until she was fairly sure no one could see her unless they bent down.

How much longer could the conversation go on? She checked her watch. Seven minutes after ten p.m. God, why wouldn't these guys get in their cars and go away? Cash and his brothers would undoubtedly be coming out soon, too.

Just as she was considering calling it quits—leaving Leslie with one tire inflated—the group members started calling goodnight to each other. She held her breath again while she listened to them walking to their cars and prayed that Leslie wasn't among them.

Apparently he wasn't, because four engines started up and four sets of tires rolled out of the parking lot, leaving only silence.

Opal sucked in a few deep breaths, then managed to maneuver her body so she could reach the fourth and final valve stem. The hissing commenced, the tire deflated, and Opal scrambled out from under Leslie's car and jogged to her own, breathless.

She considered waiting for him to come out of A Cold One, so she could see his reaction. He was going to be so mad. A grin—probably a maniacal one—spread across her face and she wished she had the guts to sit there and catch it all on video. But Pearl could never know. And how often did Opal hand over her phone to share a video or photo or a funny social media post?

No, she'd have to store these memories in her mind and use her imagination to enjoy her revenge. As if the idea of revenge had conjured him, an image of her ex-husband flickered to life in her consciousness as she started her car and reversed out of her parking spot. In a way, getting revenge on her sister's husband felt like getting revenge on Boone Getty, the lying scumbag that he was.

She glanced in her rearview mirror just before she pulled out of the parking lot. Good. The coast was clear. A Cold One's door was shut and no one else was around. Giving Leslie the biggest mental middle finger, she turned right and headed toward home.

* * *

The next morning, Opal woke up with a self-satisfied smile on her face. Deflating Leslie's tires felt so good. Countless times before falling asleep, she'd watched imaginary film of him discovering the tires, cursing, stomping around like the man-child he was. Countless times, she'd smiled and congratulated herself. *A bully gets what he deserves.*

Armed with fresh-brewed coffee, she sat down at her dining table and opened her laptop. This was it: the first day of her new life. Six months ago, her marriage to Boone started falling apart.

Three months ago, she'd felt like happiness was unattainable, unavailable to her. She *had* it. She held it in her hands for just a short time. And she during that time, she recognized it, appreciated it.

That, perhaps, was the worst part of the divorce: she'd never once taken her happiness for granted.

She *had* taken Boone's supposed virtues for granted; she'd believed he was a kind, generous person. But she'd been wrong. And the shock of that was perhaps the most devastating blow of all. She'd never let someone fool her again.

Ruminating on Boone, on the failure of their marriage, wouldn't do. This was her new life. When Opal first saw the listing for her Prescott property, she gained immediate clarity. All the chaos of the past months fell away to reveal her future: there, on a sprawling, tree-dotted spread with a barn and stables and corrals already built, she could start the animal rescue she'd always imagined. One day, hopefully soon, horses would fill the stables and dogs would run the acreage. This would be a haven for those who needed one.

She opened her email, looking for a response from the man she'd emailed about a couple of horses he was retiring from farm work. And there it was, received at six a.m.:

Hi Opal,

Yes, they're still available for rehoming. Roxy has a stiff left hind leg, but she handles it fine with medication. And Velma's fit as a fiddle ... as long as she's playing a slow song. You're welcome to come over and meet them any time. I'll be home this afternoon. Just call me ahead of time so I can meet you at the barn.

Jim

Tears sprang to Opal's eyes. Roxy and Velma could very well be the start of her rescue operation if they all got along well.

She rushed to write back:

Hi Jim,

Thank you for your speedy reply. I'd love to come meet the girls this afternoon. Would 2 p.m. work for you?

Opal

She closed the laptop and leapt to her feet, swinging her arms and head in a victory dance. "Roxy and Velma are going to love it here!"

Although she'd asked Jim about two p.m. because she hoped Pearl would go with her after the boys' morning soccer games, she decided surprising them would be more fun. So, after she watched the boys play soccer, she'd spend the rest of the day double checking to make sure the barn and corral were horse-ready, and then she'd go meet the girls.

Decision made, she went to her room to get dressed, pulling on jeans and a tank top. For just a moment when she stepped into her cowboy boots, she froze with panic. The leather was stiff, a reminder that she hadn't lived in this world in years. Was she still cut out for it? Was this really what she wanted?

She stood there in the middle of her new closet, eyes closed, waiting for the answers to come to her. Her spirit answered: *Yes.*

Sure enough, by the time she walked back into the kitchen to get breakfast, the boots had softened up and fit her feet exactly as they had before she moved across the country.

If the boots fit, wear 'em.

Fortified both emotionally and physically, she filled a water bottle and headed for the front door, only to stop short when she opened it. On the front porch sat a huge cardboard box, emblazoned with the words *Farmhouse Porch Swing: Assembly Required.*

One hand flew to her mouth. A porch swing. Exactly what she'd wanted. She should have known: of course Pearl would surprise her with a wonderful housewarming gift; she really was the most thoughtful sister. Opal couldn't wait to thank her.

The morning was sunny and bright, and dew sparkled on the soccer fields. Walking across the park to Wyatt's game on field six, Opal saw harried parents pulling wagons loaded with chairs and coolers and water bottles. All the members of one family had bright white hair, and the children followed the parents in a single file line like little ducklings. Opal's heart ached. She wanted that. Maybe not the wagon with a zillion things in it. But that exasperated-but-amused glance between the parents, the way one small girl, her long braid swishing back and forth over her jersey number, wrapped her little hand around her mom's pinky.

She sighed and decided to be grateful that, in this moment anyway, she was an aunt, commandeering only her coffee cup and her loudest cheering voice.

Her heartache turned to joy when she arrived at the edge of field six and Wyatt and Will ran up to her, arms pumping, faces alight with happiness to see her. Each one of them clung to a leg and she wrapped her free arm around both of them, kissing their heads. Then they were gone, running back to the center of the field where Wyatt's team stood in a circle, kicking the ball around.

Pearl was easy to spot. Hair in a messy topknot, brightly framed sunglasses covering most of her face, and a fluorescent pink umbrella to shade her from the sun, she sat in a camp chair near the field's halfway line. A second camp chair—empty—sat next to her. A twinge of guilt hit Opal then, and she cringed thinking her antics the night before might have made Leslie unable to attend Wyatt's game for some reason.

"I brought you a chair," Pearl patted the seat.

Relief washed over Opal. "Thank you! Is Leslie not coming?"

The sunglasses were so dark, Opal couldn't actually see Pearl's eyes roll, but she knew they did.

"No. He said he had something or the other to do. Got home late last night, left early this morning. I get so tired of hearing the details of all his excuses, I don't even ask anymore."

Opal offered her brightest smile. "Thank you for the porch swing, by the way. I can't wait to sit on it with you."

"What are you talking about?" Pearl's eyebrows furrowed.

Opal hooked a thumb over her shoulder, pointing toward home. "The porch swing that was delivered to my front door this morning."

Pearl shook her head, and her expression morphed from confused to excited. "It wasn't me. But I have my guess as to who it might've been."

"Callie? June? Lila? All three?"

Looking smug, Pearl sat back in her chair and crossed her free arm over her chest. "Nope, nope, and nope. I wasn't thinking of them."

Pearl's guess was starting to dawn on Opal. "No. It couldn't be."

"And why not?"

Opal spluttered for a second before Pearl interrupted her. "Game's starting. You might want to sit down. It's never a good idea to have your back to the field. You'll get a ball to the head."

Opal spun around and sat down. The soccer teams lined up.

"Why don't you call him?"

One of the kids on Wyatt's team kicked off, and the field became a hive of activity.

"Who?"

Pearl laughed out loud. "Cash."

Opal considered while Wyatt stole the ball from an opposing player, turned it around, and started dribbling toward the goal. She hollered for him. "Because."

"That's a great reason, Opal."

Opal sighed. "Because. What if it wasn't actually him? And then I call him, try to feel him out, get him to say something before I do, and it ends up being an awkward conversation because we have nothing else to talk about."

Wyatt passed to his teammate, who took a shot.

Pearl cheered. "You could invite him over to finish that bottle of wine."

Her sister's voice was so matter-of-fact, Opal's reluctance to call Cash suddenly seemed silly and childish. "I'll think about it."

The two of them watched for a few minutes as the kids dribbled the ball up and down the field.

"Wyatt's footwork has gotten really good."

"I know. Soccer is all he wants to do." Pearl shrugged. "He's constantly in the backyard, dribbling, doing drills, shooting goals."

"Impressive."

"I think he got his drive from you. Remember how hard you used to study?"

Opal smiled. "Of course I do. But it's a double-edged sword, isn't it? I studied, got good grades, aced my tests, got into a good college. And ended up divorced and on my own."

Pearl shrugged. "I think divorced and on your own might be better than married to Boone Getty. In fact, if you're willing to shift your perspective a bit, I'd say you ended up in a pretty sweet spot: the owner of a new, amazing property, living in the same town as your awesome sister and adorable nephews. Seems pretty good to me."

Opal nodded. "You might be surprised to hear that Cash said pretty much the same thing."

"I knew I liked that guy."

Pearl screamed for Wyatt, and Opal's attention snapped back to the field just in time to see him make a goal. She screamed for him too, and watched his teammates give him high-fives and pats on the back.

Maybe she would call Cash. But not right here, in front of her sister. Yes, she'd call him. After soccer. When she was alone.

Almost three hours, two soccer games, and a quick lunch later, Opal finally headed back toward her house, trying to work up the courage to make the call. Only, when she pulled into her driveway, she realized fate had taken the situation out of her hands.

Because Cash Wilder, clad in jeans and a tank top that showed off his rippling muscles, was on her front porch assembling the swing.

Chapter Seven

Cash heard Opal's car turn into the driveway and had to tell himself not to look up and wait for her to emerge and watch her every move. He didn't know what it was about her, but some invisible force seemed to draw him to her. Giving into that force just wouldn't do. At this point in his life—in his career—he required focus. Buying and assembling a porch swing was a friendly neighborly gesture and nothing more.

When he arrived that morning and found her car gone, he was relieved. If he didn't have to see her, talk to her, watch the sunlight dance on her skin, maybe he wouldn't be tempted to go beyond neighborly. Her car stopped, the engine turned off, and the door opened and closed.

And then she was beside him and manners dictated that he stop working and look up at her. He wished he hadn't. She wore leggings and a t-shirt that defied the laws of what was fair when a man was trying to be neighborly.

"So *you're* the mystery philanthropist."

He grinned. "Guilty."

"Thank you. I love it. I can't wait to sit in it."

"You're welcome. Should have it assembled in another forty-eight hours or so."

Her lips quirked and he knew right then he wanted to be the one to make her smile a million times.

"You don't have to assemble it. I can do that."

"I want to. You've got enough to do with moving in and unpacking. I didn't intend for this to be one more thing to add to your list."

"That's really sweet. Thank you."

"You're welcome." Because he had to, or he risked jumping up and taking her in his arms, he turned away from her and continued assembling, screwing the seat onto its frame. "Where were you off to so early this morning?"

"Soccer. I don't know how Pearl does it every week. It was exhausting, and I'm just the aunt. I didn't have to pack the wagon or anything."

"Did the boys win?"

"Wyatt's team won, but they don't keep score for Will's age group."

"That's stupid."

She laughed. "Pearl says at this age, they're just learning how to play. Winning isn't important."

He sat back again, shielded his eyes with a hand. "Winning's always important."

"That's what Wyatt said."

"Smart kid. Listen, this thing is almost done, but I forgot we'd have to buy the hardware to install it. My day is wide open, so I can run over to the hardware store to get the hooks and chain if you just decide where you want it."

She checked her watch. "That would be amazing. I have an appointment at two, so I'll make a quick decision." She must've seen the curiosity pass over his face because she said, "I'm going to look at some horses."

"To buy?" He stopped what he was doing and stood.

She nodded. "Yeah. They're retired working horses. When I found this spot"—she gestured with her arm—"I knew I'd want to do something with all this space."

For just a beat, her expression changed. He was fairly certain he detected pain there. Just as quickly as it had come, it was gone, replaced by resignation. "I guess I'm considering the place as sort of a haven. Retired horses, abandoned dogs, who knows what else?"

"Now you're speaking my language."

She wrinkled her nose. "You want animals? I thought you'd moved to an apartment."

Word traveled fast. And, she'd remembered what she heard. "I did. Well, a duplex." His nose wrinkled involuntarily. "But then Mr. Hendrickson was selling some horses and I bought them. Put them up with Travis's horses, Leia and Chewy."

"That's nice. Have you been riding?"

Just thinking about riding brought a certain sense of peace, and Cash's shoulders relaxed. "Yeah. Not as much as I'd like to, but I've definitely been spending some time in the saddle."

"Is it as fun as I'm thinking it's going to be?"

He felt himself smile—a genuine, honest-to-goodness smile born of pure joy. "It is."

She grinned back. "Hey, you want to go with me to see them? Shouldn't take too long. It's just up the street."

Cash told himself his excitement was the result of having an opportunity to check out some horses—not the result of Opal inviting him to spend time with her. He acted like he had to think about his answer and let a beat pass before he shrugged. "Sure."

"Great. Then help me decide where to hang the swing, and then we can go."

Ten minutes later, they were in her car heading north.

"How many horses are we looking at today?"

"Two. I thought that seemed like a good number."

"It's a good start. I assume you already checked the barn and fences?"

She nodded. "Everything is good to go. That's part of why I chose this property." They rode in silence for a few minutes, and Cash took in the familiar rolling hills of the ranch properties. For the first time since he moved off of Sweet Springs Ranch, he experienced regret. Something about being out in the open gave a guy the space to breathe, to think.

Opal slowed down and turned off the main road. "Here we are."

The owner of the place was already in the driveway and raised a bony hand to greet them.

Opal glanced across the cab at Cash. "I think you'd look pretty good in a pair of them overalls." Her over-exaggerated drawl made him laugh.

"I'd look like my dad is what I'd look like." The thought tasted bitter; his dad had nearly gambled away his childhood home and Cash still hadn't forgiven him, didn't know if he ever could. They got out of the car, met near the hood, and walked side by side up to the overall-clad farmer, who introduced himself as Jim.

Cash figured it wouldn't hurt, just this once, to let himself pretend he and Opal were together. That she'd asked him to come so they could decide, together, about the horses. That they would go home, together, and share a meal. It wasn't wrong to daydream, was it?

"You two looking for working horses? Because that's not what you're going to get with these ladies."

As lost as he'd been in his imagination, Cash hadn't quite realized he was following Opal and the farmer along the fence line until they came to a stop next to a couple of horses.

"Oh, no." Opal said. "This might sound silly, but I'm just looking for company."

The farmer's gaze slid over to Cash, judgmental, and then back to Opal. Cash wanted to tell him, *I'm great company!* but figured that would make things awkward.

"Well, they'll give you that." He stuck his arm through the fence rails and the buckskin horse rested her cheek against his palm. "This here's Roxy. Feed her a few treats—I'll show you which kind—and she'll be your best friend for life. Follow you everywhere. If you're not careful, she'll even check your pockets."

Opal was obviously delighted. Her grin—which, directed at Cash, felt like the warmth of the sun on a cool spring day—said, *Isn't this great?*

"This is Velma. She's not quite as outgoing, but once she warms up to you, you'll see she's always watching you. Sometimes from a distance, but she likes to know what's going on. The bay bobbed her head as if she were affirming Jim's description. "Can I answer any questions for you?"

Opal pulled a folded piece of paper from her back pocket and began reading questions. Cash took in the farmer's answers about the horses' ages, what he'd used them for, why he was retiring them, and what he fed them.

Mostly, his attention was on Opal. Even as she listened to the farmer, she moved closer to the horses. While he talked, she reached between the fence rails and let both mares sniff her hand. Then, one at a time, she stroked their cheeks, touched their muzzles, stroked their cheeks again. He could tell she was sold.

On the drive home, Opal was alight with excitement. "Those horses—both of them—were so sweet! I can't wait to bring them home! What did you think?"

Her asking his opinion made Cash feel alight with excitement. "They do seem really sweet. You might have a bit of a long haul medically with Roxy and that stiff hind leg. But if you don't mind having the vet come out, then they seem like a great fit."

She reached across the console and grabbed his arm. The contact made him shiver and he hoped she couldn't see the goosebumps rising on his skin. "Thank you so much for coming with me! That made it a hundred times more fun."

He covered her hand with his. "You're welcome. Anytime you need a second pair of eyes, I'm your guy."

She withdrew her hand and put it back on the steering wheel. Inwardly, he sighed a dreamy sigh, much like he imagined a cartoon character would when the woman of his dreams looked upon him. *Is Opal the woman of my dreams?* His phone ringing prevented him from exploring that thought any further, fortunately. Grateful for the distraction, he snatched up his phone and saw Callie's name on the screen.

When he picked up she said, "Hey, what are you doing?"

His gaze flicked involuntarily over to Opal. God only knew what Callie would say when he told her. She'd been hinting at Cash and Opal being an item, which was fine when Opal wasn't there, but now she sat less than two feet from him. He cleared his throat. "I just ran up the road with Opal to check out some horses."

To his surprise, Callie didn't say anything awkward. "Oh, she found some already? That's great news. How were they?"

Tucking away his own discomfort, Cash gave her the rundown.

"That's great," she said again, then, after a beat, said, "Listen. I'd like to say I just called to shoot the breeze, but I didn't."

"What's up?"

"I'm calling to ask a favor."

"What kind of favor?" This time, when he looked at Opal, she was trying not to smile.

"Just hear me out." Callie's loud inhale and exhale came through the earpiece as Opal turned into her driveway. "There's a fundraiser."

"Count me in. I'll donate. How much do you need?" Opal parked but left the car running.

"I love you for that, Cash. And thank you. I wish I was asking for a financial donation, but it's a little more complicated than that."

Uh-oh. "Lay it on me."

"It's a karaoke contest."

Cash's mouth dropped open. "A karaoke contest?" He turned to face Opal, whose eyebrows shot upward.

"It's a fundraiser. I should have said that first. You do it in teams."

"Teams? No problem. I'll be on your team. What do I have to do?"

"The thing is, it's teams of two. Hayes and I are going to be on a team, so you'll have your own team. Each team has to raise a certain amount of money. I was thinking, maybe you and Opal?"

He didn't dare look at Opal. What if she hated the idea of being on his team? And, karaoke? The last time he thought he was any good at singing, he was six years old, belting out "Jingle Bells" at a school Christmas concert. He closed his eyes. Maybe if he couldn't see Opal, she wouldn't know how mortified he was. Teeth gritted, he asked, "What is this fundraiser for?"

"It's for that women's shelter, the one over on the west side?"

In his head, Cash cursed. He had to say yes. The fundraiser was for a good cause. "I'll do it. You know I'm in. And you know how much I love winning." He glanced at Opal and gulped. "Not sure about Opal, though. If she gets these horses, she's going to have a lot going on."

"Thank you, thank you, thank you!" Callie sounded like she was on the verge of grateful tears. "I so appreciate it, Cash. And didn't you say you're with Opal? Why don't you ask her right now?"

Finally, he risked a glance across the car. Eyes shining with humor, she shrugged and nodded.

"I guess it's a yes."

Callie cheered and rattled off a bunch of details. After they disconnected, Cash looked at Opal again. His heartbeat pounded in his ears. "So, I guess we're partners."

Her expression gave nothing away. "Sounds fun to me. So, what's the deal?"

"Callie said she's going to email us the details. But the long and short of it is, it's a karaoke show and a fundraiser. For the next couple of months, each team will raise money, and then we'll put on a karaoke show, for which people will buy tickets."

Opal raised her eyebrows, grimaced. "I won't tell you I'm not nervous about singing karaoke in front of a bunch of our neighbors. But it does sound fun, and it's for a great cause."

An idea occurred to Cash, and before he chickened out, he decided to go for it. "I think tonight's the night we finish the bottle of wine and come up with a plan."

"Sounds great." And so what if Cash got a rush from knowing she hadn't drank the wine without him—or with anyone else?

With that, they both opened their doors and got out of the car. "You know what? I'd better run over to the hardware store now to get bolts and chain I need to hang that swing."

When he returned, Opal greeted him at the front door and led him to the kitchen, where their wine glasses from two nights before sat clean on a towel next to the sink, the mostly full bottle next to them. She turned the glasses upright, then filled them and handed one to Cash.

"I thought you might finish the bottle without me, and I'd braced myself for disappointment."

He almost couldn't believe he'd spoken that fear out loud, but Opal didn't seem to mind. "As nice as you were to buy it for me, I wanted to finish it with you."

The words made Cash feel like a little kid whose parents said "Yes" to cotton candy at the fair.

"Did Callie say she was going to email us right away?" Opal tilted her head toward the dining table where her laptop sat. "Come on, let's check."

They sat side by side at her dining room table, and again Cash let himself imagine this was their norm. She flipped open her computer, typed in her password, and waited for her email to load. He had to stop himself from commenting on how beautifully she'd grown up. She'd been pretty back then—especially in high school— but she was stunning now. Maybe it was the wisdom earned from walking a rocky path. Maybe it was the anticipation of a fresh start. Or maybe it was simply the confidence of adulthood. God, if only he wasn't starting a new career path. If only she wasn't fresh off a breakup. If only they could be more than friends.

"You look sad." Her voice pulled him out of his thoughts. Her gaze was piercing.

"I'm not. Just deep in thought."

"Yeah? What are you thinking about?"

"Just about the academy."

She'd always been able to read him, and he sensed she still could because disbelief passed over her expression before she blinked once, nodded, and said, "Okay. Anything you want to share?"

It was like she was giving him permission not to share his feelings. He took it. "Nah. I don't want to bore you with it. Thanks, though. Did you get the email from Callie?"

"I did. Here's what it says: 'Dear Singing for Hope contestant, thank you for your interest in raising money for the Hope Hall women's shelter. Since the shelter opened ten years ago, we've been able to help more than two hundred families, and that's thanks in large part to people like you. Below you'll find the schedule for this year's fundraiser, as well as general guidelines and answers to frequently asked questions. If you have additional questions or need any assistance whatsoever, please don't hesitate to reach out. This event is about raising money and is also about having fun and building community. Thank you again for your support. Sincerely, Tessa Winant, Founder, Hope Hall.'"

Opal stole a glance at Cash. "Sounds pretty simple. Here, let me scroll down." Her eyes widened. "Well. There's a photo shoot."

"Photo shoot?"

"And a video shoot. Meet and greets, dinners, a cocktail hour."

For a moment, Cash was flabbergasted. Speechless. He was supposed to be focusing on graduating from the academy and becoming a cop. Not schmoozing, wining, and dining. And *singing*. But then, his perspective shifted.

He was going to be spending so much time with Opal. Every one of the events she listed off was like a date. They had to go. Together. And, they had to practice their karaoke songs. Together. No, maybe he couldn't actually date Opal. But he could certainly make the most of the next couple of months. If he focused on raising money—not on how damned sexy Opal Houston was now—they might even be able to win.

Grinning, he rubbed his hands together as she looked from the computer screen to him. "This is going to be fun."

Chapter Eight

Opal woke up Sunday morning looking forward to the day more than she had looked forward to any day in a while. She allowed herself the luxury of staying in bed, stretching like a cat bathing in sun rays while replaying her evening with Cash.

After they both penciled in all the fundraiser events, they spent an hour discussing fundraising strategy. At one point while considering songs they might have to sing, they started reminiscing about the popular music from their high school days. They finished the bottle of wine while giggling about who they'd danced with at junior prom.

"You danced with Patsy Meadow." she pointed an accusing finger at him. He raised both hands. "Only because you were dancing with Randy Aker."

She wrinkled her nose. "Only because you waited too long to ask me."

He pointed at her again. "Only because you would have said no."

She stood up, then, faux-indignant. "You would have been more confident about me saying yes if you hadn't acted like a lunatic for most of high school." She'd wanted to say these words for years, and doing so felt amazing.

Cash gasped, his horror equally dramatic. "Well, at least I wasn't a stick in the mud."

She'd been headed for the kitchen, but she spun around and faced him again, hands on her hips. "Are you calling me a stick in the mud?"

He laughed, a great big, infectious belly laugh. "I guess I am. Only because you called me a lunatic."

And then she was laughing too and she went to the kitchen in search of another bottle of wine and something to eat. When she remembered she hadn't yet stocked the fridge or the cupboards, she feared she might have to say goodnight to Cash. After all, a man had to eat.

When she delivered the news, he picked up his phone. "Why don't we order in?" He'd been all confidence, but in that instant, he looked uncertain. "I mean, if that's okay. I just thought, you know, we're having a nice time. We're both hungry. We should eat."

Happiness bubbled up inside of Opal like a million tiny champagne bubbles. "You're right. We should eat."

"How does ramen sound?"

His eyes went round when she told him she'd never had it.

"Hold up. Are you willing to try something new?" The devilish gleam in his eye shouldn't turn her on—he was talking about *food*—but it sent a bolt of heat straight to her lady parts. Her cheeks flushed, which was probably a dead giveaway. And even though she should care, she didn't. Was it the wine or the impending teamwork, or just the fact that she'd always felt a special connection with Cash? She didn't know, but it was going to her head. And then he tore his gaze from hers and looked down at his phone screen, alternating tapping with asking questions. Beef or pork? Fish, yes or no? Soft-boiled eggs? Seaweed? After several more taps and several more minutes, he set his phone down and rubbed his hands together. "I know you're going to enjoy this."

Even now, ten or eleven hours later, Opal blushed. He definitely hadn't meant the entendre, but she'd been happy to hear it in his words. She pulled her duvet up around her face as if she could somehow hide from the fact that she was very, *very* attracted to Cash.

Although the idea of laying in bed all day, fantasizing about what they could do together, was very appealing, she was also very much looking forward to getting her horses. For the moment, she would put Cash and his dexterous hands—he was amazing with chopsticks—out of her mind and prepare for Roxy and Velma to make their arrival.

Within a few minutes, she was dressed and out the door. First stop: The Buzz. Since the divorce and move, she'd had to cut back her daily coffee shop habit and make it a weekly treat—and she looked forward to it tremendously. Her mouth watered when she walked in, heard the bell ring, and inhaled the scent of fresh-brewed coffee. She ordered her usual, a large iced vanilla coffee with cream and one sugar. She stepped aside to wait, and her stomach turned when the bell above the door rang again and she saw Leslie Marshall come in. Guilt had her turning away, facing the back corner of the coffee shop, just *knowing* that if he saw her face, he'd realize she'd been the one to deflate his tires two nights before.

He stepped up to the counter to order, his voice unpleasantly loud. "I'd like my usual."

"And what is that, sir?"

Even from her spot across the shop, Opal could hear Leslie's scoff. She stared at the paintings on the wall, cats and dogs dressed up as royalty, and listened for more.

"It's the same thing I order every single day."

"I'm new, sir. It's only my second day and I don't believe I took your order yesterday."

A loud sigh followed, and Opal imagined Leslie's great chest heaving with fury. "No one briefed you?"

What does he think this is, the military?

"No, sir. What can I get you?"

The whole scene transported her back in time, to one of the first red-flag situations in her marriage to Boone. They'd gone out to eat at a steak and seafood restaurant and he'd ordered the special: fresh red snapper.

"I'm sorry, sir, but we're out of the red snapper."

Boone's eyes had widened in surprise, like he couldn't believe the restaurant would dare run out of the special before he'd had the chance to order it.

"Out of the special?"

"Yes, sir. It's been very popular. May I recommend the flounder?"

"Absolutely not. I want the red snapper."

Mortified, Opal considered crawling under the table, but the restaurant was one of those linen-tablecloth, candles-and-flowers places. The conversation went on, Boone demanding to see a manager, who told him the same thing, before he grabbed Opal's arm and stormed out of the place, dragging her behind him.

Modern-day Opal risked looking away from the royal cats and dogs and saw the people in line behind Leslie shifting, glancing at each other, uncomfortable.

Leslie was now giving his order, very slowly, enunciating each word as if he were speaking to someone with a poor grasp of the English language. One of the baristas called Opal's name and she grabbed her coffee and fled to the parking lot.

Leslie's car was like a beacon, promising Opal deep satisfaction if only she could inconvenience her great buffoon of a brother-in-law for a second time.

I really shouldn't. But it would feel so good.

An image flashed in her mind: a tube of red lipstick nestled into the small zippered pocket in her purse. It'd been there for more than a year, since Boone dragged her to one of his work events and insisted she wear it. She *hated* wearing red lipstick, and couldn't believe she hadn't thrown it out immediately after they got home.

Before she even realized what she was doing, she'd dug that lipstick out of her purse and was scrawling *Asshole* on Leslie's windshield in angry, bold letters. Adrenaline coursed through her veins, landing coppery in the back of her throat and making her hands shaky.

While looking back at the door of The Buzz, she capped the tube and shoved it back in her purse. When she didn't see anyone coming out of the coffee shop, she fled to her car, then reversed and peeled out of the parking lot.

Only when she was safely away from the scene of the crime, body still vibrating with adrenaline, did she think of whether her nephews might see the word on their dad's windshield.

Surely he wouldn't go home with his car looking like that. He'd go through the car wash. Leslie was the kind of guy who wouldn't want his wife to know he'd earned that particular badge of dishonor. Still, guilt hung in the back of her mind as she made her escape.

Then it was time to switch mental gears: Jim would deliver her new horses in just two hours, and she had to buy them food and get their stalls set up. Within a few minutes, she'd left thoughts of Leslie and Boone behind and was standing at the counter inside the feed store. She tapped the bell for service, and smiled when the sound of whistling came from the stock room and Hank Smithfield emerged.

"Opal Houston as I live and breathe!" He rushed around the counter and opened his arms for a hug.

She stepped into his embrace. "It's been ages. How the heck are you? You look great."

"I'm good." He held her at arms' length. "How are you? I heard you divorced that scumbag Boone Getty."

She shook her head. "You've always been one to say exactly what's on your mind."

"I haven't changed. You should have married me, Opal."

She laughed. "I'm pretty sure Lena would disagree, considering she's carrying your fourth child."

The familiarity was so comforting, Opal couldn't believe she'd been afraid of running into old friends when she moved back.

"Anyway, what can I do for you?"

She told him what she needed and as he entered her order into his computer he said, "The grapevine was right. I heard you were thinking of getting horses. Sounds like it's just a couple right now?"

"Two. Roxy and Velma."

"Nice. Do they sing?"

"I hope so."

"Retired farm horses?"

"Yep. You're right—news travels."

"It does."

"How are Lena and the kids?"

"Great." He grinned, reminding her of the Hank she'd known in high school. "Growing fast. Lena *and* the kids."

"You don't stop, do you?"

"Never. Anyway, let me know if you need any help with the horses. This is prime time, before the new baby comes."

"Nah, I'm good, but thanks for offering. Cash Wilder has been a big help, and I wouldn't want to take you away from family time."

"I heard he bought you a porch swing."

Opal gasped. "You know what, Hank Smithfield? You are way too much of a cog in the gossip mill. Let me pay for my horse feed and get out of here."

He laughed as he rang her up, gave her the total, and processed her payment. He handed back her card. "The guys will bring it over in the next couple of hours. Go on, get out of here. Let me know if you need any help after all."

She rolled her eyes. "I will. Probably mucking stalls."

"You know what, actually? I'm not available."

She was still smiling as she got in her car.

Something was shifting inside her.

Realizing her husband wasn't the man she thought he was—yes, she'd fallen prey to his charm and his apparent *joie de vivre* and married him before realizing he was a narcissistic, inconsiderate jerk —was bad enough. But then she'd decided to come home. Yes, Opal Houston, who in high school was voted Most Likely to live the American Dream, was returning to her dinky hometown husband-less and jobless and without a dream to her name. It was the ulti-mate humiliation.

At least, she thought it was, until she started seeing her old friends. Everyone seemed genuinely excited to have her back. Almost no one looked at her with pity or disappointment (except maybe Mrs. Gibraltar, her sophomore-year English teacher, who was about a hundred and ten and at the news of Opal's divorce arched her eyebrows at an impossible angle before sniffing and changing the subject).

And now, here she was, she thought as she turned into the driveway, the owner of her own place finally living her dream, rescuing horses. No, she didn't have a job yet, but she would get one eventually. She had savings and Callie had managed to negotiate a wild sum for her in the divorce settlement since Boone got to keep their three-million-dollar cottage on the East Coast. That thought sent a spike of anger through her veins and she gritted her teeth and tightened her grip on the steering wheel.

Then she reminded herself Boone wasn't here to enjoy the way the morning sunlight shined through the leaves on her trees, the way the breeze made those leaves dance, casting magical shadows on the side of the house, or the way the birds sang from sun up until sundown.

She put the car in park, took a deep, cleansing breath, and got out, inhaling the scent of the fall leaves and the wet grass as she walked over to the barn. Restless—she wished Jim would deliver the horses, already—she checked the fencing and the feeders and waterers yet again before raking the straw she'd put down in the stalls.

As Hank had promised, the hay delivery arrived an hour later and the driver chatted away as he unloaded the hay and helped Opal fill the hanging feeders with it. Once he was gone, Opal felt antsy. Everything was ready—she was just waiting on the horses. She busied herself by walking the corral fence one more time, going inside to refill her water bottle, and then raking some more.

Finally, Jim's old truck came rattling up the driveway and she stowed the rake and rushed over to meet him.

Logistics took up the next few minutes, with the two of them working together to unload the horses and lead them into the corral. Opal closed the gate, and she and Jim stood with their elbows on the fence, watching Roxy and Velma. The two of them stayed close to one another, sniffing the ground, nibbling at the grass. Roxy swished her tail and Velma lifted her head and snorted.

To Opal's surprise, Jim used a gnarled forefinger to wipe a tear from under his eye. "I have to say, I'm going to miss these girls. They're good horses."

Opal put a hand on his shoulder. "They have a good home here."

He turned to her, smiling, his eyes still watery. "I know they do, honey. That's why I sold them to you."

The trailer's door squeaked as he closed it, and after his truck rattled back down the driveway, Opal stood alone with her horses, suddenly as overcome with emotion as Jim had just been. The horses seemed to sense that. They came toward her, ears pricked, eyes bright, and put their heads over the fence. Laughing, she placed a hand on each horse's cheek. Roxy's soft nose brushed against her forehead.

"I think I'm going to like having you here."

After letting them wander for a few minutes, Opal went inside the corral and led them over to the barn to show them where she'd put their food and water.

She wasn't sure what she'd been expecting, but the horses seemed perfectly at ease in their new surroundings. On an impulse, she took a picture of them and sent it to Cash. *They're here!*

His response came back right away. *I don't want it to seem like I've been waiting for your text, but I have. When can I come over?*

Opal wrote back, her thumbs flying over the keyboard. *I don't want it to seem like I was hoping you'd ask, but I was. Anytime.*

She was still tidying up in the barn when she heard his truck fifteen minutes later. He'd come straight there after she texted him. It was a small thing, but it thrilled her just the same. She rushed over to meet him. When he got out and walked toward her, she couldn't help but admire the way his jeans hugged his thighs. Before he'd made it as far as the hood of his truck, he froze, held up, a finger and turned around. Reaching over the bed of his truck, he retrieved a bag and presented it to Opal as he approached. "I come bearing gifts."

"Aw, are you trying to get in sweet with my horses?"

"Not with the horses." He held her eye contact for a few seconds longer, then winked, making her laugh.

Inside the bag, she found a package of horse treats and a caramel apple lollipop. Her heart swelled. "These are my favorite. You remembered."

He shrugged. "Yeah."

The temptation to take his hand was strong as they walked through the corral, but she stuffed hers into her pockets, instead. Hand-holding wouldn't do. Hand-holding led to touching and kissing and eventually, to bed. And getting in bed with Cash Wilder was the least prudent activity she could think of right now. Somehow, though, their shoulders ended up touching, and she wondered if their bodies had some sort of magnetic pull.

When they reached the barn, Cash inclined his head. "Can I talk to them?"

"Of course."

She let him go ahead of her, mostly because she wanted to watch him. They said a girl could learn a lot about a man by the way he interacted with horses. Five minutes later, she was weak in the knees.

Cash moved with a gentleness she'd come to expect, but the way he smoothed his hands over the horses, murmured to them, smiled at them, sent delicious shivers over her skin and had her imagining those hands on her.

"Want to stay for dinner?" The words came out in a rush.

"Actually," he said, and disappointment rushed in. She shouldn't have expected him to be able to stay. But then he continued, "I do. But only as a thank you for hanging up the swing. Oh, and repairing your roof trim."

"It's broken?"

"Yeah. I noticed it the other day when I was hanging the swing. I brought supplies. Be right back."

She watched him walk away, again admiring the fit of his jeans and wishing she could tuck her hand into his back pocket, against his muscular butt. She wanted to tell him dinner wasn't repayment for anything; that she just wanted to spend time with him, talk to him, listen to his voice, watch the way he moved.

But then he was back, a bag from the hardware store in one

hand and a heavy-looking canvas tool bag in the other. His forearms rippled. Her mouth watered.

"I'll just get started. Shouldn't take long."

She should go into the kitchen. She should drag herself away from the spectacle she was about to encounter. She should avoid temptation. With all that in mind, she followed Cash around the side of the house. He set down his bags and glanced up at the spot where, she saw now, the trim was splintered and rotting. "Now I need my ladder."

"I can grab it." She started toward the truck, but he stopped her with a hand on her arm.

"Opal Houston, you should get one thing straight right now. As long as you're in my company, you'll never carry a ladder."

He must have seen the start of her indignation—the crossing of her arms, the pressing down of her eyebrows, and the scowling of her mouth—because he held up a hand before she could speak. "If nothing else, my daddy raised me to be a gentleman. You can keep me company if you like, but I'm carrying the ladder. I think you'll find it's wiser not to argue with me."

Chapter Nine

"Daydreaming, Wilder?" Commander Mosley's bark, issued from the front of the classroom, made Cash jump.

He pictured his arms and legs flailing like a cartoon character's and felt the heat rush up his neck and into his face. Because he *had* been daydreaming. "Yes, sir." He said the words with emphasis, and his classmates laughed.

Only then did he realize he should have said, "No, sir." He rushed to correct himself, which only left him more flabbergasted.

"Come on up here, Wilder." Mosley made a show of stepping to the side and holding out a hand, palm up, in invitation.

His face at about a thousand degrees, Cash stood up and took the spot Mosley had vacated.

"At attention, Wilder."

He snapped his heels together, his left arm at his side, and saluted with his right. "Sir."

"Wilder, do you know what happens when a recruit daydreams in the middle of morning presentation?"

No idea. "No, sir."

Subdued chuckles floated up from the desks where Cash's so-called friends sat. If he wasn't so humiliated, he'd glare at them. As it was, though, all he could do was stare at the back wall.

"Wilder, do you know how I feel about recruits daydreaming in class?"

So many smart-ass comments came to mind, but Cash kept it simple. "No, sir."

"I hate it, Wilder. Hate it with a passion. So when I see it, you know what I've got to do, right?"

Oh, God. "No, sir. What do you have to do?"

"I have to punish the son of a gun who dares to do it. Who dares to daydream. Hey, that has a nice ring to it, eh?"

Silence.

"I can't let that disrespect slide. Can I, recruits?"

"No, sir." Twenty-five voices echoed against the classroom walls.

"What do you think you can do to make it up to me, Wilder?"

Oh, boy. What am I supposed to say?

"I want you to give me fifty push-ups."

Cash nodded and Commander Mosley grunted. "You agreed much too quickly. Why don't you make it a hundred?"

Cash figured a person could hear a pin drop. He didn't dare agree right away, but he didn't dare wait too long either. Someone in the front row shifted and Cash said in an even, measured voice, "Yes, sir."

His stomach churned. In just a couple of hours, all the recruits were expected to pass their final physical test, which included fifty push-ups. He couldn't remember the last time he'd done one hundred and fifty push-ups in a single day. But refusing would be disastrous. So he got in position, his palms flat on the vinyl floor, his back perfectly straight.

"The rest of you, keep him honest. Go ahead and count for him."

Cash swore there was humiliation-related steam coming out of his ears. He couldn't remember a time he'd ever been more embarrassed. He bent his elbows and straightened them and his classmates counted. "One."

He did another. "Two."

His mind transported him back in time. He was fifteen and he'd mouthed off to his dad. He couldn't recall now what it was even about. He remembered the punishment plain as day.

"You're going to start chopping wood. You're going to chop and count until *my* arms are tired."

The sick feeling in the pit of present-day Cash's stomach was reminiscent of the one he'd felt all day as he'd swung that axe, the muscles in his arms and back just *burning*.

"Five. Six."

Back when he was fifteen, Cash felt like his dad's punishment was unjustified. Now, though? He figured he deserved what he was getting. Commander Mosley had made his disdain for daydreaming crystal clear from day one. And Cash *had* been daydreaming. Or, more accurately, reliving his evening with Opal a few days before. His biceps and pecs warmed up as he continued his push-ups.

"Eight. Nine."

He was positive he'd never experienced a more perfect evening, as simple as it was. While he sawed off the rotten part of the roof trim, Opal sat on the porch, her legs dangling. They talked about inconsequential things: new restaurants that had opened while Opal was gone, the truck they'd seen around town, painted with flat earth warnings, and even the weather.

They talked about consequential things, too: Opal's sister wanting a job, but her husband not allowing it, Opal researching rescue dogs she could bring to the property, and Cash mentally preparing for his big physical test. Which he'd sabotaged by thinking about Opal. Mid-push-up, Cash let out a chuckle. He was sure everyone else assumed it was a grunt.

"Twenty. Twenty-one."

Well, thinking about Opal had gotten them through eleven push-ups almost without his noticing. There *was* an upside to daydreaming.

He finished the repair and she insisted they sit on the porch swing together. He couldn't say why they seemed to fit so perfectly there, the two of their bodies side by side like puzzle pieces.

Then his stomach growled and she insisted on making dinner. "I'll make a giant bowl of pasta. You've got to carb load, right?"

He laughed. "I think you only carb load the day or two before an event—not the whole week."

"Huh. Well, I'll make a giant bowl of pasta anyway."

If he were looking for a relationship, if he weren't starting a brand-new career, and if he wasn't afraid a distraction could derail him, Opal would be exactly the kind of woman he'd choose. Not the kind of woman—*the* woman.

That thought shocked him so much, he faltered before straightening his arms, hearing his classmates call, "Thirty-three."

He switched gears. Better to think about facts. Fact: the karaoke fundraiser required each team to do a promotional video shoot. Fact: that video shoot would require them to spend time together, again. Fact: he liked that idea very much. Another strangled chuckle escaped, earning him an admonition from Mosley. "You're only halfway there, Wilder. I recommend you don't wimp out on me."

Then he started thinking about songs. Potential karaoke duets. The first ones that came to his mind, were—of course—love songs. That would never do. If he had to stand on a stage with Opal and look into her eyes and sing a love song with her ... well, he didn't know what would happen, but he knew he couldn't risk it. What other songs were there? Hard rock. But weren't many of those sexual in nature? A specific song came to him—one in which a woman made sexual, pleasured-filled noises in between verses. And suddenly, right there in the front of the police academy classroom, with all of his fellow recruits looking on, Cash envisioned himself and Opal intertwined, moving together, sexual, pleasure-filled sounds coming from *her*.

"Sixty-nine."

No. He chastised himself. He had to get these images out of his head before ...

In a rush, he started whispering multiplication tables. Math problems could always calm a guy guy down. Or, as he was finding now, *almost* always. He kept going. *Four times eight is thirty-two. Four times nine is thirty-six.* These were too easy. He'd always been bad at the twelves. *Twelve times five is sixty. Twelve times six is seventy-two.* Wow. He'd gotten good at twelves.

Meditation. That's what he should do. He had to clear his mind. He focused his gaze on a little gray fleck in the flooring directly in front of his face. *Gray fleck. Gray fleck. Gray fleck.* That was doing the trick. It kept him from thinking about—and, there she was again. What he wouldn't give to see and touch and explore the skin under the swatch of fabric she called a pair of shorts. This time he let out a full on groan. Mosley chuckled, obviously satisfied that Cash was struggling.

"Eighty-two."

Gray fleck. Gray fleck. Gray fleck. Every push-up after that felt like a gargantuan effort. It seemed as though his fellow recruits counted in slow motion. When he got to ninety, they counted down. "Eight. Seven." Only now did Cash notice his biceps and chest were on fire. God, he hoped he'd be able to do fifty more that afternoon.

"Five. Four. Three."

A bead of sweat formed at his temple and made its way across his forehead and down his nose, splashing onto the gray fleck.

"Two. One. Zero."

At first, a dreadful silence met the completion of his task. Then, Commander Mosley clapped—slowly—three times. And then, as Cash climbed to his feet, the rest of his class erupted in cheers, whistling and hollering. For a second, he was surrounded, the recipient of back-pats and shoulder squeezes. Commander Mosley put an end to that with one sharp whistle. "Return to your seats, recruits."

Cash slogged through the rest of the morning managing to force Opal out of his mind when she popped in over and over. Finally it was lunchtime, and the recruits filed into the cafeteria. Tommy Rowland slipped in line behind Cash and they each grabbed a tray.

"What was on your mind, Wilder?"

He should have known the topic would resurface. "Nothing."

"Whatever, man." Tommy clapped him on the shoulder. They moved forward in line and set their trays on the counter. "It wasn't nothing. But I can respect your need for privacy."

Cash nodded, relieved.

"Just kidding, bro. It was Opal Houston, wasn't it?"

Dammit. His face flushed before he could even respond.

"You don't have to say anything, man. I can see it on your face. You've got a thing for Opal Houston."

Cash made a show of thanking the cafeteria worker who served him.

"I heard you bought her a porch swing. And hung it up. And sat on it with her. And fixed her roof. And then she fed you dinner."

Cash cursed the rumor mill, which always always seemed to chug along. He pictured an actual mill, smoke rising merrily, industriously, from a smokestack as it produced its product.

They moved down the line and Tommy spoke again. "You know, Bella Raney is going to be real sad to hear this news."

That got him. He wasn't even sure who Bella Raney was.

Which must have shown in his expression because Tommy guffawed. "Don't even know who she is, do you? Tall brunette? Freckles on the bridge of her nose? Long legs? Apparently a great dancer—she's been telling everybody the two of you danced the night away a couple weeks ago and she's got her sights set on you. Pretty sure her exact words were, 'I'm gonna make an honest man out of Cash Wilder.'"

Cash groaned. Now he remembered Bella Raney and that (admittedly fun) night at the Boot Scoot. "She was very nice, but c'mon, Tommy. You know nobody's gonna make an honest man out of Cash Wilder."

He tried to keep his voice nonchalant, but Tommy—having absorbed Commander Mosley's lessons about observational skills—just grinned at him. "Not even Opal Houston?"

Cash cursed and headed for a spot at one of the long cafeteria tables. Tommy slid in next to him. "Listen, man. I don't want to pressure you or anything, but just know that I saw the hearts in your eyes, man. I think you've got it bad for Opal and you're in denial."

After taking a huge bite of his food—one his brothers would surely scold him about talking with his mouth full—Cash replied. "And I'm going to stay there."

"Why?"

"Because, man! I'm finally making something out of myself. My whole life, everybody has seen me as this happy-go-lucky guy. 'The fun one.'" He sneered while he made air quotes around the last three words. "I have to prove to all of them that I can *be* something. Something else." His own conviction surprised him.

It must have surprised Tommy, too, because he held up his hands. "Okay, okay. I hear you. But I'm just sayin', policing is hard work. Having someone to come home to after every shift ... I think that's pretty special."

"But what if she doesn't *want* me to come home to her? What if she wants someone better? Someone more serious? Someone besides 'the fun one'?" The words were out of his mouth before he had a chance to censor himself.

Tommy nodded, his expression suddenly going understanding and wise. "Ah. I see the problem now."

"Exactly. And the problem is that I will never live up to Opal Houston's standards. She deserves more."

That shocked Tommy into silence, at least for a few beats. He nodded while he took several bites of his mashed potatoes and gravy. Eventually, he set down his fork, wiped his mouth (reminding Cash that Sterling had recently told him he was going to have to start using a napkin rather than his hand once he became a cop), then set down his napkin and put his hands in his lap. "Have you ever considered that maybe your desire to join the police department marks a personal transformation?"

When Cash stared at him blankly before shoveling another bite of mashed potatoes into his mouth, Tommy's eyes crinkled at the corners. "I mean it, man. I mean, maybe this is the point in your life when you blend the fun-loving side of Cash Wilder with a new, serious side. The best of both worlds. And what woman wouldn't love that?"

All he could muster up in response was a grunt, which made Tommy chuckle. "Whatever. I can see you're not ready to talk about this. But just think about it, okay? Take some time, let the words sink in. Maybe even do it today while you're taking your fitness test.

While you're running the mile and a half, doing the push-ups, dragging the dummy."

Cash grunted again.

"Wow. It's like talking to a caveman. You know what? Certain women out there, they love a caveman. Even in today's world. Maybe that's what you've got going for you." With that, he picked up his tray, swung his leg over the bench they sat on, and headed for the counter. "Good luck this afternoon, Wilder."

Cash made sure to swallow his food before answering. "Thanks, Tommy."

Even though he hadn't responded to Tommy with much enthusiasm during the conversation, he did take Tommy's advice. While he ran the mile and a half, he thought about having someone to come home to every night. So what if, while his arms pumped and his feet beat the ground, the only image he could muster up was one of Opal's face, her smile greeting him at the end of a shift? While he did his push-ups, arms absolutely on fire, he thought about how he was sick of being the fun one. And while he dragged the 150-pound dummy across the yard, he thought about how badly he wanted to combine his fun side and his serious side ... but how he wasn't sure if he could. What if he tried to make something of himself, and he failed?

What if Opal thought she was getting a better version of Cash, but there *was* no better version of Cash?

Sweating now, chest heaving, he dropped the dummy and looked at Mosley, who sat on a folding chair, a stopwatch in his hand. He clicked the button, looked up at Cash and drawled, "Pass."

Cash had expected a little more fanfare as each of them passed the fitness test. His heart did leap inside his chest, just a tiny, short happy dance acknowledging he was one step closer to finishing the academy and becoming a cop.

He told his heart to simmer down. He'd passed a physical fitness test (arguably, one almost anyone should be able to pass). That didn't guarantee he had what it took to make something of himself.

Chapter Ten

Opal rose with the sun, dressed quickly, poured some coffee, and went outside to feed her horses. *Her horses.* Having them there was a dream come true.

As soon and she closed the front door behind her, Roxy and Velma paused their grazing and lifted their heads. When they saw her, they plodded toward her, eyes bright as if to offer her a good morning. She met them at the fence, giving each of them a couple of treats before going into the barn. She pulled off two flakes of alfalfa and they rushed over, eager to nibble on the sweet grass.

It wasn't exactly how she had always imagined her life. Before—before Boone, before the long months of fighting and constant disappointment, before the divorce—she wanted all of it. The husband, the kids, the house, the pets. But maybe she could be content with this—with her own little slice of heaven.

Besides, Boone had made it pretty clear she wasn't wife material. She sighed, checked to make sure the waterers were full, and went back inside.

Afraid of whiling away her day since she didn't yet have a job, Opal had made herself a to-do list the night before. After *Feed the horses* she'd written *Check Humane Society listings*. Already imagining a canine companion hopping up next to her on the couch, she curled up with her laptop. Her phone chimed from its spot on the kitchen counter just as she typed in the Humane Society's website. Before she'd even set aside her computer to stand up, it chimed again. And again.

"Geez, must be important."

Setting her computer aside, she got off the couch to retrieve it. The messages were from Pearl. The first one got her attention. *Can you talk?* The second one made her stomach drop. *I think Leslie is having an affair.* The third message sent a mixture of dread and alarm churning through Opal's veins. *Actually, I can't talk. Leslie is gone (again) and I've hidden in the bathroom long enough this morning. I'll have to text. Leslie's car was vandalized. Someone wrote asshole on the windshield in red lipstick. Red lipstick. Can you believe that? But if it wasn't a jilted lover, who would do something like that?*

Opal sucked in her breath. Another message came through before she could even gather her thoughts to respond: *He swears he's not having an affair. Says it happened at the coffee shop. But it doesn't make any sense.*

The image of Opal's phone screen swirled in her vision. Her heart pumped fast and loud. Her sister could see she'd read the messages. She had to say something. But what?

Her fingers shook so badly, she could hardly type. *I'm sure he's not having an affair.*

Pearl's response came back right away. *But how do you know?*

Opal groaned. *Because anyone who has an affair while having you as his wife is a complete and total idiot. I think we can both agree that Leslie is not an idiot.*

"An asshole, maybe. But not an idiot."

Pearl wrote back, *True.* And then, after a beat, *But seriously. Why would someone use red lipstick to write asshole on his windshield?*

"Because he's an asshole." *I have no idea. You never know. Maybe it was some insane girl, who was angry at men. Maybe someone got the wrong car. Maybe it was one of his friends playing a prank.*

Pearl wrote back, *Okay.* Opal could picture her sister leaning against the bathroom counter, taking a deep breath. She added, *These are actually reasonable ideas.*

Opal: *You're welcome.*

Pearl: *Haha. Thank you.*

Opal: *What are you doing today?* She was desperate to steer the conversation away from Leslie, from his character, from his car.

Pearl: *After I get these hoodlums to school, I'm going to the gym. Then, I don't know. Cleaning the house, doing laundry, probably binge watching a new show.* She added an emoji with a pained expression.

Opal cringed. Pearl was the first to admit she had a pretty great life. But now that both boys were in school, she wanted something of her own—a part-time job, a volunteer job ... as she'd said recently, "Anything!" Leslie refused to entertain the idea. He wanted Pearl home and focused on the kids, the house, and the cooking.

Opal: *Want to come with me to the Humane Society?*

Pearl: *Actually, that sounds like more fun than what I have planned. Count me in.*

Pearl showed up just after eight-thirty.

"Why don't we grab a coffee and then head over there? It doesn't open 'til nine." Opal regretted the words as soon as they were out of her mouth, but Pearl was already rubbing her hands together. "I hear The Buzz has a new fall drink and I've been wanting to try it."

What was I thinking, bringing her to the scene of the crime? In the parking lot, Opal's gaze shot to the spot where she'd vandalized Leslie's car. The car wasn't there, of course, but Opal was certain her guilt would manifest in some strange way. *I should have suggested ice cream. Or donuts.*

"You okay?" Pearl's hand shot across the center console and she gripped Opal's wrist.

Opal smiled, probably too brightly. "I'm fine! Why?"

Pearl shrugged. "I don't know. Your throat just made that weird noise it makes when you're nervous. You know, when you swallow, but your mouth is kind of dry, and there's kind of this clicking sound?"

"Did it?" Her eyes went round, all innocence.

Pearl released her arm. "Maybe not. Come on. We're burning daylight."

As soon as they got in line, Pearl leaned close, so their shoulders touched, and whispered in Opal's ear. "Look around. Do you think any of these women could have written *asshole* on Leslie's windshield?"

Opal pretended to look around, entertaining Pearl's idea. "I mean, everybody looks pretty friendly."

Pearl wrinkled her nose. "You're right."

The same employee Leslie had been so rude to was working the register again. "What can I get you today?"

She wished she could tell the cashier not to worry about Leslie, that she'd gotten that asshole back, but instead Opal went ahead and ordered her usual. "I'll get hers, too."

"You don't have to do that," Pearl started, but Opal raised a hand. "At least let me treat you this once, before my money runs out."

Back in the car, Pearl said, "Is your money really going to run out?"

Following a high-pitched cackle, Opal did her best to reassure her sister. "Of course not. I'm going to have to get a job eventually. But Callie got me set up well enough that if I invest the money right, I can live off the dividends."

"Wow. That was a really great idea." Pearl sat back and crossed her arms, thoughtful. Putting the car in reverse, Opal nodded. "Callie had a lot of good ideas. Without her, I'd probably be homeless."

"I very much doubt that. But I'm glad she was able to keep Boone from taking you to the cleaners."

They both said, "Asshole," and then Opal panicked again, because she didn't know what would happen if she kept using that word and Pearl put two and two together and realized she was the one who had quite gleefully scrawled it on her husband's windshield.

She turned up the music and Pearl threw up her arms. "I love this song!"

The country song—a fast female anthem about feeling like a woman—threw Opal into the past, to dancing with her sister on Whiskey Row in downtown Prescott, sawdust on the floor, their arms above their heads, their voices raw from singing along. They'd always look at each other and smile, a silent *This is so much fun!* through the noise from the band and the chaos of countless swaying bodies.

They'd both been so carefree in those days. Opal turned up the volume on the car's stereo system. For just a few minutes, while she finished the drive to the humane society, she let her body sway, she sang to the music, and pretended they were back in college with only a few small cares in the world.

After pulling into a parking spot, she let the song finish and Pearl, apparently enjoying the walk down memory lane as well, danced along with her until the last notes faded away.

The silence blared when Opal turned off the car, and they both sighed, chests heaving, satisfied.

"Shall we?"

Still smiling, Pearl nodded. They got out and walked to the front door.

"How can I help you ladies?" An woman with striking silver hair greeted them from behind the reception desk.

"I'm considering adopting a dog," Opal said.

The woman beamed as she stood up and came around the desk to offer her hand. "I'm Kate."

"Opal." They shook. "And this is my sister, Pearl."

As people often did, Kate smiled when she heard both their names. "Pleasure to meet you. Now, do you have anything specific in mind?"

Opal shook her head. "I think I'll know it when I see it."

Kate responded with another bright smile. "My favorite kind of adopter. Come on, I'll show you the dogs."

At the back of the main building, Kate leaned against a heavy door. Just before she opened it, she told them, "Brace yourselves. It's always unbearably loud in here."

Sure enough, the second a sliver of space appeared between the metal door and the jamb, an ear-piercing cacophony of yips and yowls and deep barks filled the space. Opal and Pearl grimaced at each other and Kate laughed. "Told you."

"You weren't kidding." Opal made a show of covering her ears as they entered the kennel area, a long hallway with several chainlink doors on each side.

"So many dogs." Pearl bumped Opal's shoulder with her own. "How are you going to choose one?"

There were: big dogs and little dogs and medium dogs. Dogs with dark fur and long fur and curly fur. They wiggled and jumped and danced, vying for attention as the women passed. Except for one. Two-thirds of the way down on the right side, one dog sat calmly in his kennel, watching with bright, intelligent eyes, apparently unperturbed by all the noise and excitement. His head was big and blocky, and aside from the white patch on his chest, his fur was the color of caramel.

When Opal stopped in front of him, his tail wagged against the floor and he put one paw on the door, so his toes came through the chainlink. The name tag on his door read *Louie*.

She grinned at Kate. "Can I meet this guy?"

Kate beamed back at her. "Of course. Louie might be the sweetest dog we have in here." She pulled her keyring off a clip on her belt and selected a key. "He's been here a while, too." Louie dropped his paw and sat patiently while Kate unlocked and opened the door. He watched as she removed a leash from a hook on the wall and slipped it over his head. When she told him, "Let's go," he stood up and wagged his tail, and then he trotted alongside her like a gentleman to the end of the hall, where they all went through another door to a fenced-in area with a large swatch of grass, chairs around the perimeter, and sun shades stretched overhead.

Kate gestured at some of the chairs. "Have a seat and I'll let him off the leash."

They did, and as soon as Kate removed the leash, Louie walked over and put his head in Opal's lap. Delighted, she gasped and put a hand on the back of his neck. When he leaned into her touch, tilting his head so he could look up at her, she put one hand on either side of his face and scratched, just below his ears. Tail wagging, he groaned in pleasure for a few seconds before jumping backward and putting his butt in the air, inviting her to play.

"He likes you." Kate handed Opal a tennis ball. "Here. He loves to fetch."

Sure enough, as soon as Louie saw the ball, his ears perked up. His gaze was laser focused on the ball as Opal cocked her arm. When she let it fly, he charged after it, his stride lengthening as he blasted across the yard. Almost vicious, he snapped it up, then trotted back, his tail straight up and his ears still perked. He dropped the ball at her feet and then smiled at her, waiting. They repeated that process a few more times before Louie tired out, returning to Opal and flopping down next to her, his chin on her foot just briefly before he looked up at her, his tongue hanging out, and wagged his tail again so it thumped on the ground. Tears sprang to her eyes and emotion clogged her throat.

Pearl reached over and squeezed her leg. "I think *he's* adopted *you*."

Kate, who'd watched the scene play out, arms crossed and a smile on her face, nodded. "I was thinking the same thing."

Opal leaned down to pet Louie and he rolled onto his back so she could scratch his stomach. He groaned and closed his eyes, his tongue lolling. Then he was up, onto his feet, pawing at the tennis ball, ready for her to throw it.

"You're going to have to keep him busy." Kate's smile hadn't left her face, and again, Opal felt tears stinging her eyes.

"I will."

Twenty minutes later, Opal, Pearl, and Louie walked out of the humane society's building and across the parking lot. When Opal opened the back door of her car, Louie jumped right in and sat down, smiling at them. Opal offered him the tennis ball Kate had sent with them and he took it gently from her before she closed the door.

Louie stuck his head out the window when Opal rolled it down, and his ears flapped in the wind while they drove back to the house. She let him out, and she and Pearl stood on the porch watching him explore. He ran around the side of the house, nose to the ground, and then came back to lick their hands as if he wanted to make sure they were still there. Then he checked out the corral, running around the outside of it and returning again to check in with Opal and Pearl.

"I think he's going to like it here." Pearl leaned against Opal. "He looks so happy."

"He does."

Louie dropped to the ground and rolled around in the dirt, blissful. He got up and shook off, then sprinted across the yard and back.

"Hey. You know how, when Wyatt was born, you bought out the entire baby section at the store by your house?"

"Of course. That was the funnest shopping trip ever. And one of the most expensive."

Pearl wrinkled her nose. "I'm sorry."

"No! Don't be sorry. I loved it. It was so worth it to buy every tiny jumpsuit and the softest stuffed giraffe and do you remember that adorable little baby guitar?"

"How could I forget that?"

Opal laughed.

"Anyway. I was thinking. I know you planned to go buy dog supplies after you let Louie get used to your place, but can I go now? Can I share your title of Best Aunt Ever and go buy him all the presents?" Pearl's eyes looked a little misty.

"Oh, my gosh, of course you can. You don't have to pay for it all, but you doing the shopping would be a huge help. I almost forgot I have that meeting later, and that would save me time."

Smiling, Pearl pulled her phone out of her pocket. "Let's make a list."

Once Pearl was gone, a list thirty-two items long typed into her phone, Opal grabbed the tennis ball and threw for Louie until he tired out—letting her know by flopping down at her feet again. They went inside, where she filled one of her mixing bowls with water. He lapped up most of it before once again flopping down, this time on the kitchen floor.

She figured he'd fall asleep right away. Moving out of the shelter, exploring the property, and playing fetch 'til he dropped must have worn him out. But he kept his eyes open and his gaze followed her every move.

Then it hit her: even though he was having fun, he probably wasn't entirely certain he'd get to stay here. Her heart stuttered and she sat down next to him, sinking her fingers into the thick fur on his scruff. Sure enough, a few minutes later, he was asleep, his breath coming in little snores.

Afraid to get up and wake him, she leaned against the kitchen cabinet. For a few minutes, she thought about her to-do list for the rest of the day. She needed to set up Louie's new things when Pearl got back, and she'd have to shower and get dressed for the meeting. The meeting, where she'd be paired up with Cash as the other half of his fundraising team. Agreeing to be part of the fundraiser was among the stupidest decisions she'd made. They would now be joined at the hip for the next several weeks.

"Not that I mind being joined at the hip with Cash Wilder," she said to Louie, who slept on, oblivious. "But it's a dangerous position to be in."

Closing her eyes, she ran through her options for what to wear to the meeting. Not that she should dress to impress her partner, but— who was she kidding? She wanted to dress to impress him. Her imagination drifted to the moment he saw her. His eyes would smolder before raking over her body ...

She jolted awake when she heard the front door open. "I'm back!"

Louie jolted upright and Opal's hand dropped from its spot on his neck. He gave Pearl a half-hearted bark, sat up and gave Opal's cheek a big, sloppy lick, and then trotted over to greet Pearl like he owned the place.

Chapter Eleven

It's just a meeting. Cash had no idea why he was nervous about the introductory meeting for the Singing for Hope fundraiser. All he had to do was show up and listen.

With Opal.

With Opal, in front of everyone else. He immediately pictured her ice-blue eyes, the little lines that formed around them when she smiled, the fullness of her lips when she was thinking. God, he was going to have to get his feelings for her under control.

Fortunately, the fundraiser's organizers had made the meeting a happy hour. He arrived a few minutes early after leaving the police academy, so he was able to order a beer and gulp half of it down—liquid courage—before anyone else showed up.

A sign on the long table at one end of the bar declared it *Reserved for Singing for Hope.* He chose a seat and practiced his observation skills. He would've chosen somewhere casual like A Cold One, but this place, Skyscraper, was nice enough.

In her event planning materials, June would probably call it elevated. Upscale. Every surface shone, from the mirrored liquor shelf to the sleek black bar. Even the ceiling wore shiny black tiles, which glinted as they reflected the low lights placed all over the room.

To Cash's relief, Sterling and Hayes were the next to come through the door. They both lit up when they saw him, and he felt himself light up, too. Not for the first time since Sterling moved back to Arizona, Cash felt a rush of gratitude for how things had worked out. All four Wilder boys were together again. Each of his brothers had found someone—a life partner—and he hadn't, but weren't their women simply an extension of his family?

His brothers stopped at the bar to order drinks and Cash's heart ached just a little when June came up behind Sterling and wrapped her arms around him. He forced his attention back to the door just in time to see Callie come in. She waved enthusiastically to Cash, and joined the others at the bar. Lila came in next, with Travis a few paces behind. Cash checked his watch.

The meeting wasn't supposed to start for another five minutes, but he was getting nervous that Opal hadn't shown up yet. His brothers and their significant others joined him at the table, leaving open a spot next to him.

The other fundraiser participants filtered in, and Cash watched them with interest. He recognized many of them—apparently, the event was popular among longtime Prescottonians. Finally, when his eyes flicked to the door for about the hundredth time, Opal was there, her entire being buzzing with excitement. Her eyes scanned the room, landing first on Sterling and then seeking Cash. He knew, because when she spotted him, her mouth opened in a smile that conveyed unhampered joy. She raised an arm in greeting and practically jogged over to the table, sliding into her spot like it was home plate and she was racing the catcher to get there. She gripped his arm. "I got a dog."

His mouth dropped open and then he laughed out loud. "Congratulations. Tell me everything."

While she talked, sharing the details of her trip to the humane society, Cash found himself having to push away a sliver of disappointment. He would have loved to go pick out a dog with her. As she continued to talk, positively glowing, radiant, he reminded himself he had no business being disappointed. Picking out a dog together was something couples did. He and Opal were not a couple. No matter how much he let himself enjoy spending time with her. No matter how much he leaned into their partnership for this fundraiser. No matter how they fit together so perfectly on the porch swing.

Callie materialized next to Opal with a glass of wine, squeezed her around the shoulders, and sat back down, and all the while, Opal continued talking about the dog.

"So now, he's at my house with Pearl and the boys, just while I'm at the meeting. I can't believe I didn't think about the timing of coming here tonight."

"I'm sure Louie and the boys are equally ecstatic about spending time together." Cash grinned. "There's no better matchup than a dog and a couple of little boys."

Opal nodded and took a sip of her wine and a deep breath. "You're right. I guess I shouldn't feel too much guilt for leaving him. Besides, it's just for a couple of hours."

Before Cash could respond, Tessa Winant (Cash recognized her from the photo on her email signature) stood up at the head of the table and rang a cowbell. "Can I get your attention everyone?" The chatter died down and she rang the cowbell again. "Thank you all for coming tonight. Let this serve as an official welcome to the Singing for Hope fundraiser."

A cheer went up around the table and Cash found energy contagious. He let out a loud whoop, making Opal laugh.

"I always love to start a meeting with an icebreaker." Something in her voice—a barely restrained glee, a sort of warning—had the contestants exchanging glances. The chatter at the table quieted down. At the end of the table, Callie gripped Hayes's knee.

"Now, I know you haven't had much time to practice ..." As Tessa's voice trailed off, Cash felt a tendril of dread curling in his stomach. He didn't have to wait long to hear what, exactly, he was dreading. "Tonight, each team is going to sing its first karaoke song."

Her statement cut off the low murmur that had started, like the flipping of a switch.

Someone about halfway down the table called out, "Are you serious?"

"Dead serious."

Someone else hollered, "Do we have to?"

A few people laughed and Tessa grinned, ice cold. "Of course not. But Hank over at the feed store is donating five hundred bucks to each team who participates tonight. Don't tell me you're going to let your pride get in the way of raising five hundred dollars for Hope Hall."

Cash knew then and there that every team would participate. He risked a look at Opal and saw in her expression resignation and fear. When she saw him looking at her, she put a hand on his upper arm, then made a dismissive gesture with her other hand and whispered, "It'll be fine."

"There's a catch." Now Tessa's glee wasn't restrained at all. She looked downright pleased with herself. She lifted a bowl from the table. "Inside this bowl, I have ten strips of paper. Each strip has the name of a song on it. One member from each team will draw a song out of the bowl. That's the song you'll sing tonight."

One of the more loud-mouthed guys wanted to know, "What if we don't know it?"

"I'm fairly certain that everyone is going to know these songs. If you don't, and you can't pick up on them with the help of the karaoke screen, maybe your fellow competitors will help you out."

Another round of murmurs ran through the contestants.

"Will one member of each team come choose a song, please?" At first, no one moved and Tessa's voice became singsongy. "Come on, don't be shy."

Cash and his brothers stood up to join the line. Hayes elbowed Cash. "I can't wait to see what song you get." He wiggled his eyebrows up and down suggestively, and Cash's stomach sank. He hadn't been too worried about the song selection—until now. What if they drew an overly sappy love song? Or, heaven forbid, something sexual? The blood rushed to his face. Of course, his brothers noticed.

"You scared, Cash?" Travis wanted to know. He went so far as to elbow Cash, who elbowed him back—hard—before remembering they shared this space with eighteen other people—most of whom were not family. He quashed the urge to lash out again.

The laughter in Travis's eyes infuriated Cash, and Sterling's knowing smile exacerbated that feeling. Hayes rubbed his hands together, like he just couldn't wait to see which song Cash chose. Letting anger take centerstage—he'd rather be angry than scared out of his mind—he glowered at the three of them and pushed Sterling forward so he'd be the first of the brothers to draw.

They were at the back of the line and some of the other contestants were already unfolding their slips of paper. Some groaned, some did fist pumps, and some shrugged.

Probably because they didn't want to tip their hands to Cash, his brothers maintained stony faces as they drew, unfolded, and read their strips of paper. They returned to their seats without speaking.

Tessa grinned at Cash as he reached into the bowl. Only one slip remained. He unfolded it, saw the title, and wished the floor would open up and swallow him immediately. It wouldn't, so he refolded the paper and stuffed it into his pocket. Opal must have been able to read his expression because her eyes widened as he approached her. She held out her hand, grimacing as if she wasn't quite sure she wanted to read the song title. She unfolded the paper and he read it again, upside down, while she read it, too.

"Are You Gonna Kiss Me or Not" by Thompson Square

Her throat worked. His face flamed. She looked up at him. He held that eye contact.

She smiled.

Wrapped up in that smile was everything he dared to hope for and nothing he feared. Instead of disdain or humiliation, he saw humor and hope and maybe even excitement. Oh, yeah. Excitement was definitely in there.

Still, she sounded nonchalant when she said, "I've heard this song."

His body thrummed in anticipation, the blood flow creating a satisfying beat throughout his body.

"Do you like it?" The tension sizzled between them. The air crackled with it.

"I like it." Her eyes sparkled.

"Everyone!" Tessa rang her cowbell again and Cash had no choice but to sit down next to Opal, that electric chemistry still radiating.

"Now that you've chosen your songs, I want to go over a few important matters. And *then* we'll sing."

Although Cash listened and even took notes, his mind kept drifting. He couldn't help but hear the chorus of "Are You Gonna Kiss Me or Not" on repeat, and he told himself he absolutely wouldn't—couldn't—make eye contact with Opal. If he did, he might kiss her on the spot. His body reacted to that idea with way too much excitement, and he had to resort to multiplication tables. *This is going to be awful.*

"Well." Tessa brought her hands together in front of her sternum. "That concludes the informational portion of our meeting. I know you'll come to me with any questions." She paused, Cash assumed for dramatic effect. "And now, we sing!"

Some members of their group cheered, the fools. Finally, Cash risked a glance at Opal, who offered what he assumed was a supportive smile. He returned it as best he could.

"We'll just go around the table."

The first pair had pulled "Beer for My Horses," which Cash found totally unfair. They hammed it up, much to the delight of the other contestants—except for Cash, who couldn't seem to rise out of the dread in which he'd submersed himself.

The next pair got "I Walk the Line" and Cash convinced himself this evening was rigged. When the third pair got "Wait in the Truck," he stopped listening.

And then it was their turn and he had no choice but to stand up and face the karaoke screen and feel the heat from Opal's body nearly touching his as the music played. He cursed, in his head, as the lead-in ended and it was time to sing.

They started off facing the group, each of them gripping a microphone in their right hand. Cash wondered if Opal's palm was as sweaty as his. If the situation weren't already awkward enough, someone hollered, "Come on! Sing it like you mean it!"

Everyone else in the bar—or maybe in the entire world—cheered, a chorus rising: "Yeah! Sing it like you mean it!" "Put some feeling into it!" "Are you gonna kiss her, or not?"

If he'd thought his face felt hot earlier, it was absolutely on fire now. He wondered if his audience could see the flames.

He felt a hand grasp his and when he realized it was Opal's, the shock sent a thrill through his body. She winked at him and started belting out the lyrics while looking directly into his eyes. Her courage gave him courage, and he increased his volume just a little. The other contestants urged them on, whistling and whooping.

Cash let himself sink into that moment as if he and Opal were the only two in the room and they were honest-to-God singing to one another about how they might have a chance at being together.

The connection was so intense, he just knew she could hear his thoughts, his desire ... to secret her away, take her home and tear her clothes off.

At long last, the song was over, and the instrumentals faded away. A beat of silence passed and then another rowdy contestant yelled, "Well, go on and kiss her, then!"

The look in her eyes said, *Yeah, go on and kiss me.*

He couldn't resist.

He turned toward her, cupped her cheek with his free hand, and slid his fingers into her hair. Cradling her head, he brought his mouth to hers. A gentle sound escaped from her just before their lips touched—something like a sigh—and he swore he could sense the "finally" wrapped up in it. She tasted like wine and mint gum and he felt a tugging in his soul, a magnetic pull, and her arms wrapped around his neck and she leaned into him. Cash was only vaguely aware of the cheers and whistles that accompanied the kissing ... he was wrapped up in Opal's scent and being and couldn't get enough.

Of its own accord, his tongue brushed against hers and she melted against him. The kiss was everything he loved: country music and sizzling steak and cold beer and Opal. And then it was over.

All the contestants were on their feet, clapping, and Opal

winked at Cash again before grabbing his hand and lifting it so they could bow for their audience. He felt his famous (or infamous) movie-star grin spread across his face and decided to just go with it. After the bow he lifted his right arm, triumphant, and someone whistled.

He and Opal held hands until they reached their seats. As soon as his butt his his chair, Sterling leaned over and whispered in his ear. "That was pretty ballsy, man. I'm proud of you."

Cash wasn't sure what to call it, but his entire body vibrated with need. He was certain he couldn't look at Opal again that evening, and even more certain he needed to hightail it out of Skyscraper when the meeting ended.

Chapter Twelve

*W*ell. Opal was going to have to talk to Cash about that kiss. But not right now. Right now, her main objective was to get the hell out of that bar with whatever remained of her dignity somewhat intact. She headed for her car with the laser precision of a missile.

Singing that song with Cash, looking into his eyes while asking him if he was going to kiss her, was *hot*. And excruciating. And then ... *that kiss*.

She'd never recover. Admittedly, she always thought of Cash as a friend. Throughout elementary school, they did everything together. In junior high, when she started seeing boys as "cute" or "handsome," she figured he fit the bill ... but he also started acting out, pulling away. In high school, his movie-star looks definitely positioned him in the out-of-reach, too-hot-to-daydream-about category, and his behavior positioned him in the definitely-don't-go-there category.

But the minute they became reacquainted, when he stormed up her driveway and then offered to help her unload the moving van, Opal's brain suddenly threw him into the go-ahead-and-daydream-but-absolutely-don't-get-attached category. Where he should stay. She rubbed her arms to warm them up from the chill of the air conditioner. Her car chirped when she used the remote to unlock it, and she sank gratefully into the quiet solitude it provided. She buckled her seatbelt as if doing so would prevent anyone—especially Cash—from breaking into her bubble of solitude and forcing her to have a conversation.

She'd been unable to bear talking to Cash after that kiss. Because all she wanted to do was kiss him again. And possibly yank off his clothes and run her hands over his six-pack and kiss him some more. She rolled down the two front windows, letting the evening breeze rush over her skin.

Thank goodness Pearl's waiting at my house.

If she wasn't, Opal would have invited Cash home. Which would be a complete disaster.

As soon as she saw the title of the song they'd sing together, she began to imagine kissing Cash. Of course she did. Hadn't she taken notice of his mouth since he stormed up her driveway to yell at her when she first moved in? Her own lips quirked at that. She started the car and backed out of the spot.

"Who knew karaoke could be so sexual?"

Opal loved her nephews, but at the moment, she wished they weren't with Pearl at her house. She would love to tell her sister every single detail of the three minutes and five seconds she and Cash had sung that song. How she would love to dissect every word, every intonation, every look that passed between them. And, of course, the kiss.

She turned out of Skyscraper's driveway and headed toward her house—and squinted when she thought she saw Leslie's car parked in front of one of the newer restaurants.

"What are you doing out on the town again, you rat bastard?"

She had half a mind to tiptoe into the restaurant and see what he was up to. No, she should give him the benefit of the doubt. Pearl probably told him she was dog-sitting at Opal's, and had probably updated him that it would be even later once she knew about the karaoke.

Most likely, he was just having dinner or drinks with friends. But something seemed off. Suspicious. She knew she shouldn't compare her situation with Pearl's, but every time she saw Leslie out —and not home with his wife and children—she remembered the conversation when Boone admitted he'd been secretly squirreling away their savings, staking his claim to their money so that when he divorced her, she'd have nothing.

"Did you really think I was spending all that time with friends? I knew you weren't the brightest crayon in the box, Opal, but you didn't pick up on anything, did you?"

God, she'd been a fool. She simultaneously slammed on the brakes and yanked the wheel to the right, hitting the curb as she turned into the parking lot.

She parked across the lot from Leslie's car and backed in so he wouldn't see her license plate. There was no way to avoid him seeing her if she went in through the restaurant's front door, so she walked through the parking lot and around the side of the building, doing her best impression of an efficient person who belonged there. She wouldn't dare go through the back entrance and into the kitchen, but ... "Aha." A side door. "Perfect."

A sign on the door read *Emergency Exit Only* and Opal swore. Did that mean there was an alarm? She racked her brain trying to remember if she'd seen an alarm on that door during her previous visits to the restaurant. She had no recollection. And why would she? Nobody went to a restaurant and studied emergency exits.

"Well, probably not *nobody*." She acknowledged that she would surely start doing that herself after this. Still doing her best not to look guilty or out of place, Opal stood back to study the edges of the door, searching for any visible electronics that would indicate an attached alarm. She didn't see anything—the door looked like a regular door.

The heavy slab of metal swung toward her, hinges squeaking, causing her to jump back and yelp. A couple came out, chatting about their meal, and they both jumped when they saw Opal, in much the same way she just had. The woman put a hand on her chest and glared at Opal as she ducked into the restaurant.

And now you have your answer—this door does not have an alarm.

The restaurant was so dark, it took what felt like an hour for her eyes to adjust. She stood there, floundering, feeling like a fox in a chicken coop. She debated heading straight for the restroom, but walking through the spacious dining room seemed too risky. Perilous. Dicey. Not that she could see well enough to navigate anyway.

Finally, the customers at the tables became visible, emerging from the shadows. It didn't take long to find Leslie. His unnaturally broad shoulders stood out in any room. Just like the night she'd seen him at A Cold One, he was with a group of guys. Relief rushed through her. At least he wasn't with a woman. She wished now that she'd paid more attention to his friends, though. She couldn't remember if this was the same group.

A potted ficus stood a few feet to her right and she shimmied along the wall until she was standing as close as she could without climbing into the actual pot. From that spot, she took stock of the other men at Leslie's table. The guy directly to his right had a huge nose. *Poor guy.* Opal could only imagine how much he'd gotten teased as a teenager. She'd never forget that schnoz. The guy to his right wore a light pink button-up shirt and a bow tie. The bowtie was certainly memorable, but he might not be wearing it the next time she saw him. Her search for a distinguishable, memorable feature turned up a giant bald spot. Perfect. *Heretofore, you shall be known as Cul-de-sac.* Next up: a guy whose cheeks were so rosy, she swore he was wearing blush. *David Bowie.*

She couldn't hear their conversation, but she could see that they were all relaxed. Cul-de-sac gestured with his arms as he told some story, his expression changing from serious to smiling and back again. He must be a deadpan comedian, because the rest of the guys laughed, showing their molars. Which made Opal's anger bubble to the surface.

How dare Leslie Marshall spend so many evenings out with his friends, relaxed as could be, while his wife stayed home and agonized over whether the house was clean enough, or whether he was having an affair?

Her fingernails dug into her palms and she ground her teeth

together. She wanted to wring his neck. She pictured his car out in the parking lot, tried to think of something else she could do to it to hurt his pride. She came up empty. Besides, it wouldn't do to keep messing with his car. That strategy was too predictable. She imagined putting a rattlesnake in his trunk, so that when he opened it, the viper would jump out at him. But she quickly dismissed that idea. If one of her nephews opened it before Leslie did, she'd never forgive herself.

No ... she slithered back to the side door and slinked outside. She was going to have to be clever. As she got in her car and headed for home (again), she remembered an article she'd read one April Fools' Day. The writer included a list of pranks, and one of them was to subscribe someone to a mailing list that would shock them.

As the dense city gave way to the rolling hills of her neighborhood, she considered what would be the most shocking to Leslie. She started a mental list: a drag queen association, a ballet company, a rodeo magazine (Leslie'd told her once that he was more of a golf guy; "I prefer manicured lawns to dust and horse shit").

The prank offered only delayed gratification—she would never get to see him receiving letter after letter, but she could imagine it: his frustration as he sorted the mail and found yet another horse-related brochure addressed to him. He'd probably tear it in half and throw it into the trash. But, it's not like she'd stuck around to watch him see her ugly lipstick handwriting on his windshield or his deflated tires. Maybe next time she would. A tiny voice in the back of her mind piped up, asking her what would happen if he called the police, but she pushed it away. She'd leave before the police got there. And seeing him react to her pranks would be so satisfying. In the meantime, she'd have to think of something more immediate, as a little gift to herself.

But that would have to wait until later. Her dog and her nephews must have been actively waiting, because as soon as she cut the engine, the three of them were running out of the house—Wyatt trying to match his strides to Louie's, and Will trying to match his to Wyatt's. That sight warmed Opal's heart and (nearly) pushed the thought of kissing Cash Wilder out of her mind.

Until the dog and the boys tumbled into a messy pile of arms and legs and paws, and Pearl reached Opal, a smug smile on her face. "I heard you kissed Cash." Her voice was barely audible, but it still made Opal's face burn.

"Is nothing sacred?"

"Not when it happens in front of a whole group of people, it's not." Pearl looked so self-satisfied, Opal wanted to scream. And also go inside, dig up a carton of ice cream, and dish about everything. "Was it as amazing as I've been hoping it'd be?"

She barked out a laugh. "Depends. How amazing were you hoping it'd be?"

Pearl rocked back on her heels, arms crossed. "Pretty darned amazing."

"Then, yes."

By that time, the boys and the dog had untangled themselves and were circling Opal and Pearl, vying for attention. Opal leaned town to pet Louie, who'd leaned with all his weight against her leg, and made eye contact with each of her nephews. "Hi, guys! How was your evening?"

"It was great." Wyatt grinned from ear to ear. "Did you know that when a dog leans on you like that, he's hugging you?"

"Yeah, Mom looked it up." Will leaned against Louie and scratched his back.

"Aww, so he's hugging me right now?"

"Yeah!" both boys stepped away and started patting their thighs, calling Louie's name to try to get him to hug them.

"Let's go in." Pearl headed for the front door and Opal followed, with Louie, Wyatt, and Will close behind.

"How was your night?" Pearl wanted to know as she shut the door once everyone was inside. Her eyes sparkled with mischief.

"It was, you know, good." Opal shrugged and Pearl let loose a loud belly laugh.

"It was, huh? Boys, go clean up that game we were playing."

Calling for Louie to follow them, they scampered off and Pearl grabbed Opal's hand and dragged her into the kitchen. "First of all, if a dog makes my kids this compliant all the time, we're definitely getting a dog." She dropped her voice into a hissing whisper and locked her gaze, intense, on Opal's. "Tell me everything."

Opal shrugged, playing down the huge feelings swirling inside her body. "We kissed. But you already knew that, so … "

Her sister dropped her forehead into her hand. "That is not all there is to it, and you know it."

"Fine. You're right." Opal tugged on Pearl's hand so she was forced to stop acting exasperated. "We drew the song—"

"'Are You Gonna Kiss Me or Not?'"

"It's true. There's no privacy in this town." She'd yearned to tell Pearl all the details, but now that they were here, in the kitchen, the kids happily distracted, she couldn't bring herself to do it. Talking about it would make it present, and she wanted it to remain in the past.

"And?"

"And, we sang it, and then at the end, someone shouted for him to kiss me, and he did." She shrugged again, even as her blood heated at the memory of his mouth on hers, their chests touching, his hand resting on her cheek and his fingers in her hair.

"Huh."

"Okay, fine. It was amazing. He's a great kisser and I'm so glad you're here because I would have invited him home to find out what else he's great at."

Pearl nodded, her face saying she'd known it all along. "I wish I'd been there." Opal wrinkled her nose and Pearl laughed. "I mean, not in a weird voyeuristic way, but just to see one of the initial stages of my sister falling in love."

"Oh, no." She held up her hands. "We are *not* falling in love. There is no falling in love happening here."

Pearl shrugged this time, mimicking Opal's nonchalance from earlier.

Opal sighed. "Maybe some amazing kissing, but no falling in love."

Thundering footsteps and giggling announced the return of Wyatt and Will, who plowed into Opal and wrapped their arms around her waist.

"You're right. That—the four-letter word we're talking about—is highly overrated, anyway."

Another pang of guilt hit Opal as she thought of Leslie in that restaurant with his friends, and Pearl's concerns about him having an affair, in large part thanks to her vandalizing his windshield.

"Pearl—"

Her sister held up a hand and inclined her head toward the boys. "We can talk about this later."

Seeing Pearl's stress—those little lines that bracketed her mouth—and picturing Leslie in that restaurant, relaxed as could be, sent another searing bolt of anger through Opal's body.

Consciously, she relaxed her facial features and her shoulders, ruffled her nephews' hair, and followed them out to the car. As Pearl backed out and Opal waved, Louie sat down next to Opal and leaned against her leg.

She scratched behind his ear and when she said, "Let's go," he jumped up and trotted into the house with her. And, when she changed into sweatpants and sat down on the couch, he hopped up there and claimed the spot next to her, just like he'd been doing so all his life. He watched her as she picked up the TV remote and turned on the TV, and when she chose her favorite true crime show, set down the remote, and settled back against the cushions, he put his head in her lap. She rested her hand on his head and he opened his eyes, groaned in pleasure, and closed his eyes again.

Her heart squeezed. She loved this dog already. The urge was strong to snap a picture of him sleeping and send it to Cash. And naturally, when she thought of Cash, she thought of the kiss. And when she thought of the kiss, she experienced a hot pulse of desire between her legs and she at once wanted to banish the memory from her mind and replay it over and over.

"I need a distraction."

At the sound of her voice, Louie opened one eye to glance at her, and when he realized she wasn't getting up or moving, he closed it again.

"Research." She opened the Internet browser on her phone and typed in *Pranks to play on someone you hate.*

Was "hate" too strong a word to describe how she felt about her brother-in-law? No, she didn't think so. When she was midway through a list of pranks, her phone chimed and a notification bubble dropped from the top of the screen.

She'd received a text from Cash. Heart thundering, she tapped on the notification to open the message.

Chapter Thirteen

Cash knew the moment his lips touched Opal's that he wouldn't be sleeping that night.

Once they sat down, she avoided looking at him, and as soon as the meeting ended, she muttered a quick good-bye to everyone and hightailed it out of Skyscraper, leaving him to stew in disappointment. His brothers were eerily silent about the whole thing—they kept throwing him looks, but didn't bother giving hm any advice about what to do. Meanwhile, his body vibrated with need. The need to touch her again, the need to press his body against hers, the need to find out exactly what she thought of that kiss.

That mind-blowing, earth-shattering kiss.

By the time he got home, he was a veritable basket case, unreleased energy propelling him around his tiny living room like a jet engine.

Should he have kissed her? Someone had shouted the suggestion (more like a command), and because it aligned with exactly what he wanted to do, he went ahead and did it. To be fair, she'd kissed him right back, like she'd wanted it, too.

But he had to know: was it as good for her as it was for him? Was she still thinking about it? Was her body in overdrive, craving the finish of what they'd started?

What if her answer was "No"? That would ruin him.

Sterling. Still pacing, Cash pulled his phone out of his pocket and sent his oldest brother a text: *What do I do, man?*

Sterling sent back a laughing emoji. *I'm pretty sure you know what comes after kissing.*

Cash stopped in his tracks. *That's not what I mean and you know it.*

Sterling: *Haha. I do know it. Talk to her, bro.*

Cash: *But what do I SAY?*

A thinking emoji, followed by, *Hey, baby, want to do that again?*

Cash groaned, the sound echoing around the empty room. *I'm not saying that.*

Sterling: *Obviously.*

Crickets. Cash started pacing again. Finally, after he'd made three more laps around the living room, another text came through: *Just tell her you're in love with her and you want to marry her.*

Cash could scream. "I'm not even dignifying that with a response, you asshole."

Another laughing emoji.

Then, after two more laps, Sterling texted: *Bro. Just feel her out. Ask how she feels about what happened.*

Cash ran his fingers through his hair. *What if she hated it?*

Sterling: *Oh, she didn't hate it, man.*

Cash: *How do you KNOW?*

Sterling: *Stop shouting at me.*

Cash: *But seriously.*

Sterling: *Because, dude. She kissed you right back.*

Somehow, Sterling managed to find a gif of two people making out, the woman almost aggressive in the way she groped the man. Cash rolled his eyes.

Cash: *I don't think it looked quite like that.*

Sterling: *Pretty damned close. Just text her. I've got to go. Marital duty calls. Your display of unfettered attraction put June in the mood.*

"Oh, my God."

Cash: *Have fun. I mean, you know. Enjoy. Or whatever. This conversation just took a weird turn.*

Again, Sterling showed off his prowess around finding an appropriate gif. He sent one that showed a guy wiggling his eyebrows suggestively. Cash sent an eye-rolling emoji and stuffed his phone into his back pocket. After two more laps, he decided to take Sterling's advice. He was going to have to face Opal eventually, in person, and he'd rather get this particular conversation out of the way before he had to look her in the eyes again.

He texted her: *You up?*

Not the most original start, but it would do.

Her response: a photo of what he assumed was her new dog, its head resting on her thigh. Her very touchable thigh. He was an idiot. He couldn't think like that. Well, not until he knew how she felt about the kiss.

Cash: *I take it that's your new dog? Seems like he's pretty comfy.*

Opal: *Yep. It's Louie. I can't remember what I told you when I first got to the meeting.*

She'd brought up the meeting immediately. Cash had hoped to dance around the issue for a few minutes at least ... to ease into things. Still restless, he continued to pace.

Cash: *Me, neither.* He sank onto the couch, drew in a breath, and held it.

Opal: *So ... I guess we should talk about it.*

He exhaled, wrote back: *We should.* Then he inhaled and held his breath again.

Opal: *That was some kiss.*

He let out his breath, a smile spreading. Her response didn't sound negative. She didn't sound upset. In fact, if he was reading the mood correctly, she sounded like she'd enjoyed the kiss.

Cash: *It was.*

Opal: *I admit, I wasn't thinking our first kiss would happen in front of two dozen people.*

Cash: *You were thinking about our first kiss?*

Opal: *I can't believe I just admitted that.*

A warmth infused his blood, relaxing his limbs.

Cash: *If it makes you feel any better, I was, too.*

Opal: *That does make me feel better. Btw, does "first kiss" imply there will be more?*

His stomach tightened involuntarily. *Do you want there to be more?*

Her response was slow in coming. He panicked, wished he could delete the message he'd already sent.

Opal: *Total honesty?*

He typed *Always*, but his heart hammered away as he fretted over what total honesty might reveal.

Another long pause, his heart beating so loud, he couldn't hear the sound of the silence around him.

Opal: *I want there to be more.*

He gulped in oxygen, since he'd apparently taken to holding his breath when he was nervous. She wanted there to be more.

Before he could respond, she added, *But I'm not sure it's the best idea.*

Nothing else mattered but the fact that she wanted there to be more. He pictured more kissing—on the porch swing, at her front door, in her kitchen.

Cash: *I've heard that the worst idea can sometimes be the best idea.*

She sent back a laughing emoji. *I think we should talk about this in person. Maybe test out more kissing. But seriously. I haven't even signed my divorce papers and you're about to start a new career. I'm all for kissing, but I don't want to be a distraction for you.*

Cash: *Was that the part you wanted to discuss in person?*

Opal: *Yeah.*

Cash: *Good. Then we can skip straight to the kissing when we see each other.*

Opal: *It was pretty great, wasn't it?*

A thrill ran through him. *It was pretty great.*

Opal: *Isn't your graduation next week?*

Cash: *Yep. One week from today.*

Opal: *Let's revisit this after that.*
Cash: *Wait. So no more kissing until then?*
Opal: *I don't want kissing to ruin your focus. You have tests.*
Cash: *Aw, are you concerned about me doing well on my tests?*
Opal: *Of course I am. Haven't I always been?*

She had. In elementary school, she always asked how he did on tests. Even in junior high, before he pretended to stop caring, she looked at his scores when their teachers handed back their papers. *Yes, you have.*

* * *

The next week was the longest of Cash's life. He woke up each morning and went to bed each evening with visions of kissing Opal playing across the silver screen of his mind. His end-of-academy schedule kept him from being able to see her. He didn't know if that made the time pass faster or slower, but he did know his body—his entire being—ached for her.

He spent the entire weekend locked in his duplex, his nose in the study guides and test prep books for his upcoming exams. Whenever his mind wandered to Opal, which was frequently, he refocused himself on state statutes and law enforcement policies and everything else he'd spent the past several months learning.

Hayes brought him meals Callie had prepared—spaghetti and enchiladas and a whole host of sandwich-making supplies—and he ate while poring over his materials.

By Sunday evening, he was fairly certain he could recite the most oft-used Arizona statutes in his sleep.

Monday during the last session of the day, Commander Mosley said, "Before you go, ladies and gentlemen." Everyone paused. "Graduation's this Friday. As you're likely aware, the on-stage ceremony is followed by the badge-pinning. Remember, you can have one person, and one person only, pin on your badge. Please let me know if you don't have someone."

As distracted as he'd been with the weekend and the kissing-Opal situation, Cash had forgotten to talk to his brothers about the badge pinning. He called an emergency meeting Monday evening and they all crowded into the corner booth at A Cold One, bumping elbows so their beer sloshed onto the tabletop.

After cleaning up with a bar napkin, Hayes rubbed his hands together, eyes alight with anticipation. "Tell me this meeting's about Opal."

The others swung their heads toward him, waiting.

"Sorry to disappoint you, fellas, but Opal and I have put that discussion on the back burner until after graduation."

They all sat up straight, eyes wide with surprise. Travis spoke first. "There's a discussion?"

"Yes, and you all will be among the first to know when it continues."

"Wait." Sterling held up a finger. "This means it's started."

Cash sighed. He just wanted to get to the part where they all decided who was going to pin on his badge. But he knew from experience that they were now like the proverbial dog with a bone. He was going to have to fill them in before they'd move on from this topic. "After we kissed Friday—"

They interrupted him with a messy chorus of "Oh *yeah*," and "You sure did."

—"we had a short text conversation, basically about how we needed to have an in-person conversation."

"But what did the short text conversation entail?" Hayes wanted to know.

"Yeah," Travis said. "Like, how did it start?"

Taking another deep breath, Cash rubbed both hands over his face. "I texted asking if she was up. She sent me a picture of her new dog. I asked his name—I said I couldn't remember whether she told me at the meeting. She said we should probably talk about it. And by it, I knew she meant that kiss." Cash paused and took a moment to look around the table at his brothers, who were rapt. "She said, 'That was some kiss.'"

"That's right, man." Sterling offered a high five.

"And then she said I wasn't expecting our first kiss to happen in front of an audience. Which means she expected not only that we'd kiss, but also that there would be more than one kiss. I asked her if she wanted that, and she said she did."

His brothers all whooped, then laughed at themselves.

He held up a hand. "Don't get too excited. She proceeded to say her divorce isn't officially finalized yet, and she doesn't want to be a distraction for me as I start my police career. Which brings me to the reason for this evening's meeting."

"And that was it?" Travis's eyebrows knit together.

"For now. We said we'd revisit the topic after my graduation. Which, again, brings me to the point of this meeting."

"To graduation." Sterling raised his glass, and Cash ground his molars together, even while raising his, too. He appreciated the gesture but also wanted to get to the point—finally, he had something serious to talk about and they kept derailing the conversation.

Everyone drank and Cash set down his bottle and blurted out, "Listen."

Travis and Hayes exchanged a glance that clearly said, *What is wrong with this guy?*

"At the end of the graduation, there's a badge-pinning ceremony. I'd very much like it if one of you would pin on my badge."

"We can't all do it?" Sterling wanted to know. "I mean, I know it's not technically a three-person job, but we could each do a step, or something."

"That only seems fair," Hayes said.

"Yeah." Travis pantomimed picking up the badge. "Like, I jab you in the chest, and then Hayes removes the pin, and then Sterling clasps it."

Touched that they all wanted to be part of the ritual, Cash shook his head. "I wish you could all do it, but Commander Mosley made it very clear that only one person can come onto the stage for each recruit. And I don't think it's a good idea for me to push any more boundaries at this point."

"I'll arm wrestle you for it." Travis's eyes darted between Sterling and Hayes.

Sterling, looking bored, said, "We all know I always win at arm wrestling. Don't you want to try something where you actually stand a chance?"

"We could fight for it." Hayes looked way too excited. "I haven't had a good fistfight in years."

Travis nodded. "Yeah. Or we could do rock, paper, scissors."

Cash, Sterling, and Hayes responded in unison: "You always cheat at that."

Travis shrugged. "Believe whatever you want to. I'm just exceptionally good at it."

"How about if we take a note out of Tessa Winant's book, and I'll put three slips of napkin into a hat. One will have an X on it. Whoever draws that one will get to pin on my badge."

"I was looking forward to punching Hayes in the face." Sterling shrugged. "But I guess this sounds fair."

"Does anyone have a pen?" No one did, so Cash hollered across the bar to Jerry, who threw one over, missile-style. Cash tore three sections off his napkin, marked one with an X, removed his hat, and dropped in the napkin sections. He stirred them around and held out the hat to his brothers, who jostled each other as they stuck in their hands in and drew out the slips.

Travis drew the winner."Looks like I'm the victor, suckers!" He celebrated, raising his arms and doing a little dance, and the other two punched him on the shoulders.

Cash went to bed that evening feeling all warm and fuzzy and grateful for his brothers.

Testing throughout the rest of the week took up most of his brainpower and energy, and although he and Opal checked in with each other a few times, he mostly kept to himself so he could focus.

Thursday night, all his testing complete, he was so exhausted, he zombie-walked into his house and plopped down on the couch, his eyelids heavy.

That was it: he'd done everything he could do, and he'd find out the next morning whether he'd passed all the tests. He was fairly certain he had; he felt confident as he penciled in or wrote down his answers. But he didn't want to count his chickens before they hatched. He'd been so focused, so energized all week, and now he was ready to sleep for the entire following week.

After graduation. Assuming he *had* a graduation. He set his alarm for the next morning and fell into bed.

* * *

Commander Mosley stood at the front of the police academy classroom, his mouth set in a serious, straight line beneath his serious, bushy mustache.

"I have an announcement."

In his seat, smack in the middle of the room, Cash froze. Was Mosley going to announce that the one and only recruit to fail the testing was Cash Wilder? The other recruits must have had similar thought processes, because everyone sat up straight and went totally silent.

Cash tried to read Mosley's expression. Was he angry? Sad? Disappointed?

He's unreadable, that's what he is.

Not a single element of his expression gave away a single hint as to his emotional state. His eyes showed only calm. The lines that sometimes formed around his mouth were smooth. His mustache was completely still.

"For the first time in academy history—"

Oh, God. He was going to say everyone failed.

—"Every single recruit passed every single exam."

A collective intake of breath sounded.

"Which means I owe every single one of you a congratulations. You're all certified law enforcement officers in the state of Arizona."

A collective cheer went up then, with most people jumping out of their seats and throwing their arms up and hollering and hugging each other or smacking each other on the back.

"All right, all right. Get yourselves together, ladies and gentlemen. We have a graduation ceremony to get to. Go put on your uniforms and I'll see you in one hour at the college auditorium."

The men's locker room was a hive of activity and excitement as

Cash and his fellow recruits changed into their uniforms. Then they headed out, cheering their way through the parking lot. Typically when he was feeling celebratory, Cash would blast rock music while he drove. But not on this day.

On this day, he wanted silence. Silence to contemplate his accomplishment. Silence to sink into feeling proud of himself for taking on—and tackling—something serious. Silence to look forward to changing his life.

The lights were dim inside the auditorium, and Cash felt his nerves rev up, thinking about all the people who'd be in the audience, watching the ceremony. He and the other recruits assembled backstage, the mood a bit more subdued as they waited for the event to begin.

Mosley's gun belt and dress boots creaked as he came off the stage and stood at the top of the short staircase there, a clipboard in hand. "T minus thirty minutes, Officers. Remember, we're using the same lineup we've used throughout academy. So when we call you onto the stage, don't screw it up. Got it?"

"Got it, sir."

This particular group of people would never speak in unison again after this day, and that made Cash suddenly emotional, his throat tightening even as Mosley said, "Good grief, you all sound terrible."

The sounds of people coming into the auditorium, talking quietly and shuffling into seats, filtered backstage, and Cash's nerves revved up. Butterflies took flight in his stomach. His throat worked. His palms went clammy.

"You okay, man? You look like you just heard you're going to the torture chamber, and they haven't told you what they're doing to you, yet."

Cash's laugh came out strangled. "I'm fine. The idea of standing up there in front of an auditorium full of people is terrifying, that's all."

"I remember." Tommy clapped him on the shoulder. "Anticipating it is worse than actually doing it, though. It goes by fast and then before you know it, you're getting your badge pinned on and going out to lunch with your family."

Cash nodded. "Right."

Mosley was back at the top of the stairs. "Attention, recruits!"

Within a split second, they all faced him, heels together, arms at their sides, hands in fists. "Yes, sir."

"It's time for graduation."

No one would have dared celebrate just a day before—when none of them knew whether they'd passed their exams—but someone whooped and the whole group broke into cheers and mayhem, jumping on each other's backs, throwing a few punches, letting out loud, shrill whistles.

"Line up, ladies and gents."

They did, and he gestured for them to ascend the stairs and line up on the stage. Although the curtain was still closed, the hushed conversation sounded louder from there, and those butterflies in Cash's stomach worked themselves into a renewed frenzy. The graduates lined up in alphabetical order, which put Cash in the back row —not that he minded.

Music began to play—someone had procured a live brass band and the notes rose into the air, lending to the scene a solemn and weighty vibe.

I did it.

A sense of calm—driven by the confidence that comes from accomplishment—settled over Cash, dispelling the butterflies and igniting excitement. This was the first moment of his new career. The first moment of the rest of his life. Gone were the days when he floundered around, uncertain of what he wanted to do or who he wanted to be.

He was now Officer Cash Wilder of the Prescott Police Department, infused with determination.

The curtains opened, the metal sliding sound barely audible over the music. At first, the lights were blinding, but once his eyes adjusted, he searched the crowd—the very full crowd—for his brothers. His breath caught when he spotted them. They sat just behind the section reserved for law enforcement officers, which meant they'd shown up early to get good seats. They were dressed up, too.

They're taking this seriously. They're taking me *seriously.*

Sterling, always watchful, saw Cash seeing them and lifted his chin in greeting. Cash returned his chin lift with a small nod. Sterling pointed him out to the others, who naturally waved like lunatics. All three Wilder brothers sat in a row, with June, Callie, and Lila sitting in the next three seats. And—Cash's gasp was just this side of audible—Opal sat next to Lila.

His gaze locked with hers. Just before she smiled, a grin that showed all her teeth and likely mirrored his own, there was a moment of acknowledgement. She was here, with his family, to recognize him, to honor his achievement, to celebrate him.

Commander Mosley walked to the podium and the music died down. "Thank you all for being here today. This ceremony marks not only an important accomplishment in the life of each newly certified officer who stands before you, but also his or her commitment to community."

Applause filled the silence when he paused. Then he turned to the graduates. "Law enforcement can be one of the most fulfilling jobs in the world. Every shift, you have the opportunity to make a difference in the lives of the people you serve. You are a beacon of hope, a pillar of calm, a lighthouse in the storm on some of the worst days of people's lives. Yours will also sometimes be a thankless job, and you'll have to lean on your fellow law enforcement officers, your friends, and your family—the very people in this room today."

One by one, Cash made eye contact with his brothers, the girls, and Opal. Each of them smiled back at him as if to acknowledge Mosley's message, as if to say, *I'll support you.*

Tommy was right: the rest of the ceremony went by quickly, in a blur, and it felt like only seconds had passed before Mosley invited a loved one for each graduate to come to the stage for the badge pinning. Although Travis walked, doing his best impression of a mature adult, Cash could tell he was barely able to restrain his excitement as he took the badge from the woman handing them out. If he could have sprinted up the stairs and onto the stage, he would have. He walked up to Cash and Cash felt his life force hit him, almost knocking him back.

"Congratulations, man."

"Thanks. And thanks for pinning on my badge."

"Wouldn't have it any other way. In fact, the guys were trying to bribe me to let them do it, but I refused."

"Thanks, bro. It means a lot."

Travis pinned on the badge, then pulled Cash in for a tight hug. "I'm so proud of you. So, so proud of you."

Cash squeezed him tighter and swallowed against yet another rush of emotion clogging his throat.

A few minutes later, the official events were over and the new officers and the audience members flowed out of the auditorium and into the fall sunshine. Cash's brothers and the women—including Opal—surrounded him and wrapped him in a swirl of congratulations and hugs and smiles. Lunch was a frenzy of more of the same, and throughout the chatter and laughter and toasts, Cash couldn't take his eyes off Opal.

Only when lunch was over and everyone had gone their separate ways and the two of them were left alone did Cash feel like he could form a coherent thought. And that thought was that he wanted to have that conversation about more kissing.

Chapter Fourteen

Finally. Opal had Cash to herself.

She'd waited all week, unable to think of anything other than the conversation they were supposed to have about kissing.

Well, almost. She'd thought up what she considered some pretty obnoxious pranks to play on Leslie. She needed something to keep her busy, and when Pearl reported that he'd failed to come home to take Wyatt to soccer practice, and then failed to show up at one of Wyatt's games, Opal threw herself into the distraction.

She mailed Leslie a professional looking glitter bomb, so when he opened it his office, he was treated to a hot pink cloud of sparkly stuff that would be impossible to get out of the carpet. She sent him a gift box containing peanuts, which gave him terrible hives (nothing life-threatening). And she poured half of his fancy bourbon down the sink, refilling the bottle's contents with water. Part of her worried he'd blame Pearl for the bourbon, but the other part of her didn't think he'd notice. He put it over ice, anyway.

But now, she was with Cash again, standing just outside the restaurant where they'd all had lunch together after his police academy graduation. The two of them had casually said goodbye as everyone else left, even while they both did their darnedest to make sure they'd be the last two. Her body thrummed with anticipation, which rushed through her veins like a drug.

"Let me walk you to your car." Cash inclined his head toward the corner of the lot.

"Oh, that's awfully chivalrous."

He offered an arm. "I hope you don't expect anything less."

She wrapped her hand around his bicep. He flexed and when she smiled up at him, his eyes twinkled with pleasure.

"I've been waiting to get you alone." She couldn't believe she said the words aloud, but they tumbled out, a dam breaking after a week of waiting.

"Is it because you wanted to continue our conversation from last Friday?"

It was, but she shook her head. "It's because I wanted to tell you how good you look in uniform."

They'd reached her car and she dug her keys out of her purse to unlock it.

"Oh yeah? And how good is that?"

He leaned against the driver's door. Smiling, she put her hands on his waist and leaned against him, so they were hip to hip. Feeling suddenly quite minx-like, she leaned close and whispered in his ear. "So, *so* good."

Goosebumps rose on his skin, which made her shiver.

"How much trouble will you get in if anyone sees you in your uniform, making out with some chick in the parking lot?"

He threw back his head and laughed. "I have no idea. Probably a lot. Maybe we should go to one of our places and kiss. I mean, if that's what you want to do."

"It's what I've been thinking about since the last time we did it." God, her voice sounded so ... *sexual*. When had she become a seductress?

He glanced around the parking lot and when he didn't see anyone watching them, he ran one hand from her hip to her rib cage, where he let it rest, his fingertips brushing the side of her breast.

"Let's go to your place." His voice, a ragged whisper, was still sensual when he added, "I've been wanting to meet your dog."

A fit of giggles overcame her and she pushed away from him. "He's been wanting to meet you, too. Come on, let's go."

He stepped aside, opening the door for her. She smiled all the way back to her house and kept right on smiling when he pulled into the driveway behind her and they both got out of their cars at the same time.

"I was wishing you already had your own patrol car, so you could pull me over."

He smirked. "Wouldn't you rather wait until I'm more experienced?"

She scoffed. "Cash Wilder, I've heard the stories about you. I think you're pretty experienced."

He grabbed her hand and spun her into an embrace. "Only a couple of the stories are true."

Again, she found herself laughing, charmed by the ease between them.

Louie barked from inside the house and Cash said, "I'd better meet the man of the house before we see just how experienced I am. Let me grab a change of clothes."

In her mind, Opal raised an eyebrow at him and told him she didn't think he'd be needing clothes. But she didn't feel ready to be quite that bold yet. So she waited while he grabbed his bag and they walked into the house together.

Louie stood up inside his crate, wagging his tail a million miles an hour, beating it against the side of his crate like a crazy drum.

"Look at that smile!" Cash reached the crate before Opal did, and when she opened the door, Louie bounded out, gave her hand a cursory lick, and headed straight for Cash. Opal didn't know who was happier to see whom. Louie's whole body wiggled and he alternated between bowing and standing up straight, like he had too much energy and didn't know what to do with it.

"I guess introductions are unnecessary."

Cash used both hands to scratch behind Louie's ears and Louie suddenly stopped wiggling and leaned into the scratching. Only for a minute, though. He seemed to realize he was being tricked into holding still, and he leaped back and started wiggling again.

"He loves playing fetch. Why don't we pour a glass of wine and take him outside, so he can run off some of his excitement?"

"Let's. But I'm going to change first. Want to get one more look at me in this uniform?" He did a slow rotation and she ran her gaze from his face to his feet and back again, offering an appreciative whistle.

She poured wine while he changed. She handed him a glass on the way out, then grabbed a tennis ball from the bin Pearl had bought. She threw it into the yard before she and Cash settled onto the porch swing. Louie bounded off to retrieve it and came back to drop it at Cash's feet.

"We should train him to hand it to us," Cash said as he bent down to pick up the slimy ball between his forefinger and thumb.

She noticed his use of *we*, but told herself not to dwell on it. "That would be nice for evenings like this, wouldn't it?"

"It would." He threw the ball. They both watched, sipping their wine, while Louie scrambled after it. When he came back, Cash held out a hand. The dog dropped the ball anyway. Cash laughed. "This is going to take some work."

The ball arced through the air again and Opal figured she might as well dive into the kissing conversation while they the dog to focus on. She took a deep breath to fortify herself. "So."

Cash nodded as if he knew what she was thinking. "The kissing conversation."

Still feeling inexplicably emboldened, Opal said, "I really enjoyed kissing you."

He leaned against her. "Likewise."

"And I really enjoy spending time with you."

"Likewise."

They smiled at each other. Louie came trotting back. Cash held out his hand. The ball dropped to the ground.

Opal took another deep breath. "If I'm being honest, I'm not quite ready for a *real* relationship and all it entails."

Cash nodded and picked up the ball. "Same. I'm finally making something of myself and I want to focus on my career. Not that I'd consider you a distraction, but—"

"I *am* very distracting."

"You are. But I wouldn't want you to feel like you were on the back burner." He threw the ball and Louie tore away to chase it.

"And I wouldn't want you to feel like you were a rebound. You deserve more than that."

"I really like kissing you, though." He sipped his wine and looked at her.

"Likewise." Her lips twitched. Louie came back and ignored the hand Opal offered. She threw the ball for him.

"Do you think we could still kiss? And enjoy each other's company as we can?"

"Kind of a no-strings-attached deal?"

He shrugged. "That sounds bad. I feel like I should clarify, tell you I've never done this with anyone else. I know I've got a reputation—"

"You don't have to explain."

Louie was back. Cash threw the ball. "But I want to. I know I've got a reputation, but it all stems from me flirting at the bars. I dance with women, I buy them drinks, but I haven't dated anyone in a while. I certainly haven't gone home with anyone in a while, if you catch my drift." One corner of his mouth quirked up, and Opal wanted to kiss it. "If you and I do this ... *thing*, whatever we're going to call it, I won't be doing any *things* with anyone else."

"I'm not interested in any things with anyone else."

"Me, neither." He put a hand on her thigh. "Just you."

Louie's return was slower than it had been, and his chase when Opal threw the ball morphed into more of a leisurely jog.

She laid her hand on top of his. "I think we're going to be able to go back inside soon."

Sure enough, on Louie's return, he flopped onto the porch, dropped the ball between his front paws, and looked up at Opal and Cash, grinning again.

"What do you say we go in and consummate our non-relationship?"

Opal felt a pull in her belly and immediately drained her wine glass.

"Is that a yes?"

She stood and offered her hand. He took it and stood, too.

"It's a yes."

Knowing they were about to go inside and kiss—and whatever else the kissing might lead to—Opal became hyper aware of everything. Cash's calloused palm against hers. His clean, woodsy scent. The rhythm of their footsteps as they walked inside. The sudden halt Cash came to in front of her.

"What's wrong?"

He turned around. "Where do we go?"

As much as she had her bed in mind, the idea just now made her a little weak in the knees. "How about the couch?"

Louie, sensing it was time to settle, stepped onto his bed, turned around a couple of times, and curled up in a tight ball.

"Looks like he got used to being a house dog pretty quickly."

"He did." Opal's heart squeezed. "And I got used to being a dog owner. Which is how I knew we should play fetch with him before we consummated our relationship."

"Which," Cash said, "we're going to do right now. On the couch."

He delivered both their wine glasses into the kitchen. When he came back to where she stood just inside the door, he wrapped his arms around her waist and brought his forehead to hers. "I'm not sure how much self-restraint I'm going to have."

The words ignited a pleasant little flame in Opal's core. "I guess we've both been waiting for this."

As if to confirm it was true, he growled and brought his lips to hers. Her body reacted, making her ache for him in a way she'd never ached for anyone else—not even Boone. She banished her ex-husband from her thoughts. He wouldn't taint this moment.

Cash's mouth was gentle at first, but when she sighed and leaned into him, he parted her lips with his and swept his tongue into her mouth. Oh, how she wanted his hands on her, his skin on hers, his body against hers. Removing her arms from around his neck, she took his hands so she could tow him over to the couch. When she pulled him down next to her, their tender kisses became greedy, feverish as their hands explored. His mouth left hers and found her neck, his teeth scraping gently on her collarbone, sending thrills over her skin. He left a trail of kisses on her chest before unbuttoning the top button on her blouse. He paused and when she looked down at him, he asked, "Is this okay?"

"Oh, God, yes. I shouldn't admit how much I've been thinking about this."

Another guttural sound escaped from his throat and he rushed through the rest of the buttons, his mouth following his progress. He opened her blouse and cupped her breasts, then raised himself up so he could look at her. "You're even more beautiful than I imagined." He tugged down one lacy cup to expose her nipple, which peaked, ready for him. She strained against him as he rolled it between his thumb and finger, and she cried out when he put his mouth there.

Unable to resist, she pulled off his T-shirt and ran her fingernails up his back. "If you stop, for any reason, I might actually cease to exist."

He laughed, husky, and returned his attention to her mouth. Their lips still touching, he said, "Don't worry. I'm not nearly done with you."

He hooked a finger into the waistband of her skirt and tugged it down until she had no choice but to slink out of it. And then his hand slid inside her underwear, making her gasp as he dipped a finger into her and then began to stroke her.

"So good." It took all of her self-control not to grab his hand and move against it, but she didn't want this to end.

His finger entered her again, just a single devastating plunge. Opal heard a whimper, realized it came from herself, and smiled when Cash said, "Oh, you like that, huh?"

Desperate for something to do, some way to distract herself from what was surely going to drive her crazy, she eased his sweatpants over his hips. His erection sprang free, surprising her so much that she laughed. "You didn't tell me you're going commando."

Still working his magic between her legs, he chuckled. "I thought it would be a nice little surprise."

"It was that." She wrapped her hand around him; he was glorious. He had all the length and the girth and the smoothest skin. And he was hard. So hard. For her.

Without any warning, her pleasure gave way to release, and she was crying out, bucking against his hand, clinging to his shoulders. Apparently urged on by her orgasm, he moved against her hand, faster and harder, until he, too, shattered, his body shuddering against hers, his face buried in her neck. Neither of them spoke as the aftershocks subsided.

Finally, when they both caught their breath, Cash lifted his head and kissed Opal with a tenderness that made her wish this was a real relationship. "I'd say that was a pretty decent way to kick things off."

Again, Opal laughed. "I agree." Burrowing her fingers into his hair, she pulled him in for another kiss.

He went to get a towel and after they cleaned up, he stretched out alongside her on the couch, his head on her chest. Kissing the top of his head was automatic and when she did, he burrowed in under her chin. For a moment, she thought her heart might break. This all felt so real, so *right*.

The timing was just wrong.

For now, she bolstered herself with the idea of enjoying her time with him while it lasted. Still, as she drifted off to sleep, she couldn't help but wonder what they could be if they'd reconnected under different circumstances.

Chapter Fifteen

Monday morning, Cash blinked himself awake seven minutes before his alarm was set to go off. "It's your first day on the job, Wilder." Nerves springing to life, zipping all over his body, he rubbed his hands over his face.

He glanced at the other side of his bed—the empty side—and wished Opal were there. They'd spent the entire weekend together. He considered the fact that waking up next to her already seemed normal a warning sign.

Still, when he grabbed his phone to turn off his alarm and saw that she'd already texted him, his heart did that weird pitter-patter thing it had been doing since he saw her sitting in the audience at his graduation.

Good luck today. I know you're going to be great. Catch up with me later.

He didn't even realize he was smiling until his cheeks started aching. *Thank you. Good luck to you, too, with the horses. Looking forward to hearing about it this evening.*

She planned to ride Roxy and Velma for the first time that day. He would have loved to be there, but he supposed he had only himself to blame for missing it. If he hadn't kept her schedule packed over the weekend with kissing and cooking and watching movies snuggled under a blanket together—all on repeat—they could have found time to ride.

He got out of bed, ate breakfast, then shaved and showered before putting on his uniform. Then he stood in front of the mirror. He looked good. If his dad—the crusty old bastard—was still alive, he'd say Cash looked smart or dapper. His mom would say he looked handsome. She'd probably pinch his cheek and he'd wince and try to get away.

A rush of emotion hit him.

There he was, an official officer of the law, getting ready to head out, to protect and serve. He could only hope his parents would be proud of him. Before he could get too caught up in all the big feelings, he forced himself to go through the mental checklist. Shiny boots? *Check.* A shiny badge? *Check.* Shirt buttons properly aligned? *Check.* Handcuffs in the gun belt? *Check.*

Commander Mosley's edict, "Early is on time," echoed in Cash's mind as he drove to the police department. He was satisfied when he arrived thirty minutes before his shift started and saw he'd beat Tommy Rowland—who'd be his field training officer for the next several weeks.

Inside, the other officers greeted him casually, as they went through their own morning routines. Someone poured a cup of coffee at the counter along the south wall. A few guys sat at desks, busy with paperwork. A group of detectives gathered around a table at the far end of the room. Everyone seemed engaged, focused.

Cash wasn't quite sure what to do with himself. He found a seat at the edge of the room and pulled out his phone. On reflex, he texted Opal. *My commander spent the whole academy telling us to show up early. Well, I followed instructions, and I'm *really* early. Kind of embarrassing, showing up *too* early on my first day.*

Her reply came through right away. *See? I told you we should've stayed the night together. I would've kept you busy so you were just the right amount of early.*

Ears burning, Cash did his best not to smile and wrote back, *Next time.*

A leather-bound notebook flew through the air and landed with a loud *whack* on the desk next to Cash. He jumped, levitating about three feet.

"You texting Opal?" Tommy's singsongy voice was way too loud in the quiet efficiency of the police station, and Cash rushed to darken his screen. He fumbled the phone and it, too, levitated, spinning. In an attempt to catch it, he managed to punch it out of the air. It clattered to the floor. When he finally got a look at Tommy's face, his friend was smiling, one eyebrow raised. "I see I struck a nerve."

If Cash's face had been warm before, it was positively hot now. Tommy hooted with laughter. He slapped Cash on the back. "Put your phone away, Wilder. We got shit to do." Cash snatched his phone and shoved it into his pocket, then rushed to match Tommy's long strides as they walked out into the vehicle yard. Tommy used his key fob to unlock one of the patrol cars. Its lights flashed and its siren whooped, giving Cash a thrill of anticipation.

They got in and Tommy grinned across the console at him. "So what do you want to do on your first day, Wilder?"

Cash had no idea and he told Tommy so. "What do you usually do?"

"Depends on my mood. Obviously, when calls come in, I take 'em. So, keep an ear on the radio. But for now, we patrol." He checked in with dispatch, then turned to Cash and said, "Let's roll."

Tommy pulled out of the parking lot and headed north. "Downtown is always a good place to start. There's almost always something going on. Not what you'd expect, necessarily, but definitely keeps you on your toes."

They rolled toward the courthouse plaza. The radio chirped and buzzed and Cash listened to the dispatchers and other police officers trading information.

"All units, I'm getting a call from the donut shop on Willis Street. RP states Umbrella Jack is in the drive-thru again. They're requesting assistance."

Tommy picked up his car mic. "This is unit one-four-three-seven. We're nearby. Responding now."

"Copy that."

While Tommy flipped a U-turn, he said to Cash, "This will be an interesting first call for you, Wilder. Umbrella Jack—you know him?"

"He's been a fixture since I was a kid." Umbrella Jack made his home on the benches around the courthouse plaza. Cash remembered seeing him asleep there in the early mornings as they rode the bus to school. During the day, he walked around town, an umbrella overhead no matter the weather. Rumor had it he thought the umbrella protected him from aliens.

"Right. Well, for the past couple of years, he's been a fixture at just about every fast food joint in town. Won't go inside to order his food. He insists on walking through the drive-thru."

"I'll admit, this isn't what I pictured when I thought about our first day on the job."

Tommy chuckled. "I think you're going to find out you couldn't possibly envision even a day in the life, Wilder."

They pulled into the donut shop a minute later.

"Never go through a drive-thru in a marked car," Tommy said. "You're a sitting duck. And if you get a call, you're completely stuck."

Cash nodded. "Got it." He followed Tommy's lead as he got out of the car and headed for the drive-thru.

"So what do we do?"

"Watch and learn, Wilder." Tommy winked at him as they rounded the corner and sure enough, there was Umbrella Jack, umbrella in hand, standing at the menu.

"Jack, my man." Tommy sounded jovial and Jack (and his umbrella) rotated.

Cash had never seen him this close-up before. He had big brown eyes and a neatly trimmed beard. "Tommy. What's up, bro? You're looking good."

"Oh, you don't have to lie to me, Jack. I've heard a million times I've got a face only a mother could love."

Jack's face creased into a smile and Cash was surprised to see his teeth were clean and bright white. "It's all lies, Tommy."

"Want me to buy you a donut?"

He made a dismissive gesture. "Oh, go on now. I've got money."

To prove it, he pulled a crumpled bill out of his pocket and held it up for inspection.

"Can I walk you inside to buy a donut, then? You know you can't walk through the drive-thru, man."

"You know I don't go into these places, Tommy." Turning serious, Jack jerked his head toward the front of the building. "They make me close my umbrella."

Maybe the alien theory was true.

"What if I could convince them to let you leave it open, just while you go in?"

Eyes going round, he shook his head. "They won't. I've tried it."

"Want me to take your money, buy you a donut inside, and bring it out?"

"No, man. I appreciate it, but that's an imposition."

A car had pulled up, and the driver's expression showed a mixture of curiosity and impatience.

"Come on." Tommy gestured, palm up, toward the sidewalk. "Let's at least get out of the way, let these people order."

"I'm already here. Don't know why I can't just put in my order." Jack sounded agitated, but made his way toward the sidewalk.

"You know," Tommy said. "Company policy, safety, blah blah."

"Blah blah," Jack echoed, before lapsing into mutters about safety and a guy walking through a drive-thru and just wanting some donuts.

Cash sighed with relief when Tommy and Jack reached the sidewalk. "You know, I could go in and get you something."

It was as if Jack noticed Cash for the first time. Again, his eyes widened. "Who's this guy?"

Tommy's lips twitched, but he kept a straight face. "This is my good friend, Cash. He's new."

After giving him the once-over, Jack said, "I'll say."

The comment stung—was his newbie status that obvious?—but Cash told himself he shouldn't be offended. Tommy wore a full-on smile, then, and said, "Give him time, though, Jack. He's gonna be great. The two of you will get along just fine."

Jack looked dubious, but offered a handshake. Cash accepted, and was surprised to find Jack's grip firm and his eye contact steady.

"I'm happy to go grab whatever you'd like."

"Nah, I'd rather Tommy did it." He pressed his money into Tommy's hand. "Get me a chocolate bar, will you? And a cream-filled."

"Want coffee?"

"Nah. How about a water?"

"No problem. Be right back."

Cash didn't know whether he should follow Tommy or stay outside with Jack, and Tommy didn't say. He decided on the latter—at least he could try to keep Jack from heading back to the drive-thru.

"So. You're the new guy, eh, Wilder?" Jack's gaze was surprisingly sharp.

"I'm the new guy."

"First day on the job?"

"How'd you know?"

"You've got that look about you. I've seen lots of cops, on their first day and their three-hundredth day. The job changes a guy." He shrugged. "You've got that new-guy look about you. Buck up. Don't look so disappointed. It'll go away."

Cash shook his head. "Thanks."

Jack broke into laughter then—a big, deep belly laugh, and Cash felt his own lips twitching before Jack put a hand on his shoulder. "You're gonna be just fine." He continued to laugh, a weepy, hooting sound, until Tommy returned with a bag of donuts and a big cup of water.

With a grin and a flourish, Jack bowed to Tommy and took the bag and cup. "Thank you, my brother."

"Any time, man. You know that. Stay out of the drive-through, would you?"

Jack shrugged. "I'd like to, man, but you know I can't put down my umbrella. Aliens'll get me."

Tommy put a hand on Jack's shoulder and squeezed. "They do, call me. I'll come kick their asses."

Back in the car, Tommy said to Cash, "Well, what do you think?"

Laughing, Cash said, "Not what I was expecting. I thought we'd be fighting crime and stuff."

"Walking through the drive-thru is a serious crime, Wilder."

"Right."

"Let's roll."

They cruised around town for a while. "Not every day is like this. It's dead today, man. Maybe we should go make some of our own action."

"What do you mean?"

"Let's go run traffic, see if we can't get into some trouble."

Two hours later they'd helped someone change a tire, cleared a couch from the road (it fell out of the back of a pickup truck), and pulled over several cars: two for speeding, one for zooming through a school zone, and one for driving erratically (the driver swerved into another lane when he tried to take a selfie with his dog).

Tommy wrote tickets to two of them. "The guy with the dog? He was a jerk. And for me, school zone speeding is always a ticket, no matter how nice someone is."

Cash stayed in full observation mode, watching everything Tommy did, from the way he greeted and interacted with each person to the exact angle at which he pulled to the side of the road to the words he used when he talked to the dispatchers.

Just as they got back in the car after waving good-bye to the irate-and-muttering dog-selfie driver, a dispatcher's voice came over the radio: "All units, be advised there's a horse running loose downtown. Right now it's crossing the street near Montezuma and Willis."

Cash and Tommy looked at each other across the cab. Cash pointed at the radio. "Does this happen often?"

Tommy grinned. "Only on the most exciting of days. Let's go." He picked up his mic. "Dispatch, this is unit one-four-three-seven. We're nearby. We'll respond."

"Copy that."

"What are we going to do about a *horse?*" Cash wanted to know.

"We're going to figure it out." Tommy turned the car around and headed for the intersection the dispatcher mentioned. "That's about seventy percent of this job, Wilder. They touch on this in the academy, but you almost don't believe it 'til you see it. For every speeding ticket I've written, I've taken a really weird call. I once helped remove an old-fashioned covered wagon from the roadway when a wheel broke. I chased down a burly teenager who stole the money from a kids' lemonade stand and made him give it back. I talked a girl out of jumping off that train trestle behind the hotel."

Before Cash could respond, they spotted the horse. It stood just at the edge of the courthouse plaza, ears twitching, tail flicking.

"Doesn't look like a happy camper," Tommy said, pulling into one of the parking spots along the square.

"Agreed."

They got out and headed toward the horse, which saw them coming and immediately bolted across the lawn and came to a halt at the opposite edge of the grass, ears twitching and tail flicking.

Cash couldn't help but laugh. "We might have come on too strong. Want me to try again?"

"You think you can get him?" Tommy's eyes twinkled with a friendly challenge.

"Oh, I think so." Cash *hoped* so.

By that time, a handful of people had formed a semicircle to keep the horse from running into the street. It still seemed agitated. The whites of its eyes showed and it stepped in place, snorting.

It wasn't wearing any kind of tack. Still moving slowly as he approached the horse, Cash got out his phone and called Tommy. "You got anything in the car that resembles a rope?"

"Yeah, man. I've got a tow strap. Can you make that work?"

"Yep. Bring it to me?" He was within a few yards of the horse.

"You got it."

The horse noticed him, took a couple of steps away from him. "Hey, Tommy?" He paused.

"Yeah?"

"Move slow, okay?"

"Got it, boss."

He tucked his phone into his pocket and continued his journey toward the horse, which had stilled again. "Hey, guy."

The horse blinked and snorted but didn't back away. Cash took another couple of steps, his arms at his sides.

"What are you doing out here, huh?" He'd thought he was done with horses until recently ... and talking to this one, falling into that calm demeanor, was as natural for him as breathing. Now he was so close, he could reach out and put his hand on the horse's neck. But he didn't—not yet. "We're going to have to get you on a rope and find your owner, you know. You can't just run around town."

As he spoke, the horse relaxed. Its ears stopped twitching, its tail stopped flicking, and its breathing slowed. Tommy's footsteps sounded behind Cash, and he held out a hand for the tow strap. Once he handed it off, Tommy backed away. The horse didn't react, so Cash risked reaching out and laying a hand on its neck. Nothing happened.

A car horn blared. Everyone jumped: the people standing by, Cash, the horse ... and it was off, galloping across the lawn, back to the spot where Cash had originally seen it.

Cash swore. The others started to follow the horse, some of them jogging, and Cash called out to them not to chase it.

"If a few of you could make a wide circle, get around to its other side so it won't run into the street, that would be great."

A handful of people followed his instructions, and he started over with his approach, softening his posture, slowing his stride, quieting his voice. This time, when he reached the horse, it didn't settle quite as quickly. "Bro. You can't be running off like that. You're gonna get yourself killed."

It was as if the horse understood him. It took a step toward him, and then another, and before he knew it, his hand was on its neck again and its soft nose bumped up against his shoulder.

"That's a good guy. So what I'm going to do is tie this tow strap around your neck. Just for now. It's temporary. And then we're going to get you to a safe place."

Still moving slow and careful, he slipped the straight end of the tow strap through the loop. He held the contraption up to the horse's nose, then slipped the loop over its head. As soon as he pulled it taut, quiet applause filled the air.

Cash looked around to see that an even bigger group of onlookers had formed while he talked to the horse, quieted it, and secured it. Then Tommy was at his side, patting his shoulder. "Good work, man. Not bad for your first day on the job."

"Thanks." Cash could feel himself glowing with pride, a huge smile spreading across his face. "Only, now what?"

Tommy chuckled. "You'll find yourself asking that a lot. Someone's coming with a trailer and they'll take him to the humane society for now. I'm sure his owner will turn up."

After loading the horse, Cash and Tommy walked back to the patrol car.

"I'm beat, man." Cash leaned his head against the headrest and closed his eyes.

"And think, we're only halfway through the shift."

Cash opened his eyes looked at Tommy. "I think I'm going to need some coffee."

"I've got you, man."

They drove to The Buzz, where Cash pulled out his wallet to pay and the barista, a young man with scraggly facial hair and a nest of dreadlocks, said, "Coffee's on us, man. We appreciate you."

Caffeinated and recharged, Cash and Tommy hit the streets again. Tommy showed him the hot spots for traffic stops and drug deals and high school parties, and then they went back to the office to work on reports.

Cash was dead on his feet by the time their shift ended.

"It's quittin' time, Wilder," Tommy said. He punched Cash on the shoulder. "You did a kick-ass job today, man. We're going to have a blast together on FTO."

He tried to hide his smile as he left the building. Walking through the police department parking lot, his legs felt like lead. As soon as he got in the car though, he felt energized again—because he couldn't wait to tell Opal about his day.

She answered on the first ring and as soon as he heard her voice he knew: everything Tommy said about having someone to go home to was the truth. And he wanted Opal to be his person.

Chapter Sixteen

Opal passed the week in a dream state, working with her horses and caring for her property during the day, welcoming Cash home in the evenings, and spending the nights curled up next to him after he passed out from exhaustion.

Despite her best efforts not to get accustomed, she found herself falling into the routine, floating downward into the blissful oblivion that was domesticity with a man she really, *really* liked. When he came home each evening—correction: when he came directly to her house after work—she served him dinner and they talked into the night, trading stories and laughing and washing dishes before making their way to the porch swing to watch the sun go down, creating a silken peach-and-lavender sky that faded to navy.

They'd go into the house and get on their computers, sending emails and making social media posts to raise money for the Singing for Hope fundraiser. So far, they were in sixth place, which Opal didn't consider half bad.

Friday while she went about her morning chores, she found herself planning when she'd start dinner so it was ready when Cash got off shift.

Oh, how she already loved leaning against him, their bodies

touching from knee to shoulder while Louie ran the yard and the horses neighed from their corral.

Oh, how she wished it could be permanent. But it couldn't. She'd never put him at risk of being the victim of her certain failure. Besides, hadn't he said he didn't want a serious relationship, now that he was finally launching his dream career?

When an unfamiliar car pulled into Opal's driveway, everyone turned, ears pricked: the horses, the dog, and Opal. Louie gave a single alert bark, one that sounded like a cartoony *woof*, and then trotted alongside Opal while she walked up the driveway to meet her unexpected visitor. He looked up at her, his brow wrinkled like he was asking who the driver could be.

She placed a hand on his head. "Don't worry, bud. It's probably just someone who's lost and looking for directions."

Before they reached the car, the driver opened the door and got out. Tall and slender with a full head of slicked-back hair, he wore mirrored sunglasses and held a thick manila envelope.

She froze, just for a moment, and immediately wished she hadn't. This city slicker would undoubtedly report back to Boone that his appearance—or the appearance of the envelope, which held the divorce papers—had affected her. Taking a deep breath, she did her best to gather herself.

"Opal Getty?"

"That's me." She offered him a bright smile and held out her hand. Even if she'd shown her hand with that brief pause in her stride, she didn't have to let on any more that inking these papers and finalizing the divorce actually hurt. She took the envelope. It was cool and smooth against her fingertips.

"You've been served."

She nodded, Louie offered another *woof*, and the man (whose name Opal didn't even know) slipped into his shiny car and backed down the long driveway.

Opal no longer loved Boone—quite the opposite. She watched the stranger's car stop at the end of the driveway, then reverse onto the street, stop briefly, and then head south, back toward town.

Finalizing the divorce hurt because it was akin to admitting she'd failed. Not that this was her first failure, by any means. She'd failed her driver's license test the first time because she forgot to use her blinker for a lane change. And one chemistry test her junior year of high school. She'd *almost* failed a few tests during law school. But those were all small things.

Limbs suddenly feeling quite heavy, she turned around and headed for the front door.

Marriage—if a person decided to do it—was quite possibly the most important activity in life. And if a person failed at it—well, it was quite possibly the biggest possible failure in life. Tears blurred her vision as she reached the front door and turned the knob. She wasn't crying over Boone. She'd told herself she'd never do that again. Not after she realized he'd been squirreling away their money for months.

Louie waited for her to walk through the door and then trotted in after her. "You're more of a gentleman than Boone ever was." She dropped the envelope on the floor, then bent down, took his face in her hands, and kissed the top of his head, tears plopping into his fur. He backed up, just enough to lick her cheek, and then let her bury her face in the soft spot between his ears and cry.

Her life with Boone played like a movie reel in her mind: they met at a cocktail party and his eyes—the ice blue visible at the very edge of a glacier—captivated her right away. He was charming. So charming. *Too* charming, she realized later. He bought her a drink, pulled out a chair, asked her all the right questions. He proposed exactly six months later, at sunset on the beach in a picture-perfect moment.

Whenever she wanted to introduce him to her family, he was too busy ... and he was gone a *lot*. So much that she never questioned him. Well, she never questioned him because he used the best, sweetest, most convincing words to declare his undying love for her.

And when he was there, he was so wonderful. Cooking dinner with piano music playing in the background. Seducing her with lit candles on every flat surface in the bedroom. Bringing her fresh flowers. Buying her favorite cheese and crackers from the specialty market on the corner.

How could I have been so stupid?

"I was so smug about it too," she said to Louie, finally releasing his head and straightening up. In the kitchen, she pulled a tissue from the box and blew her nose and wiped her eyes. "I thought everything was so perfect. I thought I was being such a good, supportive wife, being so easygoing about all of his trips and meetings." She threw the tissue away and grabbed another. Louie watched her, eyes somber, while she blew her nose again and threw away the tissue. "I guess I should just get this over with." She chuckled. "But first, wine."

After pouring a glass of wine—all the way to the rim—she retrieved the envelope from the floor inside the front door and brought it to the dining room table. Louie sat beside her and as if he could sense she wasn't feeling stable just yet, he leaned against her leg. The papers slid out in a tidy, paper-clipped pile. A pen tumbled out after them. "How thoughtful. He included a pen."

A few minutes—and a few signatures—later, she blinked back another round of tears while she waited for the ink to dry. Without another look, she slid the papers back into the envelope. And just like that, it was official: Opal was no longer Mrs. Getty; she'd go back to being Opal Houston, who'd failed at the most important thing in the world.

Louie made a soft grumbling noise and rubbed the side of his face against her leg. She put a hand on his head, grateful she'd made the choice to bring him home. And the horses. Inspiration struck. She'd take them for a ride. Louie could join them. The exercise would do him good. They didn't have to go far.

Within minutes, she had Velma saddled up and a bridle, bit, and reins on Roxy. She mounted Velma, and when she started to ride, Louie stood statue still next to the porch swing. He wagged his tail when she called for him to follow, but didn't move. When she called a second time, he apparently realized he was invited, and leaped into action to follow her. She rode Velma right past the porch and to the rear of the property, where she headed north on a trail she knew bordered the creek.

"It's a beautiful day, isn't it, ladies?" She leaned forward and rubbed Velma's neck as the box horse walked along.

Closing her eyes just for a moment, Opal focused on the sunshine warming her skin. She envisioned the golden rays pushing out those heavy feelings she'd experienced while signing the divorce papers. Inhaling, she imagined breathing in only positive vibes, breathing out negativity. When she opened her eyes, she felt lighter somehow.

"I think everything is going to be all right." From his spot on the ground next to her, Louie smiled up at her, affirming what she'd said.

They reached the creek, which shone like a silver ribbon and gurgled happily over the rocks. Velma approached the water with confidence, like she wanted a drink. But Roxy pulled back against her reins. Opal knew better than to try to force her to get closer, so she dismounted and let Velma go. Louie splashed into the creek, sending droplets flying. That didn't bother Velma too much—she looked at Louie like he was an excitable little boy—but it sure spooked Roxy.

She lurched into motion, jumping forward before rearing, her eyes wild. Opal managed to hold onto her reins for a moment, but then she bolted. Her jerky movement tore the reins from Opal's hand and before she knew it, the horse was heading west along the creek. For her part, Velma simply lifted her head and watched her friend take off, then looked at Opal briefly before putting her head down to drink more.

Although panic set in fast—Opal's heart raced, her hands shook, and she tasted the tang of adrenaline in the back of her throat—she grabbed Velma's reins to keep her from taking off, too. Louie barked and took off after Roxy.

Opal had no idea what to do. Her body froze as her mind raced. Both Roxy and Louie were relatively new to her home. Would they know how to find their way back? Would Louie chasing Roxy make the horse run farther away? What if they made it to the main road? All it took was one turn.

She did all she could think to do: she mounted Velma and nudged her into a run, heading in the same direction Roxy had gone. Velma, apparently sensing Opal's distress, seemed jittery, and Opal knew that if she didn't calm down, she'd spook Velma, too. Inhaling deeply, she slowed Velma to a walk and continued to take slow breaths until her own body stopped vibrating. Meanwhile, she scanned the horizon for Roxy and Louie, but all she saw was scrub oak, grass, and rocks. After a solid minute, she nudged Velma into a run again, her eyes still scanning.

This time, the canter felt smoother and Opal was able to stay relaxed while they traveled parallel to the creek. "They must be booking it."

Over the sound of Velma's hooves hitting the ground and the thump-thump of her own heartbeat, Opal could barely make out the sound of barking. She steered Velma to the right, and every nerve ending in her body jolted when she saw Louie at a spot where a rock wall rose on the opposite side of the creek. His alarm bark, in combination with his raised tail, gave Opal the chills. He had something cornered, and it wasn't Roxy. She was nowhere to be seen. Not wanting to surprise whatever creature Louie'd found, Opal slowed Velma to a walk again and approached the dog.

"Louie." He froze, turned to look at her, and then quickly turned away again and continued to bark.

A rattlesnake. The dog had cornered a rattlesnake. It shook its rattle and lifted its head, fangs bared. Opal's adrenaline spiked again. She called Louie, but he wouldn't be deterred again. The snake lunged at him, and he leaped back, still barking.

Velma took a few steps backward, herself, while Opal's mind raced. "At least you're smart enough to get away from the deadly snake." She tried calling Louie again, and when he ignored her, she wished desperately for a rope. If she had one, she could lasso the dog and yank him to safety.

Her body swayed as the horse pranced beneath her. She had the insane thought that the snake looked just as terrified as she felt. If only she could get the damned dog away from it. Infusing her voice with as much serious authority as she could, she tried again. "Louie. Come."

To her surprise, this time he paused his barking, looked at her, and wagged his tail. Then he resumed barking again. Would it be better to get down and approach him? Maybe if she could grab his collar ... but what if the snake lunged at *her*?

And where was Roxy?

Suddenly a thought struck her: could this be karma for everything she'd done to Leslie lately? But weren't her actions *his* karma? He deserved everything he got. Didn't he? Maybe the universe was trying to tell her that she shouldn't take karma into her own hands.

She'd hate herself if she lost the dog or the horse. And if she lost them both? She didn't know if she could live with herself. Although her eyes were fixed firmly on the dog-and-snake situation, she caught a movement out of the corner of her eye. "Roxy?"

But when she turned her head, she saw that it wasn't Roxy—a plastic grocery bag tumbled across the open area, the breeze blowing it this way and that.

She huffed out a sigh and returned her attention to Louie. If she could just make eye contact with him, maybe she could get him to leave the snake alone. Still uncertain as to whether she was doing the right thing, she dismounted. Reins loose in one hand, she walked toward Louie, who continued his standoff.

Briefly, she considered throwing a rock at the snake but dismissed the idea as quickly as she had it; she didn't want to startle it into biting Louie. Maybe it'd be better to come at him from the side. Heading to the left, she passed the dog and then turned back so she was facing him. She called his name and this time, he seemed to give her his full attention for just a bit longer.

"Come *here*." She pointed at the ground in front of her and just like that, he trotted over and leaned against her leg, looking up at her in adoration, tongue lolling. All the fight had left the snake, too, and it slithered away and disappeared. "I could kill you," she told the dog in her sweetest voice. She didn't mean it, of course, and he'd never hear it in her tone. Her eyes smarted with tears of relief, but that lasted only a split second before worry jumped back in. "Now we have to find Roxy."

When she mounted Velma again and called for Louie to follow, he took off the opposite way—toward the house. No matter how she hollered, he didn't turn around. At least he was headed home.

"Fine." She took another set of calming breaths, climbed back into the saddle, and started off in the direction Roxy had run.

Finally, after what felt like hours but was probably only a handful of minutes, Opal spotted Roxy. She was standing statue-still, her mane and tail blowing gently in the breeze. Opal had Velma approach her slowly, hoping not to set her into running off again, and to Opal's surprise, the only body parts that moved as they approached were Roxy's ears, which rotated toward Opal and Velma and back toward the road.

Velma made a chuffing noise, and Roxy finally looked at them. That's when Opal noticed: Roxy's front leg had a huge gash on it, and the blood ran all the way down to the ground. Hoping Roxy wouldn't move away from the horse she'd lived with for years, she urged Velma forward until she was within arm's length, but didn't reach for the reins right away for fear of sending the horse running again.

"Hey, girl." Roxy remained in place, which Opal considered a good thing. "Want to come on home with us?"

She looked away, as if the answer was clearly, "No." Opal sighed. She had experience with horses, but not with *this* horse. She didn't know whether Roxy was an easygoing girl who would come with her when she took the reins, or if she was stubborn and wouldn't move. And who knew how the injury would affect her?

Gently, she laid a palm on Roxy's neck. Roxy flinched but didn't move away. Moving her palm up and down the length of the horse's neck, Opal talked to her in a soothing voice. "Come on now, girl. Let's go home. If you can walk home, I can take care of you. We'll call the vet, get you all fixed up."

One ear twitched, but still, Roxy didn't move.

Opal turned Velma back toward the house, hoping Roxy would follow—but she'd run so far, the walk back to the house was going to be long. It didn't matter. She didn't budge, even as Velma created some distance between them. Opal turned around and this time when she reached Roxy, she took hold of the reins and tried to lead her back toward the house.

But still, she didn't budge. The reins went taut, Roxy's neck lengthened, and nobody moved. Opal knew better than to force an injured horse to walk.

She had no idea what to do. Cash would—she checked her watch. He should be getting off work any time now. She'd just send him a quick text message, and then she'd wait. Only, when she went to take her phone out of her pocket, she realized she didn't have it. As distracted as she'd been by the divorce papers, she must have left it at home.

The smart thing to do would be to leave Roxy there, head back to the house, and wait for Cash to come back. He'd help her. But she couldn't. She couldn't leave this horse alone on the open land. If she spooked again and ran toward the road, Opal would never forgive herself. So for now, she'd wait. She'd get Velma as close as Roxy would let her, and then they'd all wait, together, until Opal came up with a better idea.

Chapter Seventeen

"I'm tellin' you, someone's messing with me."

"Maybe so, sir, but there's no law against a glitter bomb."

Cash, two hours remaining in his first week as a police officer, walked into the lobby of the police station. He immediately recognized the owner of the first voice as Opal's brother-in-law, Leslie Marshall. Leslie stood across the counter from Detective Robert Montez, who looked like he was trying not to smile. Cash exchanged a glance with Tommy, who looked amused, too.

Almost of one mind after a week of working together, the two of them stopped at the desk behind the counter, pretending to look over some of the papers there. Cash picked up a memo and pretended to read it so he could listen to the conversation.

"It's not just the glitter bomb. Are you even *listening* to me?"

Montez looked down at the notebook in front of him. "Yeah. Someone wrote 'Asshole' on your windshield. Flattened your tires. You're pretty sure they're sending you regular deliveries of dahlias, which you're allergic to."

Leslie huffed. "Right."

"Here's the thing." Montez looked at Leslie again and shifted his weight. "You washed the car immediately after finding the writing on the windshield."

"I can't have my kids seeing it, can I?"

Cash wanted to walk right up to Leslie and punch him in the face. His ego was the only reason he didn't want his kids seeing that on his windshield.

Montez held up a hand. "Of course not. But we have no way of collecting evidence. Unless the coffee shop or A Cold One have surveillance cameras in the parking lot. But I know for a fact that they don't."

Leslie sighed, his chest heaving.

"And we could probably dig in, find out who's sending you flowers, but dude, sending flowers to someone isn't a crime."

"It is if they know I'm allergic, right?"

Montez shrugged. "You'd have to prove they know. And I suppose you could get 'em on harassment, but no lawyer worth his salt is gonna spend any time on that case." He looked back at Tommy and Cash. "Rowland. Wilder. Flowers, can you imagine?" He chuckled, and Cash looked down, hoping Leslie wouldn't recognize him.

Fortunately, he now knew Leslie wasn't the kind of guy who paid much attention to anyone else—not even his own family.

"The tire flattening." Leslie gestured at the notes Montez had taken. "Surely that's a crime."

"And again. You erased any evidence. Filled the tires, went to the carwash."

Leslie ran a hand through his hair. "I've also started receiving mail from the World Drag Queen Association."

"You want me to put that in a police report?"

"I do, man, yeah. Because it's proof that somebody's messing with me."

Montez shrugged again. "Okay. You got it." He bent down and wrote it in his notebook. "Anything else?"

"Shit, I don't know. That's it for now."

Montez slid his business card across the counter. "Be sure to give me a call if anything else happens, okay? We'll add it in."

Leslie picked up the card, turned around, and lifted a hand in farewell as he walked out. Montez turned to Cash and

Tommy. "What the hell are you two doing, just standing there like that?"

Cash opened his mouth to apologize, but Tommy cut him off with a halfhearted punch to the shoulder.

"Bro, what is that leech doing in here, wasting your time over some flowers?"

Exasperated, Montez rubbed his forehead. "You heard the guy. Thinks somebody's out to get him. Flowers, glitter bombs, drag queen mailings. Can't blame the perp, if it's true. Guy's a first-rate asshole."

Remembering what Opal had said about Leslie and Pearl, Cash bit his tongue. He didn't want to risk putting Pearl under the microscope.

"Yeah, I've seen him around town," Tommy said. "Come on, Wilder. Let's get those reports done so we can get out of here on time."

Cash nodded and followed Tommy down the hall. He'd been at a wedding once where the maid of honor asked the newlyweds to look into each other's eyes for ten seconds and then said, "Just think: you're looking at the person who's most likely to kill you."

Everyone had laughed, but Cash had seen enough true crime shows to know the spouse was the primary suspect in many a murder. This wasn't a murder—these were just pranks, inconveniences.

And Pearl? *Nah.* She was just about the sweetest woman Cash knew. She was the type of student to bake cookies or bring coffee for teachers once a week in high school. And she adored her two boys. Cash couldn't think of a situation on Earth where Pearl would flatten the tires of their father's car. No, he figured someone else had to be involved.

When they reached the first patrol desk in the back room, Tommy stopped dead in his tracks. Cash almost ran into him and then saw that he'd lifted a newspaper off the desk and was holding it up.

"What's this?" Cash took it and held it in both hands.

"You made the front page, Wilder. In your first week, too. Not bad for a rookie."

And there he was, in full color, talking to that horse on the courthouse plaza when he'd caught up to it and slung the tow rope around its neck.

The headline blared *Horse Whisperer Cop Saves Equine Life.* Cash laughed. He scanned the story and was pleased to read a quote from the owner: "Fast Break lives up to his name, but fortunately, a Good Samaritan, who also happens to be a police officer, stepped in today to keep him from getting hurt or worse. I'm forever grateful to Officer Wilder. Hit me up, buddy, and I'll buy you a beer."

By the time Cash had finished scanning the article, Tommy had turned around and was congratulating him, and everyone else in the office was clapping.

"Aw, shucks, you guys," Cash said, setting the newspaper on the desk.

Tommy picked it up and handed it to Cash again. "No, no, take this home. It's yours. Show it to your brothers."

Cash shrugged. "Okay. If you say so."

Just like that, his first week was over and he was heading out to his car, his own front-page story in his hand. He couldn't wait to show Opal.

Only, when he got to her house, she was nowhere to be found. She usually greeted him at the door, but not this time. He knocked and she didn't answer, and when he opened the door and called for her, his voice echoed into the empty house.

Her car was in the driveway and the front door was unlocked, so he was sure she hadn't planned on being gone long.

Kneading the rolled-up newspaper in both hands, he called for her again, this time letting the sound of his voice flow over the property. Again, she didn't answer. He shouldn't panic—he knew he shouldn't. She was a strong, independent woman and she'd probably lost track of time while doing chores. Maybe she was in the barn. He headed over there, his excitement about getting out of his uniform forgotten. The barn was completely empty, which gave him a bit of a shock.

It was possible she'd taken the horses for a ride, but he would have expected her to come back in time to greet him. He'd just call her. He dialed and held the phone to his ear, and then heard her ringtone coming from the barn. Only, he knew she wasn't in there. He'd checked every nook and cranny.

Great. Wherever she was, she didn't have her phone. An unsettling feeling wrapped itself around Cash, heavy on his limbs.

In the distance, he heard a dog bark. He didn't know Louie well yet, but he recognized the low-pitched single, "*Woof,*" straight out of a dog cartoon. His hopes lifted. Surely Opal was with him. But when Louie came trotting around the corner, Opal was nowhere to be seen. When the dog spotted him, he ran up and then darted away, this time issuing a higher-pitched yap before running back to Cash and then darting away again.

The unsettling feeling turned to pure dread. Cash rushed to follow Louie. He wondered whether he'd seen one too many dog movies in his childhood. Was Louie really leading him to Opal, or was he just taking Cash on a wild goose chase?

Louie, his nose to the ground, ran all the way to the creek and hooked a left. "I have no idea if I'm doing the right thing, buddy." In response, Louie paused, looked back at Cash, and then put his nose to the ground again. Throwing up his hands, Cash continued to follow him.

The longer they walked, the more worried Cash became. His imagination went on its own wild goose chase, putting Opal in all kinds of precarious situations. She'd a broken leg and couldn't move. She'd encountered a swarm of bees, been stung a thousand times, and was even now experiencing an anaphylactic reaction. She'd come across a bear and was laying in a field with gashes all over her body.

Finally, after he'd walked about a million miles, he spotted Velma and Roxy, standing together in the middle of the field. And then he saw Opal, standing between them, stroking Roxy's cheek. His whole body released as relief flooded his veins. She was alive and upright and seemed more concerned about the horse than she was about herself.

"Opal!" He was running now and when she heard his voice she turned toward him, the relief on her expression mirroring his own.

They met halfway and threw their arms around each other.

"Thank goodness." Opal's voice came out in a near sob.

Hands on her shoulders, Cash held her at arms' length and looked her over. "Are you okay?" He didn't see any damage, but the fear in her eyes made his heart clutch.

"I'm okay. It's Roxy." When she stepped aside, he saw the blood right away and another spike of adrenaline hit him. "What happened?"

Together, they knelt next to the horse to examine her wound. "I don't know. Louie spooked her. Or maybe it was the rattlesnake. She ran off and by the time I caught up to her, she was bleeding." Fresh alarm made it difficult to think clearly. Cash held up a hand. "Wait. A rattlesnake? Is anyone bit?"

She shook her head and another sob, this one sounding something like a laugh, escaped. "Fortunately, Louie listened to reason before he got bit, and this doesn't look like a bite to me. But I can't get her to come with me."

Cash blew out a breath. "I guess luck was on your side today." His mind racing with thoughts of how close to danger Opal, Louie, and the horses had been, he focused again on the injury. The amount of blood had seemed alarming at first, but upon closer inspection, the cut looked relatively shallow. "She may need a handful of stitches, but I don't think she's done any real damage."

Opal licked her lips. "Just to her confidence, which I was hoping to avoid."

They both straightened up and Cash put an arm around her shoulders. "Don't beat yourself up." He kissed her temple, inhaled the raspberry sent of her shampoo, reassured himself that she was fine. "Might not have been the smartest idea to take the horses out with the dog for the first time by yourself."

Grimacing, she nodded. "You're right. That was stupid." She laughed. "But look. I got a sexy man in uniform to come rescue me."

His nervous system had calmed down enough that he was able to chuckle. "You like that?"

"More than I can explain."

Velma shifted on her feet and her movement, along with the sound of her saddle creaking, reminded Cash that they still had a problem to solve.

"What do you say one of us stays here with Roxy while the other rides Velma over to Sweet Springs Ranch to pick up a trailer?"

"That sounds like a fantastic idea. I'll stay here with Roxy. After I brought her out here, I don't want to abandon her."

Cash smiled. "You came after her. I'm sure she wouldn't feel abandoned. But I'm happy to take Velma. I'll put her up at the Sweet Springs, and we can go back for her later."

Opal nodded. "Before you go." She flung her arms around his neck and pressed her lips to his.

The kiss—an expression of gratitude as it was—shouldn't arouse him as much as it did, but Cash blamed it on the relief from the rush of fear he'd just experienced. "You're welcome. And if your gratitude means I get a kiss like that, I'll come to your rescue any time."

He adjusted the stirrups on Velma's saddle, mounted, and took off toward the Sweet Springs Ranch at a comfortable canter. He estimated the ride home would take him about twelve minutes, and he used those twelve minutes to analyze his reaction to finding Opal gone when he'd arrived at her house. The fear he'd experienced was more than what he'd feel for a friend. No, that kind of intense, paralyzing fear was reserved only for those people a guy really really cared about.

Somehow, they'd become more than just partners for the fundraising event. They weren't a couple. They were sleeping together, practically cohabitating, and he couldn't wait to get back to her house to tell her about his day. But that didn't mean he ... *loved* her. Did it?

He pulled back on Velma's reins as they reached his childhood home. "You are in way too deep, Wilder."

Sterling materialized and Cash jumped. "Talking to yourself?"

"Where did *you* come from?"

Sterling grinned. "The RV. June and I just had dinner and—"

He laughed. "And now I'm heading over to the site of the new dude ranch building."

"Dinner, huh? Is that what we're calling it now?"

Sterling's cheeks flushed. "Hey, isn't that one of Opal's new horses?" He looked around. "Where is she?"

Cash explained what had happened and Sterling said, "Shit, man," and pulled out his phone. "Trav. Give me ten extra minutes. I'm gonna help Cash hook up the trailer." He pocketed his phone again and said, "You can take my truck."

Ten minutes later, Velma was safely inside the barn and Cash was driving Sterling's truck, trailer attached, through the field to where Opal and Roxy waited. It took some coaxing and a handful of molasses treats to get Roxy into the trailer, but she walked in on her own. As soon as Cash and Opal got into the truck, she leaned her head against the headrest and sighed. "Thank you so much. I don't know what I would have done if you hadn't come to my rescue."

Even though he could feel himself glowing from her praise, he acted casual as he put the truck in gear. "You would have figured it out. You're a strong, independent woman. It's one of the things I love about you."

Right away, he panicked over using the L-word. But she didn't seem to think anything of it.

She reached for his hand and squeezed it. "Thanks."

Back at the house, they unloaded Roxy and Opal cleaned her wound. Cash was right—it didn't look deep at all. In fact, Opal doubted it would even need stitches.

Chapter Eighteen

A s she and Cash circulated throughout the main room at the swanky Skyscraper bar, Opal had to keep reminding herself that the Singing for Hope fundraiser cocktail party was *not* a date. Most definitely not a date. Still, she couldn't ignore the way their bodies kept coming together, almost as if they had minds of their own. His hand on her back. Her shoulder brushing his. Their arms touching when they stood next to each other.

The presence of everyone in their circle was at once a relief (it forced her to focus on schmoozing and fundraising) and a nuisance (she *so* wanted to be at home and in bed with him).

"Hey!" Leslie's upper lip formed the top side of a triangle and he pointed a meaty finger at Cash. "Aren't you one of the guys who was at the police station the other day?"

Drink in hand, Cash's spine stiffened. Opal felt hers stiffen in solidarity ... or fear. Leslie was at the police station? While panicking, she schooled her expression to one of curiosity. Cash paused before answering and Opal wondered if he was deciding whether to be honest. "I was, yes."

Pearl's gaze snapped to Opal's face. Opal shrugged, going for innocence, as if she had no idea why Leslie would have dropped by.

"They got anything yet?" Leslie demanded.

Cash shook his head, sipped his drink. "I don't know, man. I'm sorry. I'm on patrol and new, too, so I don't hear what's going on in investigations."

Investigations? Why hadn't Cash mentioned that Leslie had been at the police station?

"Wilder." Leslie tilted his head forward, intensified his eye contact with Cash. "Someone's messing with me." He then looked at Opal in what Cash would describe as a leer. "Aren't we practically family now?"

Pearl elbowed him. He'd gone to the police station because someone was messing with him. That someone was Opal. Surely her guilt showed on her face. She could feel her pulse in her throat. Her vision was going all black and swirly at the edges. She had to get away from Leslie.

As charming as ever, Cash raised his glass. "Cheers to family, Leslie. Let's keep tonight fun, and we can talk business the next time we see each other."

Reluctant, Leslie lifted his own glass and tapped it against Cash's. "Cheers." After draining his glass, he flashed a smile that was anything but fun. "See you around." He grabbed Pearl's elbow and steered her away. Over her shoulder, Pearl gave Opal an apologetic wave and grimace.

"You okay?" Cash's eyebrow furrowed. "You're pale. Did you eat lunch?"

Opal's nod made her teeth chatter.

"Did someone lace your drink?"

Her laugh came out way too high-pitched. "I'm fine. A little light-headed. I must have held my breath without realizing."

"Do people really do that?"

Fortunately, Tessa Winant chose that moment to tap her spoon on her glass and call for everyone to listen up. Opal made sure she was one of the first to snap to attention.

Once everyone had stopped talking, Tessa flashed her world-class smile. "First, I'd like to thank everyone who has come out tonight to help our teams raise money for Hope Hall." A cheer went up. Opal howled and clapped along with everyone else. After a few seconds, Tessa raised a hand for quiet and waited while that sank in. "Pretty great turnout, am I right?" Another round of cheers, and some of the tension left Opal's shoulders. "Now. We're going to play a little game." A low murmur traveled through the room. "You're all wondering what it is, aren't you?"

Opal glanced at Cash, whose furrowed brow indicated he was as nervous as she was.

"Before we begin, I'm going to ask everyone present to pull out a bill. A buck, five, ten, twenty—a Benjamin, whatever you've got." Tessa lifted a basket off the table next to her. "I"m going to pass around this basket."

She handed it to the person closest to her, a guy dressed in an expensive shirt and even more expensive shoes. He dug out his wallet and slipped out a bill. Opal couldn't quite make out the denomination before he dropped it into the basket and passed the basket to the next person.

"While everyone's doing that, I'll explain the game." She looked around the room, made eye contact with some of the contestants, Opal included. "I've written down several different scenarios—each one on a slip of paper. Each pair of contestants will draw a slip of paper out of this hat and act it out. That's right—this just turned into improv night!"

This time, her exclamation was met with silence rather than cheers, and she laughed out loud. "Oh, come on, you guys. This is going to be so much fun." Silence. "So. Here's what we're going to do. Everyone is going to draw a prompt. Each prompt is numbered, and that will determine the order of performance. The moment we start drawing prompts, partners are prohibited from communicating with one another. This is improv—we don't want anyone planning anything." She looked around again, serious. "Once everyone has performed, the audience will vote. The winner gets to add all the cash in that basket"—she pointed to the basket, in which a decent-sized pile of cash was visible from across the room—"to their fundraising efforts."

A few people gasped.

"Ladies! Since the gentlemen drew songs at our last event, I'll ask you to come on up and draw your scenes."

Opal made her way into the line with June, Lila, and Callie. She watched the faces of the first few women who drew their scenes. Some smiled while others looked terrified. Then it was Opal's turn. Tessa offered what was probably supposed to be a reassuring smile as she reached into the bowl.

Walking back to her spot, she unfolded her slip. *One of you has been arrested, and your one phone call is to the other. Convince your partner to bail you out of jail.* The number 7 was written at the bottom.

A shock jolted through her system. This prompt was way too close to reality. What if she slipped and let on that she'd actually been harassing Leslie? She hadn't really thought of her pranks as actual crimes until she heard Leslie had gone to the police. She shoved the slip into her pocket.

"Everything all right?" Cash took her elbow and looked at her with his eyebrows furrowed. "You look ... sick. You feeling okay?"

Biting back a sigh, she smiled. "I'm great! Just thinking. Want to see our prompt?" She pulled it out of her pocket and handed it to him, then sank into her seat and took a long pull of her drink. When she set down her glass, Cash winked at her. She could tell he thought the prompt was hilarious. "We've got this, Opal."

From her spot at the other end of the table, Tessa made a *tsk* sound and pointed at them. "Remember, teams. No talking or gesturing or communication whatsoever until it's your turn."

Within a few minutes, every pair had drawn a slip and it was time for the first pair to act.

"Pair number one, please take your places." Tessa gestured at an open space between the tables. The first couple—Juan and Rosita Corales—made their way to the front of the room. Rosita looked sheepish, and Juan, shoulders back, looked confident. "Read your slip, Rosita!"

She smiled with her lips pressed together, nodded. "You're a pair of evil villains. The wife confesses to her husband that she wants to quit the villain life and become a philanthropist. How does the husband react?"

Why couldn't Opal and Cash have gotten that one?

While Rosita and Juan acted out their scene, generating plenty of laughs from their fellow contestants, Opal tried to figure out how she could make Cash the jailbird in their scenario. Maybe if she just picked up an imaginary phone and said, "Hello?" he'd be forced to be the guy in jail.

Only, when they went up, he beat her to it. "A call from the county jail? Yes, I accept."

She had no choice but to take the role of the jailbird. She cleared her throat. "I'm in jail."

"Jail?!" His eyes went comically round. "What happened?"

Sensing her nerves, he gave her a tiny nod and an encouraging smile. "Um, I was arrested." Her eyes darted from side to side. The audience laughed, obviously thinking Opal's pause and wide-eyed look were for dramatic effect.

Cash was grinning, too. "For what?"

What was she going to say? "You wouldn't believe it."

"I'll bet. Why don't you tell me about it?"

She glanced up at the table where her sister was sitting. Pearl stared back at her, waiting, expectant. Opal could swear Leslie was glowering at her, daring her to tell Cash the truth about everything she'd done.

"Well, I was at the lake today."

Cash's eyes lit up. "Don't tell me you were skinny dipping again."

That shocked a laugh out of her—and the audience. "Of course not. Not after the last time, when those fishes bit my—"

"Honey. We have an audience."

More laughter from the audience. "Right. Well, I was at the lake today and there were these cute little ducklings, just along the shore." She had no idea where this inspiration was coming from. "You can picture it, right? The reeds, the lily pads ..."

"Oh, yeah, I can picture it. That's where you dipped your foot in the water right before the fish bit your—"

"Now, now, sweet cheeks. We have an audience."

Someone cackled.

"Well, anyway. The mama duck wagged her tail and went straight into the water. The ducklings followed her. Well, all except one. The mama duck didn't even notice she left one tiny duckling behind." Opal pretended the was seeing the duckling for the first time. "It was so cute. You wouldn't believe it. Its little quack was intoxicating."

Cash sighed. "But you know ducklings grow up, right, sweetie pie?"

"Right." She drew out the word while blinking, all innocence. "I do know that. But that's beside the point. This guy was just so adorable. And I decided I was going to bring him home to you."

In a completely different voice, Cash pretended to be a detention officer: "Two more minutes, young lady."

Opal played right along. "Yes, yes, of course. Anyway, you should have seen the chase. You'd be quite proud of my athletic prowess, dear, really. I followed that little duckling all over creation, just fawning over his *quack-quack-quack*. And that's when the mama duck came around the curve of the shore and saw her little duckling. Let me tell you, she was not happy to see this human—" she gestured at herself—"chasing her baby."

"She started hollering at me. You know how ducks do. Well, as you can imagine, as soon as the duckling saw its mama and all his duck siblings, he made a beeline—or would it be a duckline?—for the water. And I just couldn't let him go. So I dove for him, you know? And I just—I just fell, right into the mucky mud at the edge of the lake."

Cash hissed through his teeth and rubbed his forehead with one hand, like he was used to—and exasperated with—his fake wife's shenanigans. "The mud that's about fifty percent duck shit?"

"The very same."

"And then what?"

"And then—"

"One more minute, ma'am."

Opal had to bite the inside of her cheek to keep from laughing. "And then I could barely stand up, as slippery as it was."

"Because it's fifty percent duck shit?"

"Right. And so, once I finally got myself to standing, I realized—I was completely covered in mud."

Cash let an over-exaggerated realization overcome his features. "Are you about to tell me what I think you're going to tell me?"

"It wasn't my intention, dear, you've got to believe me!" She could say this part with total conviction. It had never been her intention for Leslie to go to the *police* because of some harmless pranks.

She feigned embarrassment, eyes wide, and tucked her chin. Her eyes on Pearl's, she said, "I stripped down." Cash gasped to interject and she rushed to say, "I had no choice!"

Their audience laughed, heads thrown back, glasses raised.

"So, tell me, sweetheart. How much is your bail this time?"

Cash's eyes sparkled with mirth, and Opal's stomach churned with nerves. She could actually wind up in jail. If she did, she certainly wouldn't call Cash to bail her out. But she'd have to face him eventually.

She gulped. Everyone laughed. It was no wonder she sounded near tears when she said, "A thousand."

Tessa Winant's timer went off—they were done—and all the other contestants got to their feet and cheered. A sick feeling clawing its way up her esophagus, Opal forced herself to smile, pretending to bask in the appreciation of her peers.

Cash grabbed her hand, then lifted their joined hands so they could take a bow. When they finished, he grinned at her as if to say, *Wow, look what we did—together!* Her heart simultaneously broke and responded to that connection, pulling her toward him.

Still hand in hand, they made their way back to their seats while the applause continued. Tessa called Sterling and June next, and while they read their prompt, "Your time machine has taken you to the wrong time period," Cash drained his beer.

He set his empty glass on the table as June and Sterling started acting out their skit, then wrapped an arm around Opal's shoulders and squeezed. "That was pretty awesome."

His breath was warm in her ear and goosebumps traveled down her neck, sending pleasant shivers all over her body. "It was."

"What's wrong?"

How could he read her so easily? Risking quick eye contact, she offered a tiny shrug and what she hoped came across as a genuine smile. "Nothing." She inclined her head toward the front of the room where Sterling and June had realized they were in Arizona's nineteenth-century Wild West rather than 1950s Paris. "Just watching those two."

"Right." He squeezed her thigh. "Sorry."

Throughout the remaining acts, she let herself become totally engrossed. Travis and Lila were a pair of farmers whose corn crops had turned to gold. Callie and Hayes were a houseplant and its owner, with her beseeching him to take better care of her. Opal definitely detected a hint of motherhood in Callie as she described to Hayes how she wanted him to feed her, water her, move her to another part of the house and sing to her ... "and maybe even rock me like a baby."

After they were done, Opal excused herself to go to the bathroom and as she rushed away from the table, her fear returned. Cash could never know she'd been the one to harass Leslie. No matter how much Leslie deserved it, it was illegal. Cash was a cop. Heart thumping, she pushed open the bathroom door. Her sweaty palms left marks. She rushed into a stall, her breath coming fast and hard.

"Get ahold of yourself." Her whisper echoed against the walls of the stall. Just like she'd done so many times when she fought with Boone—when he told her she was the worst wife he'd ever had the displeasure of knowing because she asked why he didn't want to spend more time with her—she focused on breathing in through her nose and out through her mouth until her heart rate slowed.

The bathroom door swished open and closed and a pair of high-heel-clad feet made their way in. Opal pulled a length of toilet paper off the roll and wiped her nose.

"Opal? Opal." She recognized Pearl's hiss and quickly dabbed at her eyes.

"I'm in here."

"What are you doing?"

Quite suddenly, Opal felt laughter bubbling up. "Using the restroom."

"No, you're not. You went right when we got here. There's no way you have to go again."

Ah. The age-old laser-focused attention, which a little sister used as a secret power ... or a secret weapon.

"That skit made me nervous. You know what happens when I get nervous."

"Oh, no. This isn't like that time you and I flew to California on our own for the first time, is it?"

Now, Opal didn't bother suppressing her laughter. "Let's not revisit that, shall we?"

"I'm not sure who was more traumatized."

"I was. Certainly. And to answer your question, no, this isn't like that."

Pearl's laugh floated through the room then, echoing much like Opal's whisper had a minute before. "Okay, good. I saw you rush toward the hallway and wanted to make sure you were all right."

Opal flushed the toilet. "Thank you. I'm fine." She emerged from the stall to find Pearl leaning against the counter, arms and ankles crossed, pretty as a picture. Only ... she had that crease between her eyebrows. The one that showed up when she was particularly stressed. Or concentrating. "Are *you* all right?"

"*Moi?*" Another throwback: Pearl slipping into French as a distraction. She put a hand on her chest for dramatic flair as Opal dispensed hand soap.

Opal pointed at her. "*This* is exactly like that time I asked you if you'd been drinking Mom's wine and you said, '*Moi?*' with that sassy blink and everything!" She scrubbed her hands under the water but kept her eyes on Pearl, whose gaze darted around the small space. *Caught.* Opal felt just the tiniest bit guilty, turning the conversation around like she was. But what else was she supposed to do, admit to her sister that she was stressed because she'd been harassing her husband and was worried she might go to jail when she was in the middle of falling for an actual officer of the law? She dried her hands.

"Okay." As usual, Pearl was ready to spill the beans the minute she knew she was pinned down.

The bathroom door opening again saved them both. Pearl mouthed "Later," and they made their way back to the bar. As soon as Opal sat down next to Cash, he rested his hand on her thigh. The contact made her warm and gooey even as anxiety churned in her veins.

A half-hour later, Tessa Winant took and tallied the vote, and when she announced that Cash and Opal had won, Cash hauled Opal to her feet, threw his arms around her waist, and lifted her off the floor.

"Congratulations," Tessa said. She pulled the wad of donated cash out of the basket and held it up, to more cheering and whistles. "This seven hundred and fifty dollars has your name on it. You've just earned three quarters of a grand for Hope Hall."

Cash set her down, grabbed her hands, and looked at her like she was not only the best partner, but also the best person he could have hoped to work with on that skit. And she vowed she'd never do anything even close to illegal again. Ever.

Chapter Nineteen

When the alarm went off, Cash silenced it before stretching and rolling toward Opal, curling his body around hers and nuzzling her neck. The weekend was here, and he couldn't wait to spend every minute of it with her. Just as he finished that thought, she interlaced her fingers with his and turned to kiss him.

Apparently feeling his arousal, she pressed her backside against him. "Good morning."

He released her hand and slid his palm up to cup her breast. "Good morning to *you*."

The sun slanted through the blinds and slivers of light played on the bedspread, shifting as she rotated to face him. "This might be weird to say, but I'm getting awfully used to waking up with a boner in my back."

"God, I love it when you talk dirty. But *boner* is such a crude word. I feel like we should call it an invitation."

A smile forming on her lips, she said, "I accept."

A while later, the two of them made their way to her kitchen for coffee and breakfast, stopping on the way to let the dog out. Cash couldn't believe how quickly they'd fallen into a routine together. As she scooped coffee into the filter, he got out a pan and started on eggs. She finished pouring the water into the coffeemaker and turned it on. He captured her in his arms as she headed for the silverware drawer.

"It's weird." He kissed her and she relaxed into his embrace. "This all feels so new and exciting and at the same time, I feel like we've been doing it for a decade."

She laid her head on his chest. "I know." Cash could have sworn she wanted to say more; she inhaled, then held her breath for a second, kissed him again, and disentangled herself when Louie barked at the door. Before she went to let him in, she gave him a peck on the lips and said, "It's the same for me."

The smell of the pan heating stopped him from asking her what she'd been about to say. He rushed to the fridge to grab eggs. "Wow, Lila's chickens are really laying, aren't they?"

Opal laughed. "Yep. She brought me three dozen today, said we might want to make a quiche or something."

Her use of *we*—especially combined with Lila's suggestion that *they* make a quiche—did something funny to his insides.

The eggs sizzled as they hit the pan. "Are you looking forward to the barbecue?"

"Yeah." She sighed as she pulled a couple of plates down from the cupboard. "It's really nice of your family to include me in all their festivities."

Cash smiled, remembering how irritated he'd been that Callie was giving Opal such a warm welcome when she zoomed onto the property in her moving truck. "They're pretty great."

After feeding the horses, they spent the day together: sitting on the couch with their laptops, catching up on bills and emails, chatting about the weather and the dog and news around town.

Instead of having lunch, they snacked, grazing on vegetables and chips and salsa, and then headed outside to do chores together. Around two, Opal said, "Do you suppose we should go in and make the jalapeño poppers for the barbecue?"

They did, standing side by side in the kitchen as they prepped the peppers, mixed the filling, and wrapped bacon around each one before putting a loaded baking sheet into the oven.

"I'm going to change into my party clothes while the poppers bake." Opal had already headed for the bedroom, and blinked at Cash over her shoulder in invitation to follow.

"Do you think we have time to squeeze in a quickie?"

She winked. "Depends how good you are, Wilder."

He caught up to her, lifted her in his arms, and tossed her down on the bed, where he showed her just how good he could be and how fast he could get the job done. She rewarded him by showing him she was equally efficient, and twenty-five minutes later they both lay on their backs, panting, as the oven timer went off.

"Now we have only twenty minutes to get dressed, fix our sex hair, and package up the poppers." Opal rolled onto her hands and knees, gave Cash another smack on the mouth, and went into the closet. She returned a few minutes later, dressed in a pretty yellow sundress and a pair of sandals.

"Wow. You look great in that dress. Think we have time for another quickie?"

Her smiling eye roll in response—which he'd seen a lot lately—sent a little thrill through his torso. "I'm afraid it just wouldn't do to show up late to your brother's barbecue. Everyone would know what we were up to."

"Nah." Cash made a dismissive gesture. "They'd just think our poppers took longer to pop."

Another eye roll. "Come on, Casanova."

Together, they pulled the poppers out of the oven and transferred them into a glass container before putting Louie in his crate and heading out.

"Is it weird we're showing up as a couple?" he asked as they walked down his driveway, their feet crunching on the gravel in perfect time.

She shrugged. "I mean ... no. Everyone knows we've been ..."

Cash's heart squeezed. Everyone knew they'd been sleeping together. Why did that give Cash such an unsettled feeling? Probably because everyone would assume they were *together* together, and they'd agreed this whole thing was no-strings.

He sighed and Opal squeezed his elbow. "Everything okay?"

Looking down at her, he smiled. "Everything's great."

Her eyebrows drew together and he knew she didn't believe him but fortunately, they'd come up the Sweet Springs Ranch driveway and reached the big house. Sterling and June were just emerging from their RV.

"Hey, guys," June said, running up to give Opal a hug, and then Cash.

"Whaddya have there?" Sterling peered into the dish Cash carried.

When Cash told him, Sterling raised an eyebrow. "Bacon-wrapped?"

"You know it." He held up the pie plate he carried, his lip forming a half-sneer. "Pie. I wanted to bring beer, but June said we had to bring *actual food*."

"June, don't you know beer is its own food group?"

She, too, rolled her eyes at Cash, who said to Sterling, "Is that eye-rolling thing something all women do?"

He chuckled. "Only when they love you, bro."

Those words sent another strange feeling through Cash and he glanced at Opal to see if she'd heard. But she and June seemed to be locked into a conversation as they all climbed into Sterling's truck.

"Travis and Lila are meeting us there." Sterling turned to Cash and grinned a wicked grin. "They were gonna ride with us too, but he texted me that their food isn't quite ready. We all know what that means."

"Right." Cash drew the word out and glanced back at Opal, whose raised eyebrow gave him an *I-told-you-so*.

Inside Hayes and Callie's house, music played over the sound system and plates of food covered the entire kitchen counter. When Opal and June immediately volunteered to help Callie with whatever mysterious activities take place in the kitchen after all the food has been cooked, Hayes beckoned to Cash and Sterling. "I've got something to show you."

He led them into the garage and over to a table where he had a set of blueprints. "I bring to you Casa Wilder. Although, come to think of it, we're going to have to give it another name. All our houses will be Casa Wilder, won't they? I'll have to think on that. But anyway, just look."

He flipped back one giant sheet of blueprint paper to reveal a rendering: a cottage-style house with flower boxes below the windows and a generous front porch.

Sterling put a hand on his shoulder. "Is this your new place, bro?"

"It is." Hayes's smile was bigger than Cash had ever seen it. "We figured we want our little munchkin to grow up on a ranch, like we did." He flipped to the next page and Cash immediately recognized the map of Sweet Springs Ranch. Hayes pointed to a spot on the outer edge of the property, back away from the main road. "So we're hoping to build here. But we wanted to get your okay, first."

"You know you have it." Emotion clogged Cash's throat and he chastised himself. Why was he having so many *feelings*? It was *embarrassing*.

"Yeah, man." Sterling held up a hand for a high five, which Hayes turned into a hug.

"Thanks, you guys. Just gotta get the all clear from Travis."

"Did someone say my name?" Travis came into the garage, arms out like a celebrity making a grand entrance and expecting applause.

"Come look at this, bro." Cash waved a hand at the table.

When Travis got a look at the blueprints, he whooped and raised his arms in victory. "You guys are moving home? I can't *wait*! That baby is going to be the most spoiled niece or nephew this side of the Mississippi."

"So it's okay with you?" For the first time, Cash saw the worry in Hayes's expression.

"Okay?! Are you kidding me? It's the best news I've heard all day."

"I think we need to toast to this," Sterling said, and they all trooped back into the kitchen where the women stood in a tight circle, talking a million miles a minute.

Cash headed for the cooler but stopped when Hayes called, "Hold up. Callie and I want to talk to you all."

Hayes's eyes darted to Callie, to his brothers, and back to Callie again. Was he nervous? The guy had nerves of steel. Callie, her smile brilliant and her posture confident, walked over to stand next to Hayes. She wrapped her arms around his waist and nodded up at him.

"You guys all came over here for a regular ol' barbecue right?"

"Right," Cash, Sterling, and Travis said, the three of them lengthening the word a couple of beats.

"Well, you're actually here for a different reason." Cash exchanged looks and shrugs with Sterling and Travis. "You're here for a wedding."

He let the news sink in, and then cheering and laughing and congratulations filled the air.

"*Now* we need a toast!" Travis said.

"Wait." Hayes grinned at Travis. "I promised Callie we'd all be sober for the ceremony. Which begins in—" he looked at his watch—"ten minutes. You ready, Cal?"

"Ready," she said. He leaned down to kiss her and Cash made a big deal of groaning. "Save it for the wedding, you two."

Only then did Cash realize Callie was wearing a white dress, which showed off her still-tiny baby bump. She was radiant.

The doorbell rang and Hayes hollered for the visitor to come in. A cheer went up when they saw who it was: Jerry, owner of A Cold One, wearing a shirt and tie and a giant smile.

"Ladies and gentlemen, I'd like to present our officiant!"

Jerry came through to the kitchen, accepting hugs and high fives before Travis opened the sliding glass door to the backyard, where a podium stood in front of a wooden archway that was heavy with flowers.

"Let's do this! Guys, out here." Travis practically bounced out to the setup, where he took his spot and held out an arm, palm up, inviting his brothers to stand beside him.

Cash felt a new emotion: pure joy. It filled his torso, fizzy like champagne bubbles, and he laughed out loud. "I can't believe you guys pulled off this surprise."

"Me neither, man. But I'll tell you, it seemed like the way to go.

Barely any planning, barely any costs, no stress. And just wait for the music."

Sure enough, a few seconds later, music—*Marry You* by Bruno Mars—started playing on the speakers in the yard. Lila came out through the sliding glass door, a big bouquet of white flowers in her hands. She walked up an imaginary aisle and then took her spot on the opposite side of the podium from the guys. June was next, also carrying a bouquet. Cash couldn't believe Hayes and Callie had pulled this off without any of them knowing. They must have done some planning to get Jerry here, get those flowers put together, and have the music playing.

Opal stepped through the opening in the sliding glass door and Cash's breath caught. She wasn't the bride, but he couldn't take his eyes off her. Somehow she looked angelic, like she wasn't even of this earth. She glowed, luminescent. And her eyes were on his. Those crystalline blue eyes were so full of affection and happiness and he almost dared to think ... but he wouldn't let himself even consider the word.

Did it matter, anyway, when a woman looked at a man like she was looking at him?

Another swift, powerful wave of emotion hit him, almost knocked him off his feet, as she walked up the aisle. He couldn't even name it. He wanted to protect her and kill for her and take her to bed, all at once. He wanted to keep her all to himself and shout his feelings for her from the rooftops. Every single love song was about the two of them. As she neared the end of the aisle he wanted to reach for her, to take her in his arms and never let go.

But this wasn't their day, he reminded himself as she turned away from him to take her spot next to June. This moment belonged to Hayes and Callie, and to their unborn baby.

When the bride came out of the house, now wearing a veil, the music changed—to the old-fashioned Bridal March—and a collective sigh passed through the air. Callie dazzled in her white dress. Just as Opal's gaze had found Cash's a moment before, Callie's found Hayes's. Cash glanced at his brother, who absolutely beamed. Sterling and Travis must have noticed, too—he heard them each give a little chuckle as Hayes wiped a tear from under his eye.

Callie reached Hayes and handed her bouquet to Opal before she and Hayes took each other's hands.

Behind the podium, Jerry stood up a little straighter and looked first at the wedding couple, then at the women, and then at the men. "I think the best way to start out this ceremony is to say, surprise!"

They all laughed and Jerry opened the binder he'd set down in front of him. "We've come together today to celebrate the love of Hayes Wilder and Callie Barrett and the precious new life they've already created together. Shall we begin?"

"Yes, please," Hayes said, producing another round of laughter.

"I once heard someone say that a couple comes to their wedding day naive. But I disagree. I believe a couple comes to their wedding day wildly in love, ready to promise one another that they'll be together forever. That doesn't mean they don't realize they won't encounter tough times or obstacles, but it means that they promise to do their best to work through those challenges, together. A promise of unconditional love is a promise to double the joy and half the sorrow, to walk side by side through the fire, to emerge holding hands on the other side, stronger and more deeply in love than ever."

Cash swallowed. He could almost hear *himself* saying some-thing about newlyweds being naive—especially in the wake of everything his own parents, his own family, had gone through. He and his brothers had started to piece together what may have gone wrong, and they believed their dad's gambling might have pushed their mom to leave. But how could a woman leave her children? They'd later learned she had tried to come back, but their dad hadn't let her.

What if Levi and Sophia Wilder were the exception rather than the norm?

"With that in mind, I'd like for the two of you to share the vows you prepared." Jerry turned to Callie. "Ladies first."

After a shuddering breath and a quick swipe under both eyes, Callie gave a breathy laugh. "Geez, this is more pressure than giving closing arguments in court." She inhaled deeply, then exhaled, then started to speak. "Hayes Wilder, if you'd told eleven-year-old me that we'd be standing here one day, about to get married, I would have said you were completely crazy. I might have even threatened to punch you in the nose. Not because I didn't like you, but because you were just one of the kids. When I first saw you at Cool Pines two Christmases ago, though ... if you'd told me then that we'd be standing here, not even two years later, I would have laughed out loud. Until I saw your abs. That morning when I caught you coming out of the shower."

Cash chuckled. He was positive Hayes had engineered that moment after Callie arrived at the camp and he saw how damned beautiful she'd turned out.

"I'm hard to resist," Hayes quipped. "Especially fresh out of the shower."

Callie gestured at her baby bump. "Obviously. But let's get back on track. The more time we spent together, the more I realized you're everything I could ask for in a life partner. You're smart and funny and dedicated. Not to mention, handsome. And you're great at arguing." She held up a hand. "I know. You prefer to think of it as healthy debate. Anyway. I know you're going to bring all of those qualities—minus the debating—to fatherhood, and I can't wait to share that with you. I orbit you now, and have since we reconnected that Christmas. You're literally the sun to my earth, and I can't exist without you. I am so excited to be your wife and start our life—and our family—together."

Cash's gaze slid back to Opal, who was wiping her eyes, as were June and Lila. Opal smiled at him again, and he felt it: she was the sun to his earth. God, this was probably wedding fever of some kind. He didn't need a woman to be his sun right now. His career was supposed to be his sun.

He tore his eyes away from Opal to look at Jerry, who was saying, "And now it's your turn, Hayes."

Hayes cleared his throat. "Callie's the orator in this relationship, you guys. Don't expect such a great speech from me."

Cash imagined him just saying, "Ditto"—it was something he would have done as a kid.

But he didn't. "Callie Barrett. I've always thought you were a real pain in the ass, and spending all this time with you over the course of the past two years has confirmed it."

Her mouth dropped open in mock indignation.

"I love it. You're the best kind of pain in the ass. By that, I mean you're hot."

She gave him a slap on the shoulder.

"I'm kidding, Cal. You know that. I love you so much. When I first saw you walk into Cool Pines that afternoon, I thought ... well, I won't say it out loud. But as you just said—and I already had this in my vows, so just know that I thought of it on my own—since I've gotten to spend time with you, I realized you're truly my other half. With you, I feel suddenly complete. I didn't know anything was missing until we reconnected, and now I understand. You're exactly who I was waiting for, all this time. You're exactly the person I need. You're funny and serious, witty and smart, devoted and free-spirited ... you're everything." His voice sounded tight and he paused. "Before we met—as adults—I figured I was fine on my own. I loved my free-wheeling life. But now? Now, I can't imagine living without you. I know now that I was incomplete, and you're that piece that was missing. You and the baby. I will love you both forever, Cal."

Cash was in serious danger of bawling like a little kid. Fortunately, Jerry said, "Wonderful. This is really special, you two. Now, I'd like each of you to repeat after me."

As he read the second part of the vows—the part where Callie and Hayes promised to take each other as their lawfully wedded spouse and forsake all others, whether they were sick or healthy, rich or poor, Cash's throat tightened again. And when Jerry said they could kiss, everyone cheered again.

Cash's vision blurred with tears as they all moved closer to congratulate the newlyweds. There were more hugs and high fives and champagne appeared and everyone raised their glasses when Jerry called out, "To the newlyweds."

Callie set down her flute and brought her hands together. "Everyone! I've been waiting all afternoon to say this. Let's eat!"

They trooped back into the kitchen and lined up at the counter.

Cash ended up behind Opal, and while they waited, she leaned against him, tucking her head beneath his chin. He wrapped his arms around her waist and inhaled the raspberry scent of her shampoo.

When it was her turn to get food, he couldn't help but watch her. Mesmerized, he found himself taking in every detail as she picked up a plate. Her perfectly rounded fingernails were shell pink and stood out against the white dish. The way she held the serving fork as she chose rolls of meat and cheese off the platter, while biting her lower lip in concentration. The toasted-almond shade of her skin where her collarbone met the strap of her dress.

At one point, she paused and smiled up at him, as if she could sense him watching her. He smiled back, his heart pounding out a whole new rhythm.

They all gathered around the table to eat, and he continued to observe her. Her eyes crinkling at the corners when she laughed at something Travis said. The way she covered her mouth in surprise— and glanced at Cash—when June said something raunchy. The golden light gilding her hair through the window as the sun descended.

"Is everyone done eating?" Callie stood and stretched, then picked up her plate. "We have some dancing to do."

Before long, Opal was in his arms and they were swaying to another love song, the sunset blazing in the sky and Cash's heart swelling in his ribcage.

"This has been a magical evening." Opal tilted her head back to look up at Cash.

"It has." He brought his mouth to hers, thinking *magical* didn't even come close to describing the evening, from his perspective. No words existed to describe what was happening to him, but fortunately he didn't have to explain. She rested her head on his chest and that song faded into another and another and all Cash could think about was how he didn't want that indescribable evening to end.

Chapter Twenty

Opal had just come down from the most romantic evening ever. Callie and Hayes throwing a surprise wedding was perfect. And spending those few special hours with Cash was ... sublime. Incredible. The absolute best time of her life.

Night had fallen and they walked hand in hand back to her house, her head on his shoulder, their steps in sync. Would it be wrong to tell him how much she cared for him? Would it be too much to tell him she *loved* him? A raw, tingling energy buzzed around her body—excitement, anticipation, love—wanting to come out. An explosion waiting to happen.

How could they just walk down the driveway like this, when there was so much between them?

"Cash, I—"

He stopped walking and turned toward her and looked into her eyes and in that moment she was terrified. And then he kissed her and it was as if the two of them were frozen in time. Surely the earth continued to spin on its axis—around them as they stood there, hearts melded together.

He ended the kiss and his gaze was at once gentle and intense.

"Me, too."

She found she no longer needed to finish her sentence. He knew exactly how she felt and he felt the same way. Nothing seemed as important in that moment as getting back to her house and taking him to bed.

Louie, of course, had other priorities, and insisted on a game of fetch before he'd let them settle down.

Just as she and Cash poured glasses of wine and made their way to the bedroom, her phone rang—Pearl's ringtone. The impromptu wedding had made it so easy to forget about her concern for her sister, who hadn't called or texted since the improv night.

Her face contorted into a guilty grimace as she picked up her phone. "It's my sister. I'm so sorry. I've got to take it."

"No problem." Cash, all easygoing sexiness, pulled off his shirt and set it on the chair in the corner, then laid on the bed while Opal tapped *Answer*.

She ran a hand over his six-pack and her fingertips under his waistband, and then winked at him and went into the living room.

"Hey." Pearl was all business.

"Hey. What's up?"

"Oh, no. Is this a bad time? This is a bad time, isn't it?"

"No!"

"It is. I can tell. You're doing that thing where your voice is all high-pitched."

Opal sighed and sank down onto the couch. "Okay. Yes. It's sort of a bad time. But I want to talk to you. It's been a few days."

"I'll call you tomorrow."

"No. I insist. I've already answered. Paused the romantic activity that was about to take place—"

"Oh, my God." Pearl's sigh came through the earpiece. "I knew I should have waited."

"Which means you had a good reason for calling and I'm even more glad I answered. The romance will be waiting for me after we hang up. So tell me why you called."

When Pearl started speaking, her voice bordered on hysterical. "I don't know what to do. Leslie—shit, he's coming back in. Hold on."

Opal's breath came short while she listened to Pearl moving

through the house. Was her sister in danger? Opal wouldn't put it past Leslie. Footsteps, the sound of fabric covering the mouthpiece, a door opening and closing. And then, in a whisper, "Okay. I'm back."

"What's going on?" Opal wasn't cold, but she shivered and her teeth chattered.

"Leslie is threatening to leave. He's packing his suitcase. Not just packing it, but slamming around, yanking his clothes out of the closet and dresser and stuffing them into his carry-on. The kids are freaking out."

"What *happened?*"

Voice shaking, Pearl said, "We were eating dinner. I don't know why dinner always has to be a point of contention. But first, I cooked spaghetti. He was already mad about that because he says tomatoes upset his stomach. He said he's told me that before, and maybe he did, but there's no way I can keep track of everyone's preferences. And anyway, isn't Leslie the one who says we shouldn't cater to the boys' preferences? That I should cook whatever I want to cook, and they can eat it or go to bed hungry?"

"So then what?" Opal clenched her teeth.

"Right. So then, of course, because Wyatt always has to act like a smart ass, he was slurping his noodles, trying to slurp as many as he could at once. He probably thought Leslie wasn't paying attention, because he was so busy complaining to me about the tomatoes. But then all of a sudden, Leslie noticed. And you know much bad manners piss him off. He stood up so fast, he flipped the table. Everything went flying. Honestly, he looked as surprised as I felt, but he just went with it. I kept thinking he was going to stop, apologize, *something*, but he started screaming at the kids, telling them how worthless they are, how they can't even act like normal human beings, and he's so sick of their behavior and he just can't stand to be around them any longer."

Opal could kill that guy. She wanted to say to Pearl, "Why don't you just let him leave? You're all better off without him." Before she blurted that out though, she clamped her mouth shut and take a deep breath. "Does he say where he's going?"

"No, only that he's leaving."

"Where are the kids?"

"I sent them to Wyatt's room for now. I told them I was going to clean up the mess in the dining room and I didn't want the broken dishes to cut them. I don't know what to do, Opal. If he leaves now, even if he comes back, he's going to traumatize the boys forever. What they're going to remember from this night is all the horrible things he said to them—and that he left—and they're going to believe it was all their fault." On that last part, she broke into a sob.

Opal wished she was there. She'd grab Pearl's shoulders and tell her to get ahold of herself. "What are your options?"

"I don't know." She drew "know" into a long, four-count note.

"Can you go talk to Leslie, ask him to settle things with the boys?"

A pause, and then, "No. Absolutely not. He's, you know, in the red zone."

"Can you just let him leave?"

"Of course. Of course I can. But the boys—"

"Maybe it's better for Leslie to go out, cool off, get out of the red zone. If you can't reason with him, maybe you can just let him leave, clean up his mess, and comfort the boys. Let him come to his senses."

Another sigh. "You're right. I'll just hunker down here until he leaves. Then I'll make the boys fresh plates and let them eat in the living room while I clean. This all makes sense now. I am so sorry, Opal. I just couldn't think clearly and I didn't know what else to do. Go back and enjoy your romantic evening. I won't bother you again 'til tomorrow."

"You can call me any time. You know that."

"I know. And I love you for it."

"Love you too, sis."

Setting down her phone, Opal closed her eyes for a moment and forced herself to switch mental gears. She inhaled, relaxed the muscles in her face—she could feel herself scowling—and put on a smile.

Cash lay on her bed, hands behind his head, legs crossed. "Everything okay?"

"Everything's fine." Remembering her fear that Cash would know she'd been the one who flattened Leslie's tires and wrote *Asshole* on his windshield, she made sure to keep any venom out of her voice. "Pearl and Leslie had an argument."

"Is she okay?"

"Yep. And while I love that you're concerned enough to ask—" she climbed onto the bed, straddling him—"I think we should get back to where we were before she called."

His hands came to her waist, slid up her torso as he pulled her forward so their lips came together. "I like your thinking."

They moved in sync, removing clothes and touching skin and sighing and whispering, until they both rose to the edge and tumbled off.

Within seconds, Cash's breathing evened out and his arm, draped over her waist, became heavy.

Opal remained wide awake, her eyes open, staring into the dark. How could Leslie blame Wyatt and Will for his outbursts? They were just kids. She couldn't let it go—she wouldn't.

Moving as smoothly and gently as she could, she lifted Cash's arm and slipped off the bed. She wasn't exactly sure what she planned to do, but she told herself she'd be fast. Cash was exhausted. He probably wouldn't wake up while she was gone, but if he did, he'd likely assume she was in the bathroom and fall right back asleep.

She grabbed some clothes out of her closet and padded to the bathroom, where she got dressed. Pulling on her leggings, she considered what she'd do. She had to show Leslie he was wrong— that he was wrong for Pearl and wrong for the boys, even if they did share his DNA. After peeking into the bedroom to make sure Cash was still out, she tiptoed out of the bedroom. On her way past, Louie lifted his head, ears perked. "Be right back," she told him. Satisfied with that, he put his head down and thumped his tail.

In the late-night quiet, Opal's car engine starting up sounded like an explosion. The tires crunching as they rolled down the gravel driveway sounded like a jet engine overhead. "Please don't wake up."

The town was quiet. Lights were turned off, livestock huddled together in fields, and the stars sparkled overhead. Opal drove to Pearl's house first and saw right away that the garage was open and Leslie's car was gone. The lights were on inside, but she didn't slow down enough to catch a glimpse of Pearl through the window. She couldn't risk Pearl seeing her.

"Where would you go, Leslie Marshall?"

The white numbers on her clock glowed 12:24. The bars were still open ... and he had been frequenting them. She went around the block and headed toward downtown.

What was she even going to do? She had to come up with something that would really get to Leslie. Why did his car always come to mind? Maybe because he loved that car more than he loved those boys. He'd even joked with his friends about preferring the vehicle to his wife most of the time. At least, Opal had thought he was joking, but maybe it was the truth.

Downtown was busy, as usual on a weekend night, and Opal suddenly doubted Leslie would come down here, fresh off a rage fest. A hotel. If he'd told the kids he was leaving, he must have in mind somewhere to go.

"If I were Leslie, God forbid, where would I stay?"

Still rolling through town, Opal considered. Just like his cars and expensive leather shoes, Leslie preferred his hotels luxurious and extravagant. The swanky Hotel Prescott was the first place that came to mind, and Opal turned around and headed there.

"Bingo." His car was parked about two-thirds of the way across the lot, straddling the line between two parking spots. *Of course.*

But now what? Surely he was already tucked safely inside his room, away from his family. Undoubtedly he wanted to be alone, away from the sights and sounds of bad manners and chaos.

Deflated, Opal sighed. "This was a stupid idea." She let her gaze roam over the hotel's ivy-covered brick façade one more time. A familiar silhouette caught her eye as she scanned the covered drive-through at the entrance. "There you are."

He wasn't alone.

Right next to his broad, beefy silhouette stood a smaller, slenderer, decidedly female silhouette.

Opal gasped and on reflex, her palm moved to press on the horn. She quickly balled her hand into a fist and pulled it against her chest. She couldn't let on that she was here. She cruised by at a snail's pace. Leslie and the woman—Opal couldn't see her face—leaned close, talking. The woman rubbed his giant back with a tiny hand.

Obviously he'd come to her with some sob story. Ice-cold rage rushed up Opal's torso and all the way to her fingertips. That rage made her want to scream at Leslie that he was a fraud and a liar. She could already feel her throat, raw from screaming.

Leslie and the woman walked into the hotel lobby, her arm linked through his like they were familiar, intimate. Opal took her foot off the brake pedal and let her car coast through the parking lot and around the side of the hotel building where it was pitch dark. Her entire body vibrated as she pulled the car up alongside the hotel, into the shadow of the giant Dumpster. Her breath was shaky. She climbed out and gently shut the car door. Her legs tingled in anticipation of fight-or-flight mode. She walked around the back of the hotel. The keys cut into her palm as she came around the opposite side.

When she spotted Leslie's car again, her gaze zeroed in on it. An idea came to her. She walked toward his car and forgot everything else.

Chapter Twenty-One

Cash woke up and realized right away that Opal was gone. The front of his body and the spot next to him felt cold—she'd been gone a while. His first thought was that something new had happened with Pearl, and he listened for Opal's voice coming from another part of the house.

But it was silent—the kind of silent where a guy knew he was alone. Except for Louie. The dog yipped in his sleep, but Cash didn't hear anything else. He got out of bed and remembered he was naked, so he groped for his underwear and stepped into it. He'd be pretty embarrassed if he walked into the living room in his birthday suit and Pearl was there.

If it were just Opal ... his dick twitched at that. He'd love coming across her if he were undressed. He was still imagining all the ways he could pleasure her on the couch, in the kitchen, on that soft rug on the living room floor, when he realized she wasn't there.

"Shit." She'd gone to her sister's, alone. Which meant whatever argument Pearl and Leslie had been in, it had blown up, and Pearl needed Opal's help. *Shit.* Cash's stomach did a somersault. During his few short weeks as a law enforcement officer, he'd quickly learned that family fights were the most dangers calls for cops to go out on. Those fights often turned violent. Which meant Opal could be in danger.

Don't panic.

He'd call her, first. But pretty much as he expected, she didn't answer. He ran a hand through his hair. He had to go to her. Within two minutes, he was dressed and in his truck, on the way to Pearl's house. He tried Opal again, and again, didn't get an answer.

He drummed his thumbs on the steering wheel as he drove, needing somewhere to displace his nervous energy. As soon as he turned onto Pearl's street, he started scanning for Opal's car. He didn't see it, but Pearl's garage door was open and Leslie's car was gone.

Nausea hit him hard. Opal hadn't come to comfort Pearl—she'd gone to find Leslie.

She'd been so quick to dismiss the content of her conversation with her sister ... was it because she'd planned to leave the house and have it out with her brother-in-law? Cash didn't know Leslie very well, but he did know his type. If Opal confronted him, there was no telling what he'd do.

Cash drove around the block and headed for downtown—he'd seen Leslie at the bars plenty of times, and wasn't it common for a guy to grab a beer after fighting with his wife? The longer Cash looked without finding Leslie's car, the sicker he felt.

What else would a guy do after fighting with his wife?

The casino. Whenever Cash's parents would fight, their dad would slam his way out of the house and head for the blackjack tables. Gambling was his vice; it was why he'd almost lost the Sweet Springs Ranch—he'd gambled away his sorrow for years after Cash's mom left.

But no, gambling wasn't Leslie's style. He was too proud of his financial status to risk losing his wealth. That's why he always bought the finer things: his car, his watch, even his house, which was located in the most prestigious neighborhood in town.

Leslie was a guy who wanted attention. Which meant it was likely he'd sought solace from someone else. But where would he go, if not to his favorite bars?

The answer came to Cash, a nebulous idea taking shape out of smoke rising from a small flame: he'd go to the fanciest place in Prescott: the Hotel Prescott. Cash huffed out a breath. He hoped he wouldn't find Leslie there. Because if he did, that meant Leslie was meeting someone. Probably a woman.

His fears came true when he pulled into the hotel parking lot and saw Leslie's car there. If he didn't dislike the guy already, he would have done so immediately when he noticed the way he'd parked, taking up two spots so people wouldn't open their car doors into his.

He'd found Leslie ... but where was Opal? Neither she nor her car were anywhere to be seen.

A movement near Leslie's car caught his eye. A figure emerged from the darkness into the orange glow of the parking lot light. A familiar figure. It was Opal. She must have parked behind the hotel and walked over.

Joy was the first emotion to hit him. He'd found her. She was alone—and safe. Then, dismay kicked in. She was safe, but she was also moving with the kind of determined energy of someone on a mission.

Oh, no.

She was moving with purpose—and she was moving right toward Leslie's car. Maybe she was just going to look inside, see if he was in there, see if she could talk to him. No. She was walking along the passenger side, one arm down. Cash didn't have to see her arm to know what she was doing. She was keying his car. He was certain of it.

"I should stop her." His voice sounded odd and hollow in the empty cab.

Options ran through his mind. He could go over there and stop her. But then what? He'd be obligated to turn her in, wouldn't he? They could always keep it between the two of them, but if anyone ever found out, he'd be fired. He'd lose the career he'd been working so hard for.

Maybe he should just leave, pretend he hadn't seen a thing.

Pretend he hadn't just seen the woman he was falling in love with—and he *was* falling in love with her—committing what was a felony.

Before he could make a decision or take action, Opal stooped, stood up, and raised her arms over her head. She clutched a huge landscaping rock between her hands.

"Opal! No!" His hands went up, as if his motion would stop her. But she couldn't see or hear him, and she swung the rock downward until it made contact with the windshield. The glass shattered, crumbling, as the rock came to rest on the dashboard.

Cash's jaw dropped. He sat there stunned while she seemed to come out of a trance. She blinked, brushed her hands together, and then turned and walked back into the shadows. Had that really just happened? Was there any way he'd imagined any of it? But no, even though Opal had faded, ghostlike, the many cracks the windshield bore were as real as the steering wheel he gripped.

What now?

If she went back to the house and realized he wasn't there, she would know he'd gone looking for her. He could probably beat her home if he rushed, but he had to confront her, didn't he? Frozen with shock and indecision, he scrubbed his hands over his face.

As if his body was moving of its own accord, his right hand grabbed the shifter and shifted his truck into drive. His left hand gripped the steering wheel and his right foot moved from the brake pedal to the gas and he drove way faster than the speed limit to get back to Opal's house. His limbs shook, vibrated with the emotions his heart was pumping through his veins: anger, for sure, but also hurt.

He parked in the same spot he had before and went into the living room to wait. He decided to leave the light off, just to see how far she'd take things (and maybe so he could surprise her as much as she'd just surprised him). He could hardly sit still.

Inside, he had to wait only a couple of minutes before she opened the front door, moving carefully, trying her best not to make too much noise. After she'd come all the way in and shut the door, she turned around and nearly jumped out of her skin.

"Cash!"

"You weren't expecting me?" Eyes wide, lips parted, she looked like she was in shock. One half of him wanted to go to her, take her hand, wrap his arms around her. The other half of him, fueled by that anger and hurt, wanted to get to the bottom of what was happening—and do so as quickly as possible.

"I was! I mean, you were here when I left—"

"Where did you go?" Asking a question to which he knew the answer was a technique he'd learned in the police academy. He couldn't believe he was using it on Opal.

"I—to Pearl's house." He didn't know if she saw disbelief or disappointment flash in his eyes, but she added, "and then downtown. And then to the Hotel Prescott." Her throat worked.

At least she's telling the truth. "Why?"

"Well." Louie had come out of the bedroom and was stretching, tail wagging. She paused to bend down and scratch his neck. "Do I have to say?"

She's not lying. Yet. "I'd like to know."

She inhaled then, a sharp intake of breath. "You're dressed."

"I am. I woke up to find you gone and I was worried."

He could almost read her thoughts. She was wondering what he'd done when he found her gone. Had he gotten dressed and looked for her? Where would he go, first? Had he seen anything?

"I'm sorry. I didn't mean to worry you."

If only she knew how very much more worried he was after finding her and witnessing her crime. "I wish you'd told me you were leaving."

"You were sleeping so soundly. I didn't want to wake you."

You being gone woke me. He didn't speak the words. He couldn't. What did this mean for them? "Why did you go to Pearl's, downtown, and the hotel?"

"I was looking for Leslie." The sentence poured out of her mouth like water tumbling down a fall.

"Why?"

"When Pearl called earlier and said they'd had an argument, she told me some of the things he'd said to her—to the boys. I just couldn't let him get away with it."

"What was your plan?" Uncomfortable, he shifted on the couch. That didn't help.

"Um, well, I didn't have one."

"Did you find him?"

Her eyes darted to the left. "Do I have to say?"

"Of course not." His gaze locked with hers and he waited.

She shifted her weight, looked at her fingernails. "I don't think I can say. I mean, not to you. I didn't endanger anyone's life." She barked out an awkward laugh. "So you don't have to worry about that."

"Did you break any laws?"

She closed her eyes and tilted her head back. "See, this is the part I don't think I can say. To you."

He sighed and pinched the bridge of his nose between his fore-finger and thumb. "Why not?"

"Could this be, like, one of those 'don't-ask-don't-tell' things?"

"You have to understand how this"—he circled his finger in the air to encompass the situation—"feels to me."

He could hear tears threatening when she said, "I do. And you don't know how much I regret not telling you. But I think it's better —for both of us, but especially for you—if I don't."

Cash couldn't believe this. On one hand, it felt like she was protecting him. But on the other, it felt like she'd betrayed him. He knew the question he had to ask ... the question she had to answer. But he didn't want to ask it, and he didn't want to hear her answer, even though he already knew. "Opal, have you been harassing Leslie for the past several weeks? Flattening his tires, writing on his wind-shield, sending him glitter bombs ..."

Her mouth formed a little *o*, and the guilt was written across her face.

"I think I should leave." He stood up.

With one arm, she reached for him, but she didn't move her feet when he headed for the front door. "Cash."

Hand on the knob, he turned to look at her. God, she was so damned beautiful. He couldn't believe he'd fallen in love with her, and he hadn't even suspected she'd been the one harassing Leslie.

This was exactly the reason he couldn't have a relationship *and* a career—love had made him blind to what was right in front of him. He shook his head, turned the knob, and walked out into the night.

Chapter Twenty-Two

Opal stood in her living room, her body frozen in place while her mind whirled with thoughts. *Stupid. Idiotic. Asinine. He deserved it. I did it for Pearl and the boys. Cash hates me.* Even while she felt satisfied about smashing Leslie's windshield—the adrenaline rush when she saw the glass shatter was such a thrill—she felt sick with regret that she'd betrayed Cash.

And that regret pulsed through her body, washing away the momentary satisfaction. She was a criminal, and he'd never see her as anything else. All along, she'd felt like she was avenging her sister … but now, she realized she was an actual criminal. Even if Leslie never figured out it was her, Cash knew, and that was the absolute worst-case scenario.

When her body finally kicked into motion, it was to call Louie, lock up the house, and head out to the car. They drove straight to Pearl's house, where the garage was still open and the lights were still on, just as they had been thirty minutes ago.

As if the entire world hadn't just changed.

Without knocking, she went in through the garage, Louie at her side. Pearl jumped as the door opened, then put a hand over her heart when she realized who it was. "What are you doing here?"

Her accusatory tone, paired with her accusatory eyebrows, made

Opal's chin wobble just as it had when she was a little girl. Louie licked her hand. "I—I came to check on you, make sure you're all right."

Pearl sighed and her hand dropped to her side."I'm sorry. You scared me." And then, after giving the dog a quick pat, she was in Opal's arms, but only briefly before she stepped back and rubbed her eyes with her knuckles. "Thank you for coming. I feel like I ruined your night."

"You didn't," Opal said, her shoulders slumping. "Where are the boys?"

Pearl hooked a thumb toward the living room. "I shouldn't have called. I—"

"It wasn't that."

"What happened?"

Oh, shit. Telling her would mean admitting Opal had been terrorizing Leslie. Which was bad enough on its own, but his suspicions of Pearl had caused even more friction between them.

"Don't worry about it. You've got enough on your mind. Let me help you clean up the dining room." Opal walked past Pearl and what she saw stopped her in her tracks. The table still stood on one end, the dishes on the floor forming a misshapen semicircle. Noodles and tomato sauce and red wine coalesced. The white tablecloth, stained with various shades of red, lay on the floor by the wall. None of it seemed to bother Louie, who launched forward to explore, gobbling up spaghetti.

"He did this in one fell swoop? Louie! Go lay down!" The dog slinked of, licking his chops.

When she turned to look at Pearl, Pearl deflated and offered a weak shrug. "I mean, no. He flipped the table, then got pissed about it and yanked off the tablecloth and sent all the dishes flying a second time." After a pause during which Opal rotated back to look at the scene again, Pearl's hooting laughter filled the space. "You should have seen it, Opal. It was quite a scene. He slammed his fists down on the table, like a toddler, you know? With a knife clutched in one and a fork in the other. Then he stood up, so fast. I've never seen him move that fast. And then, bam! He'd dropped his silver-ware and tipped the table right over."

She sounded hysterical, and Opal glanced at her again to see tears leaking out of the corners of her eyes. "Should we clean it up? Or are you saving it?"

Pearl went from hysterical to forlorn in a split second. "I'm not saving it. Unfortunately, it's etched into my mind permanently. I guess we should clean it."

Opal nodded, all business (and relief; it seemed Pearl wasn't going to push her for details about her argument with Cash). "Okay. Let's start with the dishes."

Pearl moved robotically, body stiff, and Opal followed her. They knelt side by side and began collecting plates—some still intact and others broken—and silverware. Pearl sniffled while they worked and Opal's thoughts drifted to Cash.

How could she have been so stupid? She should have known Cash would figure it out eventually. He was a smart guy and they were spending so much time together. His new career made the situation even worse. There was no way he could be with her now. And they still had to finish the fundraiser. She groaned.

"I know," Pearl said as they both stood up to carry their dishes to the kitchen. "It's bad."

It *was* bad. "We'll take care of it." *I wish I could say the same for Cash and me.* "I'll start rinsing these and loading them into the dish-washer if you want to gather up the rest and throw the tablecloth in the wash."

Pearl nodded, left her stack on the counter, and returned to the dining room. Opal turned on the hot water and set her stack in the sink. She picked up the sponge, grateful for the scalding water, which felt like a punishment—one she deserved. The rhythm of the chore soothed her, momentarily, but her mind continued to race.

She had to tell Pearl what she'd done to Leslie. Pearl would understand. And she'd be able to help Opal figure out how to make Cash understand.

Even if he understands, he can't be with a criminal. It's not even personal. But it *was* personal—because Opal had put him in a terrible, terrible position.

Her eyes burned with the start of tears and before she knew it, she was in a full-on cry right there at her sister's sink. And then Pearl was back, her arms wrapped around Opal's waist, and they were both crying like little kids.

"It's going to be okay," Pearl was saying, her hand making comforting circles on Opal's back. "I've known this was coming for a while. You don't have to worry about me."

That only made Opal cry harder.

"Come on. Let's turn the table over, mop the floor, get the boys to bed, and then have some wine."

The boys came out of the bedroom and greeted their Aunt Opal with so much enthusiasm, her eyes stung again, and they greeted the dog with even more. Within another half-hour, the women had gotten the kids to bed, and they settled on the couch.

"So now are you going to tell me what happened with Cash?"

Opal tamped down her panic. *Redirect.* "What I have—had—with Cash is so much smaller than what you have with Leslie. I think we need to talk about what happened with you two more than we need to talk about what happened between Cash and me. You said you've been worried about this happening for a while?"

Eyes downcast, Pearl nodded. "Yeah. It started a few months ago. Little things, you know? He started making less eye contact, calling and texting less during the day. Shorter responses. Coming home later—first it was ten minutes, then twenty, then an hour."

Opal gulped.

"Then he missed dinner a few times. Always had an excuse, you know? Lately, he's been getting frustrated with the kids a lot. And since I brought up wanting to get a job, he's been dismissive, telling me I can do whatever I want, but obviously not interested in talking about it. Plus, he started asking me to do extra errands, things he used to do. I kind of felt like he was just trying to keep me busy." She sighed and took a long drink of her wine. "And then, with all this weird stuff happening to him. The tires going flat. 'Asshole' on the windshield. I started thinking he was having an affair—and the affair went bad, you know? Why else would someone want to mess with him like that?"

Opal acted like she thought that was a rhetorical question and didn't answer.

Pearl plowed on. "Did you know someone signed him up for some kind of drag queen association mailing list?" Her lips twitched at that.

On the outside, Opal smiled, but inside, she screamed.

"That whole thing caused a lot of friction. He swore he wasn't have an affair. 'Pearl, I'm just busy at work,' or, 'Pearl, I'm just trying to close this deal so we can take that Alaskan cruise you've been wanting to take.'"

The image of Leslie and the woman at the hotel flashed into Opal's mind. She pressed her lips together. Next to her feet, Louie stretched and grunted before settling back into sleep.

"I've been feeling like our marriage is a ticking time bomb. And the way he left tonight, I think I was right—I think he *is* having an affair. He ran off so quickly, like he knew exactly where he was going and he had someone to go to."

Neither of them spoke for a few minutes. The clock ticked, Louie snored, and Opal geared herself up to tell her sister the truth. Eventually, they both spoke at the same time.

"Tell me about you and Cash," Pearl said, at the same time as Opal said, "I have to tell you something."

Pearl raised an eyebrow, smiling. "You, first."

In that moment, Opal felt like she was twelve years old again, poised atop the jumping rock at the swimming hole along the Verde River where they went every summer. The anticipation of jumping was petrifying. The water always felt freezing on that first jump, and she dreaded it with all her being. Only, she knew she had to do it because all the other kids would chastise her if she didn't. *Jump, jump, jump.* She remembered the chanting—they'd all chant for one another until everyone had gone once.

Jump, jump, jump.

"It was me. I flattened Leslie's tires. I wrote on his windshield. I sent him the glitter bomb and the drag queen brochures. And that's what Cash and I fought about. Well, we didn't really fight, actually—"

"Wait." Pearl held up a hand. "It was *you?*"

Gulp.

"But, why? *Why*, Opal?"

She'd never be able to explain why she got defensive in that moment. "Because he's an asshole, Pearl. Because he deserved it. I see how he treats you and the boys and the barista at The Buzz."

"But, flattening his tires, Opal? Couldn't you just talk to him about it?"

"I—"

"You don't know how much we've argued about these things. Our marriage was on shaky ground before your—I don't even know what to call them! Stunts?" She threw up her hands. "Crimes, I guess. But those pranks you pulled pushed our relationship from shaky ground right off the edge of a cliff. What made you think it was your place to do those things?"

A fresh round of tears filled Opal's eyes and spilled over her lower lids, running hot down her cheeks. "I'm sorry, Pearl. I was doing it for you."

"For me?" Pearl's eyes went wide, her cheeks flushed, and she sat up straighter. "Let's be honest with each other, shall we? You were doing it for *you*. You were so hurt over your divorce from Boone, you wanted to get revenge somehow. Only, Boone is all the way across the country, so you had to take out your anger on *my* husband, tear apart *my* family."

Opal opened her mouth to speak, but Pearl held up a hand. "You know what? I don't even want to hear what you have to say right now. I think it's best if you leave." She stood up, gestured to the front door. "You can see yourself out."

Opal stood, woodenly, and Louie lifted his head, his eyes drowsy. "Come on, Lou." Forcing her mouth to move felt like a gargantuan task, as dry as it was. He got to his feet, stretched, and padded alongside her to the front door. Neither she nor Pearl said goodbye before she walked outside to her car.

Chapter Twenty-Three

If Cash had learned anything during the past several months since Sterling returned to the Sweet Springs Ranch, it was that family could heal. They could heal each other, and they could heal together, as a group.

Which was why he'd asked his brothers to meet up at A Cold One. He showed up early and sat in their normal booth, watching the other patrons with about as much interest as he'd give a fly on the window.

Five days had passed since he saw Opal smashing Leslie's windshield, and the two of them hadn't spoken. He'd spent those five days in physical pain, as if he'd lost a part of himself.

"You okay, Wilder?"

Cash jumped at Jerry's voice and did his best to smile. "I'm fine, man. Thanks."

"You sure?"

"Of course!" He lied through his teeth. "Why do you ask?"

Much to Cash's dismay, Jerry slid into the booth across from him. "For one, you didn't come up to the bar and order a beer." Only then did Cash notice Jerry held a frosty bottle in one hand. He slid it across the table and Cash nodded his thanks. "Two, you've been watching those ladies with about as much interest as a cow gives a cow pie."

Cash shrugged.

"Now, I've heard through the grapevine that you and Opal Houston are—you know."

"We're not."

"Well, now. I think I've just uncovered the answer to my first question. Wanna talk about it?"

"I want to drink about it." Cash lifted the bottle to his lips, took a sip, and winced. Drinking about a woman didn't feel as good when that woman was Opal and he didn't want to get over her like he had others before her.

A group of guys walked into the bar then, and Jerry knocked on the table. "I've got to go sell some drinks. But you know I'm always here to talk if you want to."

"I appreciate it, Jerry."

His brothers were the next to walk in, and each of them greeted him—Sterling with a tip of his hat, Hayes with a salute, and Travis with a finger gun—as they walked to the bar. They slid into the booth a couple of minutes later, each with a drink in hand.

"What's the word, bro?" Sterling slid his bottle across the table to tap it against Cash's.

"Yeah, why the long face?" Travis asked. "Remember when Mom used to say that?"

"I remember," Cash said. He gulped his beer, hoping it would give him the courage to tell his brothers what was going on.

"So?" Hayes pinned Cash with an intense stare.

"You guys have to promise not to tell anyone what I'm about to tell you."

Sterling used a forefinger to cross his heart.

"Sworn to secrecy, bro," Hayes said. "You know you don't have to tell us that."

Cash sighed. "I know. But you can't even tell the girls."

"Pinky promise?" Travis held up a pinky and Cash just shook his head. "Geez, must be serious."

"Have you guys heard Pearl's husband, Leslie, talking about

how someone's been harassing him? Flattening his tires, writing on his windshield, stuff like that?"

"I heard it in passing." Sterling sipped his beer. "But I wrote it off. Figured the guy deserves it."

"Yeah," Hayes said. "Because I've also heard he's basically a chump."

"Right." Cash pressed the heel of one hand against his eye, hoping to stave off the headache that was brewing.

"I heard he chewed out Marcy Winant at the coffee shop because she misspelled his name on his coffee cup." Hayes grinned. "She insisted on getting him a new cup, spelling his name correctly, and remaking the drink—because she knows how much he hates waiting for his coffee."

Cash felt a flame of satisfaction at that.

"Back on track," Sterling said. "What's the word and why the long face?"

Another hefty sigh made Cash's chest rise and fall. "It's Opal."

"What about her?" Travis wanted to know.

"It's her. She's the one who's been doing all that stuff to Leslie."

All three brothers' jaws dropped and the table was silent for a full three seconds before they all busted into laughter.

"Are you serious?" Hayes said. "That's hilarious, dude."

One corner of Cash's mouth lifted. "I know." He let them laugh for another minute before he interrupted them. "But you know what that means, right?"

"It means he finally got what's coming to him!" Sterling raised his bottle and the others clinked theirs against it.

"It does. But it also means I can't see her any more."

That sobered them up.

"But—" Hayes looked at Sterling and then Travis. Then understanding dawned. "Ohhh. It's because you're a cop now. And she's—she's committed some real, actual crimes."

"Ding, ding, ding." Cash scowled. "You got the right answer." He smiled. "But wait. There's more. In the game of what Opal did to ruin our relationship, there's one more really big thing. She went to the hotel where Leslie was staying and threw a rock the size of her head through his windshield."

Another stunned silence followed.

Sterling was the first to speak. "She *did* that?"

Cash nodded and took another pull from his bottle. "She did. She doesn't know I know, but I saw her do it."

"How did you see her do it without her knowing you saw her?" Hayes said.

"Well, after your wedding, we went back to her house. We were feeling all lovey-dovey, you know? Inspired by your and Callie's vows and everything. Pearl called, and Opal went into the living room to talk to her. She came back into the bedroom, acting like everything was normal—"

"You mean, you boinked."

Cash threw Travis a look. "Afterwards, we fell asleep. Well, I did. I woke up a little while later and she was gone. Not just in the bathroom or the kitchen, but gone from the house."

"So you freaked out because if Pearl's fight with Leslie was bad enough for Opal to head over there, you didn't know what he'd do." Hayes's summary was surprisingly accurate. "You went after her."

"Exactly." Cash nodded. "She wasn't at Pearl's—but neither was Leslie's car. I figured, either she'd gone there and he'd killed her and was taking her body somewhere, or she'd shown up and he wasn't there, so she went looking for him. Long story short, I found his car over at the Hotel Prescott. I was just sitting there, thinking about where to look next, when I saw her come out of the shadows like some kind of weird apparition."

All three brothers stared at him, rapt. He told them how he'd debated getting out of the car and going to talk to her, but she'd keyed Leslie's car before he made a decision—and then picked up a giant rock and heaved it through the windshield. They stared at him, still silent, as he described how they both ended up back at her house, and how he'd ended up leaving—and they hadn't talked since.

"Wow," Sterling said. "This is …"

"Messed up," Travis finished.

"I think we need another round." Hayes slid out of the booth and returned to the bar.

Cash, Sterling, and Travis sat without speaking until he came back and distributed the beers.

"I have no words," Hayes said. "Drink." They all drank.

"So what are you going to do?" Sterling said.

"There's nothing to do. I ended things. I had to, didn't I?"

His brothers exchanged glances.

Hayes shrugged. "I mean, I'd like to think there's another option. We just have to think of it. Isn't that why you called this meeting?"

Was it? Cash wasn't sure. He'd known only that he needed his brothers. He needed to sit with them, drink with them, talk to them, and spill his guts. "I'm not sure, actually. I just needed to talk it out."

"Come on, gentlemen!" Sterling's tone had shifted to rousing. "We're the Wilder boys. Superior in physicality and intellect." He cracked his knuckles. "Surely we can devise some sort of solution."

"Nah, man. We can't. Technically, I should report her for everything, most of all smashing that windshield. If anyone ever finds out I knew about it, I'll be fired. You all know how hard I've worked."

"Could she go to jail?" Travis looked like he'd taken a drink of sour milk out of the carton.

The thought of Opal behind bars made Cash sick to his stomach all over again. "I don't think so. Maybe? I don't know." He dropped his head into his hands.

"Well, if she couldn't go to jail," Hayes said, his voice authoritative, probably thanks to listening to Callie talk about legal stuff for the past few years, "couldn't she do some kind of, I don't know, agreement or something? Like, she turns herself in, pleads guilty, and her lawyer gets her probation or community service. Yeah. I think that could work."

"Either way, we can't be together. She broke the law."

"Ha!" Travis whacked his fist on the table. "Against a guy who deserved it. That guy's a dick, man. I feel like that's an extenuating circumstance."

"Yeah." Hayes shrugged. "A judge would definitely take one look at Leslie, hear him talk for ten seconds, and throw out the case."

"Not gonna happen," Cash said, hearing the gloom in his own voice even though his lips twitched again.

"Never know." Sterling pushed his empty beer bottle aside. "So what's your plan, bro?"

"What do you mean? There is no plan. I'll finish out the fundraiser and then I'll cut ties."

Travis bumped his knuckles against Cash's. "You don't have to finish out the fundraiser, bro. You've already raised a lot, done your duty, you know?"

"Are you kidding?" Hayes punched Travis on the shoulder. "It's a competition. Have you ever seen Cash back down from a competition?" Using his best caveman voice, he added, "'Me Cash. Me. Must Win.'"

Cash smiled. "Right. So like I said, I'll just finish the fundraiser and then cut ties."

With a kind smile, that brought Cash even closer to tears, Travis said, "Why do you sound like you're *this* close to crying?"

"Shut up, man. Because it sucks, okay? I've never felt this way about a woman before. It was like she became part of me. All day long, I thought about her. I wanted to tell her stories and thought about how she'd react. I wondered what we'd have for dinner, or whether we'd go out and play fetch with the dog. I was thinking long-term, man, for the first time in my life. Like, weeks and months and years ahead. We walked about restaurants we wanted to try and goals we had and trips we'd take. And I can't believe I'm about to tell you guys this—it never leaves this table, you hear? But I thought about asking her to marry me. I know. It's crazy. You guys are thinking I've lost my mind. I've lost my touch. And maybe I have. But I think that's why this is all so devastating." He paused only long enough to take another drink of his beer. "But you know what? This is probably all for the best. She was a distraction, just like I said she'd be. Well, not her, but a relationship. I said a relationship would be a distraction and then I went right ahead and dove into one. And the water was deep."

He took another drink and was vaguely aware that his bottle was empty. Someone pressed another cold, full bottle into his hand.

"In a way, though, Tommy Rowland was right. He said it's so nice to have someone to come home to and share your day with. I thought he was full of it. That's what I have you guys for. At least, that's what I thought. But Opal changed things. It's like—"

"Bro." Sterling held up a hand, bringing Cash to a halt.

"I was rambling, wasn't I?"

"You're in love with her, man." Sterling's grin was huge. "You know how I know? That's exactly how I felt once I'd spent some time with June."

Cash threw up his hands. "Well, it doesn't matter now, does it? Things are over between us."

"Judging by everything you just said, I think you'd better find a way to make sure things aren't over." Hayes held eye contact with him while he turned the idea over in his mind.

"This kind of love is once in a lifetime, bro," Travis added.

"You can't just let it go," Sterling said.

They all sat in silence while Cash stewed some more. He wanted to find a way to make sure things weren't over, but he didn't know if it was possible. The thought of losing Opal tore him up, but the thought of losing his job did, too. And apparently, Opal and law enforcement were mutually exclusive.

"I just don't know what to do."

"Fortunately," Sterling said, "You don't have to decide right now. Give it some time. An answer will come to you."

"Besides," Travis said, an evil gleam in his eye as he hooked a thumb over his shoulder and leaned in closer to his brothers, "there're other fish in the sea."

Cash's gaze followed Travis's thumb to a group of women who'd gathered around the pool table and were giggling as they racked the balls and chalked the cues. When he rolled his eyes in response, his brothers laughed.

"You'll figure it out, bro." Travis grabbed his shoulder and squeezed before sliding out of the booth. "Listen, I've gotta go. I've got some paperwork I need to finish tonight. Let me know if you need to schedule another meeting."

Cash thanked him, and Sterling and Travis stood to leave, too. "He's right," Sterling said. "You'll figure it out."

"Yeah," Hayes said. "What they said."

And then they were gone and Cash was once again alone with his thoughts. The guys were right: maybe he just needed more time. When they were little and struggling with a decision or a problem, their mom would tell them to ask themselves a question before going to sleep, and then let their brain work on answers overnight. That's what he'd do. After one more beer.

As if he could read Cash's mind, Jerry came over with one and plunked one down on the table. "Feeling any better, son?"

Still miserable, Cash shook his head. "Not yet. But I'm getting there, I think."

"I'll leave you to it. Busy night."

He walked away, only for a busty brunette in short shorts to replace him. "Hi, Cash."

Scouring his memory for her name and coming up empty, he smiled. "Hi."

Chapter Twenty-Four

The days passed without much structure and Opal floated, untethered and miserable. How could she have been so stupid? How did she not consider the impact of her actions on Cash? On their relationship? And how had she ever thought the situation would end with Pearl not knowing Opal had been behind all the stuff happening to Leslie?

The truth, she realized now, as she prepared to see Cash for the first time since their falling out, was that she hadn't thought or considered anything other than her own misguided sense of justice, her misplaced idea of vengeance.

Almost a week had passed since she'd smashed Leslie's windshield and all the satisfaction of that moment had melted away. Only a crushing disappointment in herself remained. Without really seeing her clothes, she moved them along the rod in her closet and eventually picked something at random. She tossed it on the bed and walked outside to feed the horses.

Overwhelming dread was her constant companion. Surely Leslie would call the police and turn her in. Would Pearl stop him? Opal wouldn't blame her if she didn't. The best-case scenario would involve Opal taking some kind of action, herself.

But she didn't know what to do, and she spent many of her

waking hours considering while she worked with Roxy and Velma and played with Louie, and even while she binge-watched her TV shows. She had to pay for her crimes, didn't she? The easiest solution was to go to the police, confess, and let them throw her in jail. A rueful smile came to her lips as she thought about Cash throwing her in jail.

Although that was the easiest, and possibly the best solution, Opal found herself waiting for Pearl to call—she'd know what to do to make things right. Only, Pearl didn't call. They'd never gone this long without speaking, and Opal felt like she was missing an actual piece of her being.

She kept right on thinking about solutions—mostly as a way to ignore the fact that she'd have to see Cash again soon. Now, "soon" was tonight. Through a series of terse text messages, they'd agreed to finish out the season of Singing for Hope together. It was too late for either of them to find a new partner and besides, they were in second place for team fundraising. It'd be a shame to let all their hard work go to waste.

The horses greeted her with bobbing heads and friendly sounds, and a rush of gratitude produced another round of tears.

While they were able to complete most of their fundraising communication and tasks through text and email, they couldn't get out of attending that night's in-person dinner.

After feeding the horses and the dog their evening meals, she returned to her bedroom to get dressed. Cash's undershirt still lay on the chair in the corner, and she resisted the urge to pick it up and bury her nose in it like she'd done the first few days after he stormed out of her house that night.

Instead, she put away the shirt she'd chosen a few minutes before and returned to her closet with determination. The idea may be childish, but she wanted to look *good*. She wanted Cash to want her when he saw her. She wanted him to miss her, to ache for her the way she ached for him.

Dressing up to impress Cash was probably pointless—he'd made it clear he'd never be with her again now that she was a criminal. But still. She was holding out a tiny sliver of hope that she might be able to find a way to make him see they were meant to be together.

She selected a pair of tight black pants and an ice-blue top that showed off her shoulders and arms, and made her eyes look crystalline. Pearl had called it her man-killer top, and she summoned all her feminine energy as she applied her eyeliner and mascara and put on a pair of sparkling, dangly earrings.

That night's dinner was scheduled to take place at Lethal, the newest restaurant in Prescott, already making a name for itself as the city's hot spot. Opal hadn't been there yet and didn't know the layout, but when she walked in, it was as if her soul was a heat-seeking missile—she zeroed in on Cash immediately.

Lust and something else, something much more powerful, flared in his eyes before he shut it down, and a flame of satisfaction ignited inside her. Hope wasn't completely lost.

"Hey." She sat down next to him at the long table, and he straightened up as if she were a stranger occupying his space. Her heart broke, yet again.

"Hey."

A server came to take her drink order and despite an intense urge to ask for several shots, she ordered a Shirley Temple. A strange silence stretched between her and Cash once the server walked away. Just a week ago, the two of them would have been chatting, laughing, sharing stories about the day. But now, they sat there, Cash on his phone and Opal staring straight ahead, barely registering what under any other circumstance would surely feel like a classy and comfortable ambiance. Emotion tightened her throat and she bit the inside of her cheek to keep herself from crying.

Finally, the other Wilders started to filter in and Opal nearly *did* cry from relief when June sat down next to her and asked about her day. Not that she'd admit it was terrible, but talking about the horses and the dog and the property helped to pass the time.

Tessa Winant stood up from her chair at the head of the table and tapped her spoon on her glass. "Welcome, everyone!" She waited for the chatter to quiet and then said, "As you know, this is our final dinner before the big event next weekend. Before I talk about what we're going to do tonight, I have some news." The silence stretched. "Just before I came here, I checked the latest numbers. This year is already our best *ever* for fundraising—and we haven't even done our main event. You guys, we are on track to *smash* all previous records for Singing for Hope!"

That announcement broke the silence and everyone cheered. Most of the contestant couples exchanged high fives or hugs or kisses, but Cash and Opal avoided eye contact as they applauded, their arms and hands as stiff as their smiles. Completely heartsick, Opal could barely maintain a semi-smiling expression when Callie gave her a thumbs-up from across the table.

"Anyway. Because tonight is the last dinner before the main event, it's also the last opportunity to raise some money in person. The owner of this restaurant, Sam Killian, has offered not only to sponsor Singing for Hope, but also to fund the prize money for tonight's competition. He is a master restauranteur *and* a philanthropist, folks!" More applause. "He's also humble as all get out and wouldn't come out of the kitchen so we could give him a round of applause. Let's give him one anyway!"

Everyone cheered again, and Opal wished with all her being that she could enjoy this moment. Here they were, raising money for a good cause, and all she could think about was how much she missed Cash. And how terrified she was of what this competition would entail.

Tessa tapped her spoon on her glass again and waited for everyone to settle. "I hope you came hungry, because tonight is all about eating."

Opal's stomach responded to that announcement with a growl so loud, June laughed and elbowed her. Cash closed his eyes, and Opal wondered whether he did so because he was put off by the stomach growling or because, like her, he couldn't stand the two of them not sharing that moment.

"So. This is going to be fun. What we're going to do is taste some of Sam's newest creations."

A murmur ran through the contestants, the general consensus

that tasting food sounded great, but no one was sure how that could tie into earning money.

"Ah, yes. You're probably wondering how tasting food could be an opportunity to earn money. You all know I can gamify anything. Due to time constraints, all teams will play at the same time. You'll each receive two separate dishes, two sets of silverware, and a pair of blindfolds."

A collective groan sounded. Tessa looked more thrilled than ever. "That's right. Blindfolds." She paused. "Each person will take a turn wearing a blindfold while his or her partner feeds them one of the dishes. The blindfolded person will get to take five bites of the food, and try to guess all the ingredients in the dish. Then the partners will switch places. Whichever pair guesses the most ingredients correctly wins the prize money."

"How much is it?" someone called out while Opal tried to come to terms with the idea of Cash feeding her. It seemed so intimate, so erotic. God, she wished she could hide under the table and never come out. Maybe she could just leave. But winning was so important to Cash. Maybe it wouldn't be that much money.

"It's one thousand dollars." A hush fell, and then the chatter rose again. Opal had to do it. She couldn't bow out. "Actually," Tessa said, her voice full of barely contained excitement, "I've just received word that Sam has decided to double the purse. The prize money for tonight's event is now *two thousand dollars.*"

Someone let out an ear-piercing whistle and the group broke into yet another round of applause.

"This could make a difference in the rankings, folks. Some of you are within five hundred bucks of moving up a spot."

More chatter. Anxiety zipped around the inside of Opal's torso like a colony of ants. *I don't know if I can do this.* Beside her, Cash sat statue-still, staring at the water glass on the table in front of him. Despite the awkwardness boiling between them, Opal couldn't help but admire his strong jawline—the jawline she'd never again get to kiss or run her fingers along.

"The first step is for everyone to be blindfolded. After that, Sam's staff will deliver your dishes. No peeking, you guys!"

A couple of members of the restaurant's staff—dressed in black and white uniforms resembling tuxedos—came around the table to blindfold everyone. The wait felt interminable. Opal yearned for normal circumstances, under which Cash would say something to her, make some wisecrack.

Cash's turn to be blindfolded came before hers. He remained motionless, stiff, as the server tied the fabric around his head. Opal was next, and not being able to see Cash—his posture, his demeanor —was a relief for about a split second until she realized the two of them would have no choice but to talk to each other and, worse, touch each other during this challenge.

Of its own accord, her body leaned toward him. When her shoulder touched his, he jumped, the movement almost imperceptible. Then he shifted just slightly so they no longer touched.

"Everyone blindfolded? Great!"

Opal didn't know how Tessa could sound so happy about that.

"Next, someone will place a dish in front of each man, and a notebook and pen in front of each woman. Women, you'll feed the men first, so go ahead and pick up your silverware." Opal felt in front of her for a knife and fork. "Good. I'll let you know when everyone has their food, and we can begin. Once you've fed your partner five bites, you'll write down his guesses about ingredients."

"While we're blindfolded?" one of the women called.

"Of course. After you feed the men, the women will receive their dishes and have a chance to guess ingredients. Whichever team has the most correct guesses, combined, wins! Now. Are you ready?"

A murmur went around the table, a little bell jingled, and Opal's entire body went alight with nerves. She hadn't spoken to Cash in a week and now she had no choice but to do so ... and feed him a mystery food while they were both unable to see? It it were at all possible, she would have crawled under the table.

The plates thumped softly onto the tablecloth as servers deposited them on the table.

"Everyone is served. Women, go ahead and feed your men."

Opal used one hand to locate the plate, and then used her fork to explore the food. Pasta, maybe? With meat.

"I'm cutting the food," she said to Cash.

"Okay."

That was it? Suppressing a groan, she finished cutting a bite. "Ready?"

"Ready."

"Where's your mouth?"

"Same place it's always been."

If she wasn't mistaken, she heard a bit of humor in his voice. Which was an improvement from the silent treatment. "Very funny."

"I try."

"Can I feel for it? This food seems saucy and I don't want to get sauce all over your face."

"I guess."

Holding the fork in her right hand, she touched his arm with her left, making her way up to his shoulder and tracing his jawline. Even though she was the one touching him, goosebumps rose on her arms. This activity was just as erotic as she'd anticipated and now she was imagining being naked and blindfolded with him. And then her fingers found his mouth and God she wanted to put her lips there. "Here it is."

He didn't answer and she lifted the forkful of food. Once it was inside his mouth, she felt a tug as he removed the food. He made an appreciative sound, which emanated pleasure and sent another round of shivers rushing over her skin. *Get it under control, Houston.* A few seconds passed and his voice was low and close to her ear when he said, "Skirt steak, parsley, red wine vinegar, garlic, pasta." How that list of ingredients sounded so sexual, she didn't know, but she nodded before remembering he couldn't see her.

"Got it." Setting down the fork and knife, she felt for the pen and notebook and did her best to write down his list. "Want another bite?"

"Sure." His voice sounded like he hadn't used it properly in a while, and that extra scratchiness turned her on almost as much as him listing off ingredients.

Sighing, she set down the pen and pad and picked up the silverware again. One hand holding the fork, the other grazed his jawline again so she could locate his mouth. *This is torture.* He took another bite and she waited.

"Cream ... hmm. I don't know." His hmm thrummed in his throat. "Probably a marinade for the steak. Would you give me another bite, please?"

She did, and he listed off a few more ingredients: soy sauce, black bean sauce, salt, pepper.

A bell rang at the end of the table and Tessa's voice rang out. "Okay, ladies! You have one minute to finish writing down your partner's guesses, and then you'll switch." A minute later, Opal felt someone reach between Cash and her to set down a plate. "All right, gentlemen. Start feeding your ladies."

Your lady. Opal could only wish she were Cash's lady.

Just as she'd done, he found her face with one hand. His fingers were rough against her skin and she resisted the urge to lean into his touch. "Ready?"

"Ready."

A forkful of food touched her lips, so gently, her heart ached. How badly she wanted to fix things between them. She had to find a way. As she chewed the food, images of their whole future danced in her mind's eye: a wedding with cheerful orange flowers, sunset games of fetch with Louie, long trail rides through the forest, babies. She wanted babies with Cash Wilder.

"Any guesses?"

She jumped, not just because of the words, but because of the shock of hearing him speak to her, his voice gravelly. *Shit.* As flooded as her senses had been by being in close proximity to him once again, she had forgotten to pay attention to the flavors of the food. Inhaling, she considered. Cumin, definitely. Sour cream, cilantro, corn. She listed those off and asked for another bite.

"Open."

The fork slid between her lips neatly and it was all she could do to avoid making a pleasure-filled sound because this whole exercise was just so *sexual.*

He waited for her to chew for several seconds. "Anything else?"

So many things.

Black beans, chicken thighs. He wrote those down. "Another?"

She could decline. She'd made an honest effort and listed a decent number of ingredients. Was it wrong that she wanted him to feed her another bite?

"Time's almost up." Tessa's singsong cut into Opal's stream of consciousness.

"No, thank you. I'm not sure I have any more guesses."

Because they sat so close together, she could feel his shrug against her shoulder. "Suit yourself."

A cowbell rang and Tessa clapped three times. "That's it, folks! You can remove your blindfolds now. I'll come around to collect your guesses, and while I tally, you can finish your food. There are no rules against sharing tonight."

The table once again erupted in chatter as everyone removed their blindfolds. Cash set his between their two place settings and Opal almost cried again—it looked like he was putting up a barrier. While the two of them stabbed at their own dishes without speaking, the rest of the contestants tasted each other's entrees and laughed and compared notes.

After a few miserable, awkward minutes, Tessa rang her cowbell again.

"Well, you guys are just not going to believe this. Not only do we have two winning couples—a tie—but one of them is a repeat! Our winners are Mike and Sheila—" she paused while everyone else applauded and Mike and Sheila raised their arms in victory—"and Cash and Opal."

More applause while Opal's face ached from fake smiling. She didn't dare look at Cash—she didn't want him to know how much she was hurting. When the clapping finally died down, Tessa beamed at them from the head of the table. "Cash and Opal, you two must be the dream team!"

Opal felt sick to her stomach.

"The two winning teams will split the prize money. Great job, and thanks to everyone for coming."

People stood up to leave and Opal decided to make a mad dash for it. She and Cash *were* a dream team, and she had to figure out how to fix things. If she didn't, she'd never forgive herself.

Chapter Twenty-Five

"You're not yourself today, man. What's up?" Tommy Rowland raised an eyebrow at Cash across the cab of the patrol car, half curious and half concerned. He started the car.

Cash sighed and rubbed his forehead with one hand. "Nothing. I'm fine. Just tired."

"Okay. Whatever you say." His right arm across the back of Cash's seat, he backed out of their parking spot. Hand on the shifter, he winked at Cash. "I don't believe you, but I won't force you to talk about it."

Cash couldn't decide whether to be relieved or disappointed. He wanted to talk about Opal, wanted reassurance that maybe everything could be okay. At the same time, he didn't dare reveal what she'd done in case Tommy told him he should stay away from her forever.

They pulled onto the road behind the police station and Tommy turned up the scanner. "Let's see what we can get into today. Take your mind off things."

The morning was slow. As the weather chilled into full-scale fall, people stayed inside, warm and cozy, until the later hours.

Cash's mind refused to stop thinking about Opal, despite Tommy's best intentions. That ingredient-guessing game had been pure torture. Imagining her lips wrap around the forkfuls of food, tugging the food off the tines—he'd better stop envisioning that right away. He adjusted his pants.

The scanner squawked with hot tones. "Here we go, Wilder." Tommy turned up the volume again and snatched the mic off the unit while he waited for information.

"All units, we have a robbery in progress. It's at the Rusty Spur, two-ninety West Pleasant Street."

Tommy flashed a grin at Cash, but sounded ultra-serious when he responded. "Dispatch, this is unit one-four-three. We're close and en route." He flipped the car around, tires squealing, and jammed down the gas.

That worked to get Cash's mind off Opal. Questions rushed through his mind, rapid-fire. What was he supposed to do when they got there? How many people were doing the robbery? Was he supposed to pull his gun right away?

Deep breaths, Wilder.

"You okay, man? Looking a little green around the gills. It's my driving, isn't it?"

"I'm fine," Cash lied, hastily running through everything he'd learned during the academy about what to do on a call like this.

The dispatcher's voice came through the scanner again. "Be advised, RP states he's in the kitchen. Robber is behind the bar, stealing liquor."

Cash's heart rate slowed, just a little. A guy stealing liquor didn't sound very dangerous.

"RP states the assailant has a rifle on a sling."

"Hear that, Wilder? Get your game face on. Whatever's been eating at you all morning, it's time to let it go. Hear me?"

Cash nodded and he swore he could feel his eyeballs rattling around in his head. "I hear you."

"Good." He replaced the mic and gave Cash a good whack on the arm. "This is what it's like to feel *alive*."

Laughing now, Cash shook his head. "I feel it, man."

And he did. Every sense went on high alert. Colors looked brighter, the engine's revving was nearly deafening, and he could taste metallic adrenaline in the back of his throat. Although he was laser focused on the road in front of them, he also saw the buildings blurring by on either side. His armpits prickled and he could smell his deodorant.

The tires squealed again as Tommy veered into the alleyway between two downtown buildings. "Game time, Wilder. Follow my lead, do what I say, and with any luck, we catch a bad guy."

A rifle-toting bad guy. Cash gave Tommy a quick nod and they were out of the car and running toward the back door of the Rusty Spur. When they reached it, Tommy stopped and looked through it. "Can't see him from here. Hallway looks clear, but don't take it for granted."

The hinges creaked and Cash winced at the sound as he followed Tommy in. Keeping his back to one wall, Tommy motioned for Cash to do the same. When they reached the end of the hallway where it opened up into the restaurant's dining room, they both stopped and listened.

From the other end of the room came the sound of glass bottles clinking together and what Cash thought was the crunching of footsteps on broken glass.

Then a man speaking: "... thinks he's above everybody else. Doesn't want to help anybody, not even a guy he's known for years."

Tommy threw a look over his shoulder and Cash shrugged.

What happened next? They'd practiced scenarios like this during the academy, but this was different. This was real life. They were about to walk into a room towards an angry—and drunk—guy with a gun.

Tommy's shoulders rose and fell with a deep breath, and Cash took one, too. Before he could ask Tommy to wait or slow down or rethink what they should do, Tommy was walking around the corner and into the restaurant, his footsteps practically silent on the laminate flooring. As soon as they had a clear view of the bar and the tall, lanky, scruffy-bearded guy behind it—who did have a rifle slung over his shoulder—Tommy pulled his gun out of its holster and aimed.

"Prescott Police Department." He sounded deadly calm and even though he spoke quietly, his command rang through the empty restaurant, causing the perpetrator to jump and grab his rifle with both hands.

"Set the gun on the floor."

"I can explain." The guy sounded breathless, shaky.

"You can explain all you want as soon as you set the gun on the floor and slide it over to me."

"You don't understand, man."

Cash's brain couldn't even keep up as the man, all elbows, grabbed the rifle in both hands, the barrel pointed toward the ceiling. Just in front of him, Tommy's shoulders tensed and his grip on the gun tightened. Cash froze, uncertain of what to do. Should he draw his own gun? Run up to the guy and grab his? Scram back down the hallway and outside? No, Tommy had told him to follow his lead, and he was giving the guy more time.

"Put it down."

In another motion so fast, it scrambled Cash's brain, the guy jerked the gun off his shoulder and threw it down. It clattered on the tile behind the bar. Tommy's shoulders released on his exhale. "Good. Now kick it over here."

A strangled sound, something between a sob and a yell, came out of the guy's mouth as he swung a leg back and kicked.

Out of nowhere, Cash pictured him as a little boy on the soccer field, winding up for a pass or a goal.

The gun slid across the floor and Tommy nodded. "Thank you, man. Wilder, wanna grab that?"

"Sure thing."

Tommy continued to point his gun at the robber as Cash retrieved the rifle. Once he was safely behind Tommy again, Tommy told the robber to step out from behind the bar with his hands in the air, to walk toward them, and to turn around.

"Go ahead and cuff him, Wilder."

Cash set the rifle on the floor next to Tommy and approached the robber. "Hands behind your back, please."

The guy chuckled. "I never had a cop tell me, 'please' before."

"What can I say? My mama taught me manners."

Feeling the guy's wrists, bone and flesh like his own, Cash wondered how a person went from being an innocent little kid on a soccer field to stealing money from restaurant registers and ripping off liquor. As soon as the cuffs snapped into place, Cash's body sagged with relief. He couldn't believe how close they'd come to getting shot. *This* close.

The sound of Tommy holstering his gun snapped Cash out of his shock, and he took a deep breath before reciting the Miranda rights.

Tommy put a hand on his shoulder, a silent *good job*. "Take him out to the car. I'll find the owner."

"Come on, man." Cash wrapped a hand around the guy's elbow and led him down the hallway and out the door. Before he opened the car, he said, "You got ID on you?"

"In my wallet. Back left pocket."

"Willard Brewer." Born the same year as Cash. "What are you doing here, Willard?"

"I don't know." He turned around. "It sounds so stupid when I say it out loud."

Cash shrugged. "You can tell me. I've done my share of stupid stuff."

Willard looked like he might cry. "My girlfriend and me—we had a fight. It was over something so ridiculous. Anyway, she ended up kicking me out. I needed money to get a new place. I can't crash at my friends' houses, you know? They all think Christie and I are meant to be. The power couple. Whatever. I can't let them know she kicked me out, can I?"

"No, I guess not."

"So I came here—to her dad's restaurant—to borrow some money. Only, he didn't want to lend me any."

"Why did you have a rifle, though?"

"What?" Understanding dawned. "I didn't. That's his rifle. Keeps it behind the bar." He slapped a hand over his mouth. "Don't tell anyone, though. I don't think it's actually legal. But he does it for protection. 'Kids get rowdy,' he says. I thought, if he doesn't want to lend me money, I'll take the rifle to the pawn shop. Get some cash for it, get a place to stay. I can buy him another one later. I wasn't going to *shoot* anybody."

"Sure scared the shit out of me."

"Sorry."

"Well, I hope things work out with Christie. But you're going to have to go to jail, first."

Willard deflated, shoulders slumping. Cash felt almost like he should apologize, but Willard saved him from that. "I just wish I'd ended things differently with her, you know? The last thing I said to her was that I was glad she kicked me out—a total lie. I wish I'd told her I loved her. That she was the best thing that ever happened to me. That I couldn't live without her. But I was so pissed, you know? And now I've done this. He tilted his head toward the back of the restaurant. "She'll never forgive me. And she'll never even know what she meant to me."

Cash felt like he'd been punched in the gut. What was the last thing he'd said to Opal? It was nothing about how much he cared for her, how much she meant to him. Yes, she'd committed a crime—a series of crimes—but he *loved* her.

"Load up!" Tommy's voice, sharp, came from the doorway as he emerged.

Cash opened the back door of the patrol car and helped Willard lower himself into the seat without hitting his head on the doorframe.

When he closed the door, Tommy said, "Having some girl talk out here?"

"Shut up, man. I got a lot of info out of this guy. Girl problems."

"Ah, so you could relate. I knew something was bothering you today." He flashed a shit-eating grin and headed around to the driver's side. Once they were in, he looked at Cash across the cab.

"We were lucky today. I don't think this guy wanted to shoot us, but do you see how fast shit can go south?"

"I sure do."

Tommy was referring to work, of course, but Cash was realizing just how fast a person could do irreversible damage to a relationship ... and just how much he wanted—no, *needed*—to fix things with Opal.

Chapter Twenty-Six

If Opal was going to convince Cash to take her back, she first had to make amends with Pearl—who was the only one who could convince Leslie not to press charges.

Her sister couldn't stay mad forever. Years and years, and countless arguments, proved that. As she put on her shoes, Opal chuckled at the memory of the time in high school when she'd borrowed Pearl's favorite yellow cashmere sweater without asking. Pearl had forgiven her—eventually. But just in case she was inclined to hold a grudge this time, Opal called Louie to follow her to the car. She definitely couldn't stay mad forever if Louie was there.

Pearl's house was quiet. The garage was closed and for once, the sounds of boys hollering or laughing didn't come through the front windows. Opal checked her watch. Pearl, Wyatt, and Will should be home—the soccer schedule showed their games started in two hours, which meant they'd be eating and getting ready.

Louie looked up at her with curiosity as she shook out her hands and blew out her breath before knocking.

A shadow passed over the covered window and Pearl's voice called out. "Boys, come answer the door. It's Aunt Opal."

Fear pierced Opal's heart. Pearl wouldn't even answer the door? But then there were thundering steps and the door swung open and two little faces smiled up at her. "Aunt Opal!" All at once, their arms went around her waist and they squeezed her and started chattering about a game they were playing. Something with aliens and puppies and kings. Two kings, because they both wanted to be king and were arguing about it so long and so loud, their mom said that if they couldn't come to an agreement, they'd have to go to their separate bedrooms for the rest of the day. For his part, Louie danced around them, tail wagging, tongue lolling, happy to be part of the boy crew.

Giving their story only half of her attention, Opal used the other half to try to figure out where Pearl was. A utensil clanked against a dish in the kitchen and Opal began moving that way, the boys now detached from her waist but still talking. Louie followed, doing his absolute best to remain in the mix.

Pearl was at the counter, whisking something in a bowl, her back to Opal. When she heard them all come in, her spine straightened and she told the boys she'd seen some aliens in the backyard. Whooping and yelling, they ran for the sliding glass door and out into the yard, leaving Opal in the kitchen with Pearl, who'd turned around and leaned against the cabinets, the heels of her hands on the counter.

"I assume you came here to apologize."

Opal swallowed. "I did."

"Apology not accepted."

So. She wasn't going to make this easy. "Pearl."

"Opal." Pearl turned away and continued whisking.

"What are you making?"

"Muffins."

"Pearl, I—"

She spun around, the whisk still in her hand. "There's nothing you can say, Opal."

"So you're just going to be mad at me forever?"

Pearl sighed, and in that sigh, Opal could hear all the weariness of the past several months. The weariness of a rough patch in the marriage, the weariness of raising two energetic boys, the weariness of wanting more for herself. "Not forever, okay? But it's like, you're supposed to be the one I can count on. When everything else falls apart, I need my sister. And as my marriage has fallen apart, what do you do? You make it worse. I wouldn't have believed it was possible, but you—" she pointed with the whisk—"you made it *worse*. You gave Leslie a reason to stop trusting me, a way to blame me for everything that was going wrong."

Opal nodded. She deserved this, and she said so.

"You're right! You do deserve this! You probably deserve more than this, but I don't know what." She turned around again, kept whisking.

"You're going to over-mix your batter."

"You're right." She huffed and got out the muffin pan.

Opal found the liners and started putting them into the pan. She'd done about five before Pearl realized she was letting her help and snatched them away to do it herself.

"Listen. I'm sorry, okay? I know you don't accept my apology. But I really am sorry. The way Leslie was treating people—not just you but also all the people I saw him interact with—reminded me so much of Boone. And even though I shouldn't, I put you in my shoes. I felt so bad for you, Pearl, and I felt like you wouldn't stand up for yourself, so I needed to stand up for you. I didn't realize that in doing so, I'd only be creating more havoc."

"Well, that's exactly what you did."

"I know, and I'm sorry. I'll say it a million times if you want me to."

"Please don't." She picked up the bowl, took a small measuring cup out of a drawer, and started scooping batter into the lined pan.

"A thousand?"

"No." The cups full, Pearl groaned when she realized she hadn't preheated the oven. "You're distracting me."

"Sorry."

After turning on the oven, she faced Opal again, just long enough to make eye contact, and then started washing the bowl.

"What's going to happen with you and Leslie?"

"We're getting divorced, Opal. I'm sure that's what you wanted to hear."

"It's not! I mean, I think you're better off and you deserve more, but I'd never wish a divorce on you."

Pearl's anger gave way to grief as she broke into tears. "It's not your fault. I'm just so *mad*. At Leslie, at you, at myself."

Opal opened her arms and Pearl stepped into her embrace. For a few long minutes, Opal held her while she cried, rubbing her back and doing everything she could to absorb her sadness.

Chapter Twenty-Seven

ash swore when he pulled into Opal's driveway and her car wasn't there. He should have called or texted before just showing up. The horses perked up when they saw him get out of his truck, and hope flickered in his chest. A week ago, he would have let himself into the house and poured himself a drink.

But today, he waited outside despite Louie's protests from just inside the front door. So Louie wouldn't be watching him, wondering why he wasn't coming inside, Cash wandered over to the corral, where Roxy and Velma came to greet him.

By the time Opal turned into her driveway, tires crunching, Cash had almost forgotten they weren't speaking and he turned around, a smile already forming. He had to force it from his face when he saw her. Her lack of a smile didn't look forced. She was probably afraid he was there to tell her she needed to turn herself in, pay for her crimes.

"Hey." Hands in her pockets, she walked toward him.

"Hey." In his mind's eye, they embraced, so glad to be reunited.

They both spoke at the same time. "I owe you an apology."

Her mouth dropped open. She closed it and tilted her head. *"You* owe *me* an apology?"

Hooking a thumb toward the house—where Louie had started his barking anew—Cash said, "Can we take this inside?"

They walked in, side by side, as they had so many times over the past several weeks. Louie greeted them both with a wiggling body and a wagging tail, and Cash thought he detected an extra dose of excitement in his whine. Just as they had so many times over the past several weeks, they both leaned down to pet him and scratch him behind the ears.

Opal straightened first, leaving a hand resting on Louie's head. "Want a drink?"

"Sure."

She poured herself a glass of wine and dropped ice cubes into a bourbon glass before pouring him a healthy shot.

"Thanks," he said and she said, "Me, first. Let's go outside."

Cash was grateful for the chill in the air—he hoped it would keep him sharp. He could already feel himself softening around the edges, just being near her.

She gestured to the porch swing and they sat, but she stood up almost immediately and began pacing. If he could, he'd catch her hand on the way by, stop her, settle her. But he knew he needed to let her do this her way. After a couple of laps, she stopped in front of him and looked into his eyes. "First of all, I have to tell you the whole truth. I created all of those small annoyances for Leslie. And I also ... I also smashed his windshield." She winced. "I can't believe I'm admitting it. That night when I left the house without telling you, I tracked him down at the hotel and threw a giant rock through his windshield." A pause and then, "Wait. You don't look surprised. Did you know? You knew. He must have reported it."

Since she was going full honesty, he might as well, too. "I knew."

She threw her head back. "I'm sorry. I'm sorry I didn't think about your new career when I was getting my revenge on Leslie. I was only thinking of myself and my sister, and I was blind to what I was doing to you. And that's not fair."

She paused just long enough for him to say, "My turn?" but she shook her head and went on. "I love you, Cash. We started out just having fun, but you're hard to resist." The corners of her mouth tilted upward. "I went ahead and fell in love with you."

His heart was waking up, fluttering around in his chest at her words.

"Anyway. When I realized that, I should have started putting you first—immediately. Even before myself and my insane need for revenge. And from now on, if you'll have me, I promise to put you first, always. That's what you deserve."

If he'd have her? He wanted that more than anything.

"I will never make that mistake again, Cash. Living without you this past eleven days? It's been torture."

He opened his mouth to respond, to tell her it had been torture for him, too, but she held up a hand.

"Wait. I have to tell you what I did."

His eyes widened. Had she done something else worthy of a confession?

"No, it's not what you're thinking. Don't worry. I worked things out with Leslie. Long story short—because he was real mad about his car—he agreed we could settle everything privately. We wrote up a contract. I'm going to pay for the damage to his car, clean up the glitter from that glitter bomb I sent, and get him removed from the drag queen mailing list, and he's not going to report me to the police or press any charges."

Again, he started to speak and again, she lifted a hand to stop him. "I know. You are the police and you already know what I've done. But I'm hoping that you'll overlook my transgressions this one time since I'm paying restitution."

Setting down his drink and standing up from the porch swing, he took her free hand in both of his and looked into her eyes, which sparkled ice blue with tears. "I'll overlook your transgressions this one time." She smiled and he said, "But only this one time."

"There won't be another time, I promise."

He nodded. "Good. Now, is it my turn?"

"Sure."

Still holding onto her hand, he said, "Okay. Like I said, I owe you an apology, too." She looked at him, listening, and her expression was so open, so loving, it almost brought him to tears. "Since you came roaring into Prescott again, playing your music way too damned loud, I've been completely hooked. You became like another element for me, like oxygen or sunlight or water. Like steak."

She smirked at that, just as he'd intended.

"When we first started talking, I thought this was all just for fun. My career was the most important thing to me and I'd somehow convinced myself I couldn't have both. Especially with everything my parents put us through." He waved a hand. "But then, during Hayes and Callie's wedding, I realized how special it is, what they have. I realized it's possible. I want that with you. I want forever. And that realization scared the shit out of me. Because I'd never wanted anything that badly—not even my career. But when I found out you were behind that string of crimes, I panicked. I thought you'd proven me right about not having a career and a relationship. I thought my relationship was putting my career in jeopardy."

Her forehead wrinkled, like that idea physically hurt her. She looked like she wanted to speak, but he held up his hand just as she'd done.

"Being a good cop, it was—well, *is*—so important to me. Because I wanted to prove myself as worthy. To my parents, to my brothers, to myself. To you, too. I didn't want anything to threaten my ability to do that. Over the past few days I realized, I'm *going* to be a good cop. I don't *need* to prove myself. And I should have talked to you. Figured out why you were doing what you were doing. But like I said, I was panicking. And I put my career before our relationship. That won't happen again. I promise you that."

She withdrew her hand from his and wrapped her arm around his shoulders, pressing her lips to his. God, how he loved this woman. He brought both arms around her waist and took the kiss long and deep, pouring in every last drop of love.

After a few minutes, she ended the kiss. Her forehead still resting against his, she said, "I love you, Cash Wilder."

"I love you, too, Opal Houston." And just like that, everything in Cash's world was right again.

Later that night, they lay together in the dark. Cash used his fingertips to explore Opal's body as if for the first time, touching the soft skin on her chest and breasts and stomach, and sliding into her warm folds before using his mouth to trace the same path. He entered her a moment later and her eyes flew open to meet his.

She smiled at him as if she were seeing him for the first time and recognizing him as her long-lost soulmate, and he came undone as they both tumbled over the edge and into oblivion.

Chapter Twenty-Eight

In her bedroom, Opal put the finishing touches on her outfit for the grand finale of the Singing for Hope fundraiser and took a moment to look herself over in the mirror. The little glacier-blue cocktail dress she'd selected made her waistline look trim and showed off her collarbones. The diamond drop earrings and necklace dazzled, and the jet black mascara brought out her eyes. She'd swept her hair into a high bun.

"I dare say, Opal Houston, you look pretty damned good." Her reflection smiled back at her.

"You look so good, I wish we had time for a quickie before we leave for the big show." Cash came up behind her, wrapped his arms around her waist, and kissed her neck.

She leaned into his embrace. "Well, we can do that when we get back—and we can take our time."

"Sounds good to me. Are you ready? You look ready."

"As ready as I'll ever be."

"You nervous?" He turned and offered her his elbow. "Remember, Tessa called us the power couple."

"I remember, and I'm *still* nervous." Opal laughed as they walked to the front door. "What if we get a terrible song?"

"We won't. I may or may not have slipped Tessa a hundred the last time we saw her."

Opal swatted his arm as she passed him to go through the door. "You did not."

"I didn't. But I'm fairly confident we'll get a song we know."

As they drove, Opal ran through the list of potential songs Tessa had emailed out a couple of days before. Each team would draw one when they arrived at Lethal for the karaoke contest.

Inside, festive sounds greeted them: laughter, glasses clinking, jazz music playing. Hand in hand, Opal and Cash approached the check-in table, and she couldn't help but compare how she felt in that moment to how she'd felt at the last fundraising event. She glanced up at Cash, who grinned at her and winked, and she knew he was thinking the same thing.

"Look who it is!" Tessa Winant beamed at them from behind the table. "Prescott's very own power couple. Have you guys been practicing your harmonies?"

"You know we have," Cash said, deadpan, and Tessa laughed out loud. "A great sense of humor, too." She looked at Opal and said, "You'd better hang onto this one."

"I intend to."

"Which one of you wants to draw your song?"

They looked at each other. Afraid of choosing a song neither of them liked, Opal grimaced.

Laughing, Cash raised his hand. "I guess I will."

Tessa held up the bowl and Cash made a big show of lifting his arm to draw a slip. "Do you want to see it?" He held the folded paper close to his chest.

She swiped for it. "Of course I want to see it!"

He backed away from the check-in table, holding the paper out of her reach while she continued to grab for it. Within a few minutes, he'd backed himself all the way into the corner of the restaurant.

"Cornered!" She grabbed for the paper again and he handed it over.

"I was trying to get us out of earshot of everyone else," he told her, obviously pleased with himself. "I think we'll score higher if we surprise the audience. Go ahead, open it up."

As she did, he chuckled. "Your hands are shaking!"

"I know. I'm so nervous."

"What is it?"

She inhaled, looked down at the slip, and read the song title on her exhale: "Happily Ever After."

For a moment, he didn't speak—he just looked at her, his eyes slightly squinted like he was thinking. Then he smiled broadly, squeezed her shoulder and said, "That's a great song."

He spun on one heel and headed back toward the check-in table and the other contestants, hands in his pockets.

It *was* a great song.

It was also one of the biggest love songs of all time.

And they were about to sing it in front of a live audience comprising people they knew as well as strangers.

Running through the lyrics in her mind as she followed Cash, Opal knew she was going to feel like she was baring her soul right there in the spotlight. Some of the other couples were just friends, and some were mere acquaintances who'd met only when they joined up for the fundraiser. The other Wilder boys, of course, would sing with their significant others ... but to Opal's knowledge, she and Cash were the only pair who had recently declared their love for one another. And she was pretty sure the whole town knew it.

If she thought she was nervous before, she was petrified now. So petrified, in fact, that she decided she'd better get herself a drink from the bar. She ordered a vodka tonic with two lime wedges and while the bartender went to work, she scanned the crowd. The fact that Cash was watching her should not have come as a surprise. The way he was looking at her—with fierce desire and tender affection— gave her heart a little jolt and forced her to turn away. If she maintained eye contact, she might run up to him, strip him down, and make love to him right there in the restaurant.

He materialized beside her and ordered a bourbon. "You okay?"

"Of course. Why do you ask?"

With the same tenderness she'd seen in his expression a moment before, he reached up and brushed a loose lock of hair out of her face. "For a minute there, you looked—oh, I don't know. You looked like you'd rather be anywhere but standing at this bar."

She laughed. "I was thinking that if you kept looking at me like that, I was going to have to leave this bar—with you—and head straight home and to bed."

"Well. That's better than what I was thinking."

"What were you thinking?"

The chime of Tessa's cowbell cut through the din and Cash winked. "You'll never know."

"Everyone take your places! It's time to begin the Singing for Hope fundraiser's main event!"

The contestants found their seats and everyone who'd come to watch situated themselves in the booths and tables surrounding the temporary stage.

Tessa rang her cowbell again and waited for everyone to get quiet. "You'll be performing in order of who's earned the least donations to who's earned the most."

"I can't handle the suspense," Opal whispered in Cash's ear.

He put his hand on her thigh and then slid it upward, so his pinky brushed the spot where her thighs met. "I can think of some ways to take your mind off of waiting."

His breath, close to hear ear, made shivers rush over her skin. She parted her legs just a bit to allow him to move his hand even closer to her center. "You won't find me complaining."

Taking her cue from him, she nestled her hand between his legs. He stirred against her, igniting twin flares of satisfaction and desire in her core. Opal could hardly focus as Tessa explained the rules. She wondered if anyone would notice her eyes glazing over as Cash worked his magic between her legs.

By the time the first pair of contestants finally took the stage, Opal was certain she'd be unable to walk if they went on that way, so she gently pushed Cash's hand back toward her knee. He gave her a devilish grin in response, and they both tuned in to watch their competition.

The first couple did a fun rendition of Sonny and Cher singing, *I Got You Babe* and received a healthy round of applause.

Cash leaned over to whisper in Opal's ear. "I think we can beat those guys."

Something about the camaraderie, the sense of pairing up against the others, made Opal feel all warm and fuzzy. She wished they could skip the karaoke contest and go straight home to spend the evening together on the couch.

Then she chastised herself, told herself she should soak up every detail of this evening with this man. Looking around, she took in the colored lights flashing across the stage, the audience dancing in their seats, tapping their feet and singing along. She noticed the warmth of Cash's arm against hers, the way he leaned into her to give her different looks during the different songs. She caught June's eye during a pair's singing of *Don't Go Breaking My Heart*, and June winked at her.

A few minutes later, Lila and Travis went onstage to sing *Endless Love*, nearly bringing Opal to tears.

June and Sterling went next, then Hayes and Callie. Finally, it was time.

Tessa, who stood at the side of the stage, spoke into her microphone. "I'd like to introduce the reigning champions, Opal and Cash, as they take the stage with Happily Ever After."

Mingled in with the sound of applause, Opal swore she heard June, Callie, and Lila croon, "Aww," as they took the stage.

The first strings of the song came through the speakers and Opal looked up at Cash. In that moment, when their eyes met, she felt it all: the biggest, most vast love she had ever experienced. So much, it bubbled up inside her body. She felt like she could float or fly ... like she could do anything.

And then it was time to sing, and they were singing about forever, and she'd never sang anything so true and real. She wanted happily ever after with Cash, and she couldn't wait to get started.

By the time the song ended, every single audience member was standing. Some clapped and others hollered, and they all smiled. Cash took Opal's hand and they bowed, to even louder cheers, before putting up their microphones and heading back to their seats.

The other Wilder brothers and their women gave Opal and Cash extra congratulations, but all Opal saw was Cash, looking at her with the biggest smile on his face.

Chapter Twenty-Nine

"Where are you in such a rush to get to, Wilder?" Tommy Rowland threw Cash a look as the two of them walked out of the police station's back doors and Cash picked up his speed.

"I'm on a mission, man."

"Yeah? Have anything to do with your teammate in the Singing for Hope fundraiser?"

Caught, Cash paused mid-stride. "Maybe. Why do you ask?"

"You've got that look in your eye, man." Tommy caught up to him, motioned for him to keep walking. "When are you gonna do it?"

They'd reached Cash's truck, and Cash's nerves jangled as he considered the answer. He hadn't talked about it to anybody, and doing so made his plan feel even more real. "I don't know yet. I'm going to pick up the ring now."

"You've already got it picked out, huh?" Tommy wiggled his eyebrows up and down, making Cash laugh.

"I do."

"Hey, that sounds great coming out of your mouth."

Cash clapped him on the shoulder. "Thanks, man. I hope you'll be hearing it again in a few months."

"I'm sure I will. Good luck, man. I know she's gonna say yes."

Cash's stomach lit up with butterflies as he imagined that hopefully infinitesimal moment between his asking the question and her answering. That split second he had to wait. She'd say yes, wouldn't she?

"Oh, man. You look like you're about to puke."

"What if she doesn't say yes?"

Tommy laughed out loud, grabbed his shoulder, and gave him a little shake. "Why wouldn't she, bro? She loves you. It's all anybody's talking about in town. 'You should have seen the way they sang that song together,'" he said, batting his eyelashes. "'They're going to have their own happily ever after.' Shoot, Wilder, I've heard it so many times, I want to tear my own ears off."

"Really?" If everyone was saying it, maybe it was true.

"You know what, Wilder? You're a damned idiot. Where's your confidence? You told me once how you became a cop because you wanted to make something of yourself. Being a cop takes guts, right? Proposing? That takes guts, too. So gut up, my man. You can do this. Of course she's going to say yes. If she doesn't, *I'll* marry you."

Cash laughed and Tommy held up a hand. "Wait. I'd better see the ring, first."

"It's nice, Rowland. You'll like it."

"Which is unfortunate, because you're going to go pick it up, track down Opal, and ask her to marry you. She's going to accept, and you're going to have to give her that ring."

Cash gave him a single nod. "Okay. I like the sound of that."

Tommy gave him a double thumbs-up. "Go get 'er."

"Thanks. I appreciate it."

"No problem. But, Cash?"

"Yeah?"

"Bring it in."

Before he realized what was happening, Tommy was pulling him in for a hug and smacking him on the back. Quite bolstered by the whole interaction, he hopped into his truck and drove, whistling all the way, to the jewelry store.

Thirty minutes later, he pulled into Opal's driveway. She came running out the front door, the smile on her face saying she had something to tell him. He tucked away his own excitement as she threw herself into his arms.

"Guess what?" she said as he spun her around.

"What?"

"My dog rescue opens tomorrow!"

"What?" He set her down.

"My dog rescue starts tomorrow!" Her smile was so big, he couldn't help but smile, too.

"I mean, I heard you, but what do you mean?"

"There's a litter of puppies, and I'm going to foster them. Actually, I'm glad you're here, because I was planning to bribe you to help me."

His original plan for their evening going right out the window (and a little bit of disappointment setting in), he said, "Of course I'll help you. What do we need to do?"

"I love you." She raised up on her toes and gave him a loud, smacking kiss. Then she proceeded to list off all the steps they needed to take that evening to prepare for the puppies. Caught up in her enthusiasm and her beauty—her sheer effervescence—he stopped listening after she mentioned clearing out a spot in the barn and then going to the feed store to get supplies. With their whole future ahead of them, he'd do whatever she wanted.

At some point, she seemed to realize he wasn't quite tuned in because they'd made it inside and she said, "Well? Aren't you going to go change?"

"Oh! Yes." He kissed her and went into the bedroom, mentally scrambling for Proposal Plan B. He should really just hide the ring for now and try again tomorrow. He started to undo the Velcro on his vest. He'd take the ring out of his uniform pants pocket and put it in a vest pocket. That way, there was no chance of her seeing it. Het set his vest on the bed.

Just as he pulled the ring box out of his pants pocket, she bounced into the bedroom, that same giddy smile on her face. He froze, standing there next to the bed with the box in his hand.

She saw his expression first and froze, too, and then her gaze made its way to the box. Her eyes went round. "Oh, no."

His heart sank. "'Oh, no?'"

She reached out a hand. "Wait. No. I didn't mean, 'Oh, no,' like *that*. I meant, 'Oh, no, like you had something planned and I ruined it. But now I'm thinking maybe you didn't? Have something planned?"

Wow. This was not going anything like Cash had expected or planned. He sighed. "I did, actually."

Her eyebrows shot up. Her grin returned. "You did?"

"I did."

Her shoulders slumped. The rapid change in emotional states was almost comical. "And I ruined it."

"You didn't! You just had your own exciting thing to share, and I figured I'd come up with Plan B. I was just working on that when you—"

"When I busted in here."

He shrugged, grinned. "You did. Which means Plan B is now in full effect." He opened the box, dropped to one knee and Opal gasped before covering her mouth with both hands. "Opal, you are the world. You are *my* world. I know now that I can't live without you. Will you do me the honor of marrying me?"

The wait really was infinitesimal. "Of course I will."

She took his face in her hands and kissed him, long and deep, while relief and gratitude and excitement pumped through his veins. Then she pulled him to his feet. He took the ring from the box and went to put it on her finger, but she stopped him.

"Wait. Let me see that thing."

He handed her the box and she turned it this way and that. He experienced another moment of waiting, breath bated.

"It's beautiful," she breathed. "It's exactly what I always wanted for an engagement ring."

He let out his breath. "Good. I spent a long time researching. Believe it or not, I read several women's magazine articles about what your ring says about you."

Laughing, she said, "What does this say about me?"

"Says you're just the other side of practical—even though you appreciate the simple things in life, you also want to dazzle, just a little."

"Perfect." Beaming, she handed it back and held out her hand. He slipped the ring onto her left ring finger and she held it up. "How does it look?"

"Perfect." Taking her hand, he kissed her knuckles. "Mrs. Wilder."

At that, she threw her arms around his neck and squeezed. "I love it and I love you. I can't wait to marry you."

He squeezed her back. "I'm so glad."

After disentangling herself, she said, "I hate to say it, but I almost wish we didn't have to get ready for these puppies. I'd almost rather stay in and celebrate."

"We have a whole lifetime to celebrate. And if we hurry, we can start tonight."

"Okay, but just for the record, I had no idea you had plans for this evening. If I had, I would have put off the puppies for a day."

Charmed, he leaned in to kiss her cheek. "I know. But this is life, right? Whatever comes up, we'll handle it. Now, shall we go to the feed store, Mrs. Wilder?"

"Yes, Mr. Wilder. Let's go to the feed store."

Chapter Thirty

A month later

"Thank you for helping me plan this wedding," Opal told Pearl for what she figured was the hundredth time.

"Any time." Pearl reached across the dining room table, over the piles of flowers and curls of ribbon, and squeezed Opal's hand. "I mean that literally, since this is the second wedding I've helped you plan."

Opal rolled her eyes. "And this will also be the last."

"I know it will. Thank goodness, because I never liked Boone."

"You didn't?"

The boys chose that moment to come flying in the back door and skid to a stop next to the table, Louie bringing up the rear. "You didn't like Uncle Boone?" Wyatt wanted to know.

Pearl shrugged, wincing. "I never thought he was good enough for Aunt Opal."

"But you like Cash, right?" Will's brow creased. "Because I already called him Uncle Cash. It just slipped out."

"I *love* Uncle Cash," Pearl said, smoothing his hair.

Opal, not wanting to have to discuss what she thought about the boys' dad, changed the subject. "How are the puppies this afternoon?"

Both boys lit up and Wyatt spoke first. "They're great!"

Louie barked, then plopped to sitting when Opal shushed him.

"They're getting so big," Will said, "and they're so funny. One of them, the spotted one, keeps tripping over his own feet." He pantomimed that, putting his brother in stitches.

"Do they still have food and water?"

Both boys became all business, nodding. "Yep. We checked both and topped off the water," Wyatt said.

"Hey, why don't you two go feed the horses for me? That way, I can start cooking dinner right after your mom and I finish up what we're doing."

"What are you doing, anyway?" Will's nose wrinkled at the sight of all the flowers on the table.

"Making bouquets," Pearl told him, holding up a finished one for him to see. "Want to help?"

"No, thanks." Wyatt answered before Will could. "That's girl stuff. We'll go feed Roxy and Velma while you ladies do the flowers and cooking. C'mon, Will."

As they trooped out with Louie, Opal told Pearl, "You're raising a real feminist there."

"I know. It's pretty great, right?"

"Why don't you guys stay for dinner?"

Still tying a length of ribbon around the stems of a bouquet, Pearl shook her head. "No, we shouldn't. Aren't you and Cash celebrating his getting off of field training?"

"We are," Opal said, "and that's why you should stay. The more, the merrier. He loves having the boys around."

The front door opened then and Cash came in, Tommy Rowland right behind him. "Oh, hey, ladies."

"Hey, yourself." Opal got up to give him a kiss.

"I invited Tommy to dinner. I figured, he's probably celebrating as much as I am—he won't have to train me any more."

"Great," Opal said, and she meant it. Tommy had done so much for Cash during and after the academy, and feeding him dinner was the least she could do.

Tommy closed the door and gave Opal a hug. "Thank you. And just for the record, I've enjoyed having Wilder attached to my hip. He's a good cop. A good man. But you know that, right? Since you're getting hitched tomorrow."

"Yep." She winked at Cash, who looked adorably embarrassed. "Come on in. As luck would have it, I invited my sister to stay and eat with us, too. And my two hoodlum nephews, who are feeding the horses."

"We saw them when we came in." Cash was taking off his vest and gestured for Tommy to do the same. "They really have the hang of taking off those flakes now."

"They do. Come on into the kitchen, get a drink."

They set their vests on the back of the couch and walked toward the kitchen. Pearl had stood up, and when Tommy saw her, he stopped in his tracks. She, too, looked like a deer in headlights.

Opal wanted to laugh out loud, but she held it together. "Have you two met?"

Pearl jumped into action, heading for the kitchen. "No, I can't say that we have."

Tommy nodded, licked his lips. "We haven't."

Opal swore he was thinking, *I'd remember if we had.* She glanced at Cash, whose eyes twinkled.

"What does everyone want to drink?" Pearl had beat everyone to the kitchen and was taking out a bottle of wine, her movements urgent.

"I'll take a glass of wine," Opal said, her tone overly helpful.

Seeing Opal's knowing smile, Pearl shot her a look and then turned her attention to Cash. "Gentlemen?"

"I'll take a beer, thanks," Cash said, and Tommy cleared his throat. "Um. Me, too. Please."

Once everyone had a drink in hand, Opal sent the guys out to check on the kids and horses while she and Pearl made dinner.

As soon as they were out of earshot, Pearl hissed, "Where has that tall drink of water been all my life?"

Smiling, Opal sipped her wine. "Well, for the past few years, he's been right here in Prescott."

"Why have I always insisted on being a model driver? I could stand to be pulled over, you know."

"I wouldn't recommend breaking any laws if you want to date a cop."

"Ha. Good point from someone who knows." Pearl drained her glass and refilled it. "Okay, put me to work. We'd better cook something good."

Opal set her up with a knife and a cutting board, and she started dicing potatoes while Opal mixed up a sauce for the chicken.

"I have to ask." Opal kept her back to Pearl while she stirred. "Are you really ready to date again?"

Pearl paused her chopping and looked at Opal. "Judging by my reaction to Tommy Hot-Pants Rowland out there, I'd say so."

"Okay. I guess you have a point."

Throughout the dinner—which they all ate scattered throughout the living room, since flower bouquets took up the entire surface of the dining table—Pearl and Tommy barely made eye contact, but Opal could feel the tension between them. She kept catching Cash's eye, and he kept catching hers.

When dinner was over and they'd cleaned up and Pearl and the boys and Tommy had gone home, Cash and Opal stood in the driveway with Louie.

"So, Pearl and Tommy, huh?"

Opal wrapped her arms around his waist. "Maybe. They would be cute together, wouldn't they?"

Cash grunted. "It wouldn't be very manly of me to agree that they'd be cute, but yeah, they could hit it off."

"That's what I thought. Especially after the way they reacted to each other when he came in."

"I saw that. And you know what? It reminded me of the way I felt when I first saw you."

"Back in elementary school?"

He laughed, kissed the top of her head. "No. When you first came roaring back into Prescott. I was completely flabbergasted."

She dropped her arms, grabbed his hand to lead him toward the front door, and called Louie to follow. "I thought you were flabbergasted due to anger at my too-fast driving and my too-loud music."

"That, too. But mostly due to your smokin' hot good looks. And that was before I realized you're the same smart and compassionate person I knew back in elementary school."

Opal closed the door behind them. "Yeah, I guess I'm pretty amazing."

"You are." He took her into his arms again. "And I can't wait to marry you tomorrow."

"I can't wait to marry you, too. And for the record, I think *you're* amazing."

Because his chin rested on her head, she could feel his nod. "I am. What a pair we make, Mrs. Wilder. Now, shall we retire to the porch swing?"

"Absolutely."

The last rays of the setting sun shot up from the horizon and cast a soft purple hue over the backyard and the rolling hills that lay beyond. They sat, and Opal took Cash's hand, interlacing their fingers. "This is the first night of the rest of our lives."

Still holding her hand, Cash stood up and pulled her to standing. "Then I think we should dance."

And they did.

The End

About the Author

Hilary Dartt loves great adventures, whether she's writing, reading, or living them. The author of twelve novels, Hilary lives in Arizona's high desert with her husband, their three children, and her Weimaraner, Leia. She loves camping, exploring in the Jeep, and dance parties with her kids. Learn more and sign up for her newsletter at www.hilarydartt.com.

www.ingramcontent.com/pod-product-compliance
Lightning Source LLC
Chambersburg PA
CBHW061803190726
48289CB00007B/2051